Paris,
RUE DES MARTYRS

A Novel

ADRIA J. CIMINO

Published by Velvet Morning Press

ISBN-13: 978-0692335079
ISBN-10: 0692335072

Cover design by Cooper Copetas
Author photo by Didier Quémener

Discover more by
ADRIA J. CIMINO
BESTSELLING AUTHOR

For new releases, deals and a free
ecopy of *Flore*, sign up here:
http://bit.ly/cimino-news

To Mom, Auntie Jean and Grandma,
the trio who encouraged big dreams

Chapter 1

Rafael

Rafael Mendez arrived like a thief in the night at 120 Rue des Martyrs. He ran all the way from the train station, where he had left one small, ragtag suitcase in a rented locker. His sneakers slapped noisily along the cobblestones, then pavement, in time with his own tears and the rain falling from a grim Parisian sky.

It was as if each minute lost counted for everything in his 23-year-old life. He pushed past umbrellas that seemed to tango as they bobbed against one another, old men who chatted with no one in particular, couples laughing, and a few sidewalk café tables left behind to weather the storm.

He was nearly blind to this first vision of the city, and only looked up now and again at the street signs to reassure himself that—yes—he hadn't lost the Rue des Martyrs.

And then he stopped. He pushed wet strands of long, black hair back from his face, wiped away the silly tears of that odd combination of desperation and excitement, and sank down onto a bench facing the address he had imagined all of his life in Colombia.

Now, as the rain soaked through his jeans and his gaze

traveled across the street to the only lighted apartment in building 120, his mind returned home. That's where his quest began, after all. In Bogotá.

As a child, he would play with the emeralds. That was his first memory. Not mother. Not father. Emeralds. Because that was how his life began. His father never wanted to tell Rafael that the French jewelry designer gave birth to him on a trip for those precious stones. He only said it once—grimly—shaking his head and staring at the dark sand under their feet. Rafael remembered looking up at him with widened 10-year-old eyes as they plodded along the dusty trail to where his father would buy the stones. It was Rafael's first trip there with his father, and in the young boy's mind, it became a sacred place.

But he couldn't think of that story right now or those fucking emeralds. It was over. He had to erase every memory from his mind, the images that haunted him at night.

The one remaining light in 120 snapped off, leaving the building in darkness. It would be too late. He was wasting time. His heart raced as he crossed the street between the cars that kicked up muddy water onto his jeans. He ignored the honking horns. He wanted to move forward, and all at once he wanted to travel back. Rafael was frightened. Afraid of what he might learn or might not learn. *Never be afraid,* his father had hissed into his ear on that first trip for emeralds.

Before he could let his worries swallow him up with one great gulp, he pounded his fist on the heavy, brown-lacquered door that like a clamshell closed the apartments to the world. Nothing. The sound of his fist against the wood reverberated through his entire body, but no one responded. He scolded himself for his own impatience. How could he possibly have expected someone to answer that door at 11 o'clock on a Thursday night? He placed his hand softly against the handle and sighed, knowing he should leave, yet not able to abandon the glimmer of hope that his problems would be resolved in a matter of hours.

The door creaked open suddenly, and he jumped back.

"There's no need to be startled, you know. When you knock on a door like a maniac, you should expect it to open."

A wispy redhead slipped through the doorway and onto the sidewalk. She gave him a crooked grin, lit a cigarette and leaned against the cool brick.

"So," she said, blowing smoke to the sky, "who do you want to see that badly?"

Something about the young woman struck him. She wasn't beautiful, with her almost pasty complexion and skinny figure in oversized jeans, but she had an assertive air about her that was much more impressive.

"It must be pretty serious," she continued, taking a drag. "Why don't we talk about it?"

"Do you know a woman named Carmen?" Rafael asked, his voice shaking.

"No."

"Someone named Carmen lives or lived here…" he said, his words trailing off. He felt ridiculous and unprepared as he faced such inquisitive eyes.

"A lot of people have been around here," she said. "I need specifics."

"That's the problem. I don't have any."

"What have you come here for anyway?"

"Answers."

She flicked her half-smoked cigarette into the gutter and with green eyes paler than any emerald gazed up to the sky.

"What are your questions?"

A window flew open from above and a woman's voice called out: "Laurel? Laurel…"

The person who had to be Laurel pulled Rafael against her and ducked into the shadows. She grinned mischievously.

"I've got to run."

His heart skipped a beat as her hair brushed against his cheek. But he kept any flicker of sentiment in check. He didn't have time for distractions.

"Meet me back here tomorrow—same hour," Laurel whispered. "I'll see what I can find out. I have some connections…" And then she slipped away from him and into the night.

Chapter 2

Cecile

Cecile de Champigny had lived on the Rue des Martyrs forever—or at least that's how it seemed to her as she sat on a wrought-iron bench and stuffed one sugar-coated beignet after the other into her dissatisfied mouth. She chewed numbly, methodically, and hated herself with every gulp. *But it was his fault!* A life of monotony suited Manu just fine. They had enough money to live in a lovely, four-bedroom apartment overlooking the rooftops, and she had plenty of time to spend with the two teenagers she had given birth to way too young.

Yet she wasn't satisfied. Manu said he didn't understand her. No one did, as a matter-of-fact. Cecile told herself that she didn't care. She didn't need their sympathy. She could find tranquility on her own, at least for a little while.

It was the only moment she had to herself. This late-afternoon hour that beckoned her to sit outside and gaze longingly at an interesting world that somehow excluded her.

A ten-minute walk brought her far from home to this bench half-hidden by shrubbery and facing the Sacré-Cœur Basilica, where tourists mounted the God-only-knew-how-many steps to see Paris from the heart of Montmartre, the city's highest point. But Cecile never looked down at the narrow cobblestone streets below. She preferred looking up at the sky.

She was about to lick the last bit of sugar off her fingertips when a strange feeling traveled up her spine. She wasn't alone. For the first time in the years she had been visiting this spot, someone's eyes were on her.

He didn't seem to realize that she had noticed, his gaze moving lithely from her face to his sketchbook. And then his slim fingers tracing patterns onto the paper.

Cecile pushed her greasy napkin away in shame. She suddenly felt undressed, knowing that he had been watching her during this private moment. She wanted to snatch another glance at the artist's large, light eyes. But it was too late. He was gone. In a matter of seconds, he had slipped away. But he had left something behind. Cecile slowly rose from her bench and crossed the uneven patch of stones to the grass where he had been sitting. She dropped to her knees, not caring about the mist from an afternoon shower that soaked through her stockings. She picked up the thick, white piece of paper dancing in the breeze only to look into her own charcoal eyes. The sadness scared her. Not the fact that it existed, but the fact that the artist had noticed it. What else had he seen as he studied her? Cecile shuddered.

Her limp blond hair looked a little fuller than in reality, and this version of herself lacked those little wrinkles that fanned out from the corners of her eyes. She wanted to rip up this testimony to her private moments, but something stopped her as she gripped it between clammy fingers. Who was this artist? Why did he spend this time tracing her face only to leave his work behind?

Probably disappointed in his decision of what to draw, she thought to herself. She sank her heels into the grass and glared with disgust at the thighs that were rounder than they should have been in the thin, white skirt clinging to each curve.

Cecile got up decisively and brushed off her bottom. A woman who could stuff that much sugar into her mouth in a matter of minutes only could be regarded as a disgusting curiosity. A slight flicker of anger rose from within. What right did this stranger have to document her weakness? If she saw him again, she would give him a piece of her mind. She certainly wouldn't have a problem recognizing him. Those eyes couldn't be forgotten. Hastily, she stuffed the drawing into her purse. With reluctant steps, she returned to her daily life.

Chapter 3

Andre

"You stupid son-of-a-bitch!" Andre Wren shouted into his cell phone, causing a start at the next table. But he didn't notice or care as he lunched at his usual, rather unremarkable bistro on the Rue des Martyrs, where everyone had learned to put up with his eccentricities.

The waiter didn't seem to hear the carryings-on as he placed a plate of *coq au vin* in front of the agitated actor. Andre, who had lost all interest in food for the moment, pushed the fragrant dish aside and hunched over his telephone.

"You're out of your fucking mind! That has to be it. You actually thought that you could get me on stage for 12 weeks in a bit part? I don't even waste my time with TV cameos, so why would I take this piece of shit?"

"Look Andre, calm down … I know things haven't been easy since the accident," Jack's smooth voice said from his early-morning breakfast spot on Seventh Avenue and 55th. "But your dancing career is over. You have to understand that! How can I get you a decent part in a musical? It's time to make some concessions!"

"That word isn't in my vocabulary and it shouldn't be in

yours either if you want to keep making money off my back like you've done for the past 25 years!"

Jack sighed into the phone.

"Andre, come on, think it over a bit," he said. "I've never steered you wrong. This will lead to more film roles. Victor plans on making the show into a movie... What you're doing is committing career suicide, and the worst thing is that you know it!"

"I don't give a damn about film! I never have—so I don't see why things should change now..." Andre's rising voice gave his neighbors another start, but he continued without missing a beat. "You tell the crook that I refuse to take part in his show—I've made my decision. At least I'm still capable of doing that!"

With shaking fingers, Andre smashed the "off" button on his phone and stuffed it into his pocket. He looked out at the same view as always—the flower shop across the street, the bakery with apricot tarts in the window—but he saw nothing. He ran a hand through his perfectly groomed silver-blond hair, and cursed Jack and the fucking accident, which had left him with five fractures in one leg and a screwed-up back.

That was six months ago, when the doctors told Andre his days of tap dancing his way through one hit musical to the next were over. From now on, his legs would only carry him with the support of this wretched cane that made him feel as if he had been on earth a lot longer than his 50 years. He thought of his Harley—his baby—sitting untouched in the musty garage for way too long after that goddamn accident had crushed its twin into dust. "Off limits," the doctors had said.

"Is everything OK over here, sir?" his usual waiter asked in that familiar tired-sounding voice.

Andre nodded solemnly.

"I'm not hungry," he muttered, prying himself off his seat with one hand pathetically gripping the fine, wooden cane Clarisse had specially ordered for him. He ignored the eyes that followed his every move, the fans who yesterday applauded and today shrank away in disappointment at the mere sight of him.

Of course he still had his voice. The perfect tenor that rang out strong and clear without the slightest strain. But Jack said it never would be enough. There were plenty of others who had the magic voice along with the whole package. Deep down, Andre Wren knew Jack was right—and right about everything. His agent had guided him without a hitch since the beginning and wasn't about to slip up now. Andre had performed the best roles on the Paris and New York stages as a result of Jack's efforts. But the idea of giving in was impossible for this actor, who didn't exist without his pride.

The warm, late-summer air rustled through the trees lining the Rue des Martyrs. Andre made his way farther up the street to his building. He winced with nearly every step. He didn't see the trees, the men in suits hurrying by, or the motor scooters as they tilted so close to him to make the turn.

It was almost as if Andre Wren, who had been living on the Rue des Martyrs for 20 years, had never opened his eyes and looked around. Andre realized this but didn't care. The only things that ever had brought him happiness were those moments on stage. That was why the idea of losing them terrified him.

Andre was so deep in thought when he rounded the corner into the courtyard of the 1930s brick building that he almost impaled the concierge's foot with his cane. She yelped in surprise and then blushed several shades of red.

"Mr. Wren, it's you... I was hoping to find you, as a matter of fact!"

She had been watering the yellow and orange roses that grew so well in the sunlight coming from the east. He glared impatiently at her round face and over-bleached hair as she set down the tin watering can and stood up.

"You had a visitor earlier," she said. "He left, oh, about fifteen minutes ago."

"I wasn't expecting anyone, so it can't be important."

Andre was very particular about his time. He didn't allot much of it to anyone. He knew that was one of the reasons why Clarisse was leaving him, but he refused any form of change.

He was just about to mount the three little wooden steps

leading to the elevator when the concierge placed a hand on his arm.

"Wait, this note was left for you."

"I'm not interested! Just throw it in my mail slot, and I'll get to it later."

"Sir, it's from a young man… your son."

Andre felt as if his heart—and the entire world—had stopped as the woman pronounced those words imploringly.

"I didn't know you had a son, but he said…"

Andre no longer was listening. He snatched the envelope out of her hands and pushed his way through the door to the stairwell. Hugo. The son he hadn't seen in perhaps a decade. He had to be… let's see… about 20 by now. Andre stumbled over his cane and into the elevator, pushed the button for the top floor and took slow, deep breaths. What did this young man want with a father who had rejected him so long ago? Andre's heart beat faster. Maybe he'd come to gloat after having observed the great fall of Andre Wren.

Sadness gripped Andre's heart each time he thought about the boy, but he had never let it win him over. June tricked him into fatherhood. He had always told her he never would be suited to raise a child… and then Hugo came along. In the end, Andre didn't completely shirk his responsibilities. He did the right thing, of course. He sent them money as any responsible man would do, but that was that. Andre didn't want any further involvement.

The elevator stopped on the fifth floor. Andre quickly unlocked his door and made his way through the clutter of the front hall. He still held the note in his hands.

Chapter 4

Mira

Mira Galino's usually steady hands shook as she tore her handbag off the coat rack that teetered precariously before crashing to the hardwood floor. She stepped over it, yanked open the door and pulled her overnight bag across the threshold. Tufts of mohair were caught in the zipper, and a corner of her favorite black sweater was slipping out the front pocket, but she didn't care.

"Mira, you can't leave! You don't understand!"

Antonio grabbed her arm, but she broke free. Wild, dark eyes caught his desperate, light ones.

"Don't understand what?" she hissed. "The fact that you've been sleeping with my business partner? And to make matters worse, a person who was supposed to be my friend... I think everything is pretty damn clear!"

Images from only moments ago flashed through her mind. She was working that afternoon in the art gallery she and Clara had started with faith, a dream and a few canvases only a year ago. Mira couldn't even remember why she ran home a half hour or so earlier. A haze clouded her normally clear thoughts. Maybe it was to drag more supplies to the gallery from the storage room in the apartment she shared with her fiancé. But all of the trivial details disappeared from her mind when she opened the door and heard cooing voices that nearly made her heart stop.

Then she walked in on them. The scene was a blur. Clara crying, saying she was sorry, running out the door with a white, cotton sheet around her middle. Antonio saying the typical "it's not what it seems" when really it couldn't be anything but what it seemed. At first, she was silent. She didn't say a word as she randomly threw bunches of clothing into one simple bag and then wheeled it into the front hallway. She didn't listen to his endless excuses and apologies.

Then, in one great fit of anger, she slapped him and headed for the door. Now, she glared at those red marks that her slim fingers had left on his pale cheek.

"You really are a bastard," she said with the pure disgust that overflowed from her heart. Tears had been forming in the corners of her eyes, but she wouldn't let them fall. She yanked her pink, leather bag over that annoying bump in the building's vestibule and headed out the main door even as he followed her.

"Go away!" she yelled, not caring if she was providing entertainment to the passersby who stopped and looked at them hurrying along the sidewalk. Antonio followed her for several blocks through the noisy streets of Naples until she finally managed to lose herself in a group of tourists, duck into a small alley, and watch him continue eagerly in what he thought was the right direction. She waited there for a few moments, her heart pounding, tears falling.

In a matter of minutes, love had turned to hate. Antonio and Clara betrayed and humiliated her. Mira suddenly felt nauseated as she thought of how she had trusted both of them. She placed a trembling hand on her stomach and took deep breaths. Some women learned to accept these kinds of situations, but Mira refused to do so. She would rather be brokenhearted. She would rather be alone forever than swallow her pride. It was all she had left.

Mira took a deep breath and emerged from the humid alley. The scent of spicy sausage and peppers mixed with automobile exhaust filled her lungs. Ignoring the bus driver's curse words as he screeched to a stop inches from her, Mira dashed across the busy intersection. Gypsy children pulling at pockets didn't stop her as she moved quickly through the ever-crowded streets, her white ballerina flats turning brown in the dust.

A feeling of strength filled her heart as she pressed on to the station. Antonio never would guess that she was leaving the country. He was probably heading for her parents' house right that very second. *Good for him!* she thought smugly. The rhythm of her footsteps accelerated. She walked past the *Buona Notte* hotel with its gold-gilded windows, the Tivoli's bakery that rivaled her father's with crackling bread in the window, and the tacky little tourist shops with postcards flashing "Kiss me, I'm Italian." Mira drank in everything. She gazed at the world she knew so well as if for the very last time.

The train pulled out of the station. Mira's reflection in the grease-streaked window showed bloodshot eyes and curly, short dark hair that stood on end. Would Tatiana recognize her in such a state? She didn't care. She turned away from that vision of herself. Tears spilled out of the corners of her eyes. She thought of how Antonio slept with an arm around her and his cheek against her neck, of how he kissed her softly and whispered little "I love yous" in her ears... Everything had been a sham. And the wedding... They would have been exchanging vows in two months.

Mira shook her head bitterly. It was funny how in a matter of hours, one's whole life could be turned upside down. Her relationship with Antonio was over. Her all-important gallery now meant nothing. Clara could have it. Let her recruit some other artist as a partner. Mira never wanted to set foot in that place again.

She faced forward during the entire trip. She didn't want to look back at what she had left behind.

Chapter 5

Rafael

Darkness engulfed the Ford Explorer as it plunged into the depths of the forest. It was an eight-hour drive turned into six with Diego at the wheel. Rafael was used to the long, gut-twisting ride out to the mines where his parents would buy the brightest emeralds for cash. They were *comisionistas,* or those who bought stones directly from the mines, shaped and polished them into perfection, and resold them to the world's biggest buyers.

Instinctively, Rafael touched the front pocket of his jeans, where he had a wad of hundred dollar bills totaling ten thousand dollars. He glanced at his mother and she smiled at him reassuringly with glamorously drawn fuchsia lips. She always told him that she had to sparkle just as much as the emeralds. Tina was there to make the best deals with the men who called her "the diva." After more than 20 years in the business, she knew her stuff. Diego was there to examine the stones with those keen, dark eyes that could turn from angelic to diabolic in minutes. He carried a 9-millimeter pistol and wasn't afraid of using it.

Rafael became part of this world at age 16, when Diego

announced that his only son would carry on the legacy. But instead of dropping out like his father, Rafael finished high school and went on to college. With the experience and a degree from business school, he would have everything he needed to make it in today's emerald world, his father had said.

Rafael thought of those words as the truck bumped along through the underbrush. Humidity and the damp smell of greenery seeped in through the window that Tina always cracked open a few centimeters. Rafael took a deep breath. He had accepted his fate with a solemn sense of responsibility. He couldn't disappoint his father.

Again, he brushed his hand along the pocket hiding more cash than most 22-year-olds ever see. He closed his eyes. He wanted to doze off. It had to be past 1 o'clock in the morning. They soon would arrive at their destination.

A flash of light, then a popping noise broke through the rhythmic humming of the motor. Rafael felt his heart leap. The Explorer spun out of control. He reached forward clutching the blood-stained denim jacket as Diego fell into his arms. The truck had jolted to a halt along with the rest of Rafael's world.

"Go!" Diego hissed. "Get out of here... You have to find Carmen..."

Rafael remained frozen in horror as he watched his mother's slim silhouette slump like crumpled silk. The windshield was riddled with bullets. But no one came to finish off the job. Diego breathed raggedly for a few moments, struggling for that once rich-sounding voice, but Rafael couldn't understand the final words his father tried to pronounce.

He hid his face so that Diego never would see his adult son cry.

The words of his father echoed in Rafael's head. He had to escape. He pushed the door open and jumped into the spindly branches that scraped his bare arms. And then he ran. So close. They were so close to the village. He could feel it.

Rafael woke up with a start in an unfamiliar bed.

"So close..." he mumbled, shaking his head. But it didn't

matter. His parents were gone. Rafael stumbled out of the damp sheets and made his way desperately to the window.

Yes, he really was in Paris in the small room he had rented until he could find those much-needed answers. Rafael rubbed his eyes and leaned out the window. A church bell rang eight. Passersby hurried along—the workers in suits and the students in jeans. The scent of fresh bread wafted up from the bakery below. But the only thing Rafael could see and smell was blood.

Carmen. Who was the woman important enough to come to his father's mind at such a moment? She wasn't in Bogotá. He was convinced that she represented something far away and essential to Rafael's happiness in life.

Rafael had found one small clue that day after returning home and ransacking the house in a quiet rage. It was a yellowed postcard with crackling edges that somehow made the sparkling lights of the Champs-Elysees on the front look rather sordid.

"Carmen wants to see you. Please come. Marie."

Marie. The French woman who had given birth to him.

So that was why Rafael hurried along the streets of Paris looking distractedly at his map now and again. After his parents' death, he had spent months absorbing the shock and settling their affairs. Then, one day, when he had accomplished the painful and necessary tasks, he allowed himself to look at that postcard once again. He spent weeks studying the careful handwriting before making a decision. But the decision was obvious: Rafael had to find this woman who agreed to have a child for his parents. He didn't even know what he wanted to say to her, but she was all he had left. This trip to Paris couldn't be avoided. Diego wanted him to find Carmen, who would then somehow lead him to Marie. That had to be it.

But Rafael developed another plan—one that he hoped would be the easiest possible path to Marie. He would pay a visit to Paris' top emerald seller. Seeing the man wouldn't be a difficult task. After all, Diego and Tina had spent years cultivating relationships with industry contacts around the world.

He arrived at 11 a.m. sharp at Monsieur Francois-Xavier Le Rocher's office in the opulent Place Vendome. Diego, who often made business trips to Paris, had spoken to his son about this particular part of the city. His descriptions had been so vivid that an immediate sensation of déjà vu overcame Rafael as he studied the vast, open space, contained by a rectangle of austere historic buildings. They housed mainly elegant jewelry shops and offices that had welcomed Diego more than once.

Rafael passed through revolving glass doors and into an austere reception area. His sneakers squeaked along the marble as he approached the front desk. He told the doubtful-looking secretary who he was, and she made a call to somewhere above the stone arches that decorated the ceiling.

Rafael chewed on his lip nervously and then sighed with relief when he saw the woman's expression change.

Monsieur Le Rocher would see the son of Diego Mendez immediately.

"Tina Mendez sold me this emerald." Those were Le Rocher's first words to Rafael as he stepped into the large corner office with a view of the slim column that rose from the square below.

Le Rocher, a tall, severe man who looked no younger than 75, offered him a leather chair so that he could sit down and examine the emerald.

It was encased in glass, almost like a paperweight.

"This way I can look at it whenever I find the need to appreciate beauty," Le Rocher said.

Rafael swallowed hard. The stone was exactly the sort that had attracted his mother's sophisticated eye. But looking at emeralds, even ones she had chosen, no longer interested him.

"Now, what can I help you with?" Le Rocher asked, leaning forward across the oak desk. It was the sole piece of furniture in the rather lifeless, empty space. Only an immense mirror that covered one wall reflected the brightness of the world outside.

"I'm looking for someone. A jewelry designer... She's an old friend of my parents, or so I've heard." Rafael said the words hurriedly, ashamed to approach a stranger for assistance of any kind. He stared into the dim, gray eyes that now returned to the emerald.

"The important ones who have dealt with emeralds have been through this office, but I can't divulge names of course."

"Her name is Marie... She must be about 45 or so..." Rafael closed his eyes. He realized the near impossibility of his quest. But he couldn't give up. It was too soon.

"You're searching for your real mother, aren't you?"

Rafael's eyes flew open. No one knew that Tina hadn't given birth to him. She had left Bogotá and returned nine months later with a baby. No one asked questions. Diego wouldn't have answered anyway.

"It's common knowledge that Diego Mendez was having an affair with a very discreet French woman..." Le Rocher said, with a hint of a sly grin.

Rafael was silent for a moment, as if he had been slapped in the face. Then, all at once, he lost control.

"No!" Rafael felt as if his voice had reverberated through the entire building. Le Rocher sat up with a start, and then settled back into the black, leather chair. His smug expression made Rafael's blood boil.

"You're wrong! She helped them have a child... because my mother couldn't. Nothing more." Rafael was ashamed of himself for letting those words slip out of his mouth. He didn't owe an explanation to this man or anyone else.

"It's best that you know the truth..."

"No. They're lies! Who is this woman?" Rafael stood up defiantly and paced behind the chair. "I want to hear what she has to say."

"I don't know. I doubt anyone would. She wasn't a classic designer or we would have met her at one point or another."

"Then how can you be sure she existed?"

"You exist, now don't you?" Le Rocher said. The sly look moved from his lips to his eyes.

"What are you trying to tell me?"

"That you should continue the search, but I can't help

you. Your father—even now—is the only one who can."

"There aren't any clues…"

"Yes there are… You haven't learned how to interpret them."

"Why did you agree to see me?"

"To point you in the right direction," he said in a matter-of-fact voice. "To deliver a message to you. That's my piece of the puzzle."

Rafael took a deep breath. He couldn't believe such a thing about his father. He never would have cheated on Tina. They had the perfect life together. Just the thought of Le Rocher and others denigrating his father's memory made him tremble with anger. But striking out wouldn't help anyone or anything. He had to maintain his family's honor.

Rafael firmly shook the old man's hand.

"Thank you for your assistance."

He hoped that he never would return to Le Rocher's office or the Place Vendome, which both left his heart as cold as stone. It seemed as if his only chance of finding Marie was through Carmen. And that led him back to the young woman at 120 Rue des Martyrs.

Chapter 6

Cecile

Cecile hurried along the rue Berthe, one of the narrow, winding Montmartre streets leading up and away from the city. She was annoyed with herself for being so distracted by the artist who had sketched her portrait that she had completely forgotten a meeting with Vivienne's ballet teacher. She didn't know what to expect from the woman she only saw from afar at recitals. Cecile didn't want any part of the group of ballet moms who wished they could have lived the dreams they pushed on their daughters. Viv was different from the other girls. At the age of six, she secretly started taking ballet lessons from a 12-year-old who lived across the hall. Cecile, astonished to find out that her daughter's allowance was funding little Sophie's college savings, was immediately shamed into enrolling Viv in a real class.

Cecile didn't like ballet, and as much as she attempted to show Viv otherwise, her true sentiments shined through. But what amazed and scared Cecile the most was that Viv didn't seem to care about the lack of attention. She lived in her own world—this beautiful, thin brunette of 14—and every once in a while, she afforded a solemn glance in Cecile's direction.

It was almost as if she wondered how she, the graceful Vivienne de Champigny, could have such an ordinary and often rather pathetic mother. Cecile never could call her on such thoughts because along with her other fortitudes, Viv chose her words with care. Every neighbor, her teachers, and just about everyone who ever had come into contact with this girl clapped their hands together with enthusiasm and told Cecile how very lucky she was to have such a child. Cecile wanted to scream at them. How would they like having a daughter who didn't need her mother? Cecile was of no use to Viv. That was an invisible wound.

She arrived at a narrow, stone building, pushed open the door, and made her way through a dark hallway, clogged with giggling girls in tights. They and those overjoyed mothers chitchatting a mile a minute didn't seem to notice her.

In a studio at the very end of the hall, she saw Viv, alone in front of the mirror and *barre*, turning one pirouette after the next with graceful, spindly legs. She was in her own world as usual.

"She's quite impressive," a voice right beside her said.

Cecile looked up into the dreamy blue eyes of Madame Vasseur, Viv's teacher. "That's why I wanted to talk with you."

"All right…"

"Please, follow me," she said, her turned-out feet padding softly into her office, a broom closet with ballet posters and show schedules covering the walls. Like a hummingbird, she flitted over to her desk and leaned ever so slightly against it.

"It's as simple as this," she began. "A highly respected ballet company is having auditions for a young dancer apprenticeship program, and I want Vivienne to audition."

"Do you think she has enough…" Then Cecile stopped right before pronouncing the word "talent." She must have sounded as if she had just arrived on the planet. She was embarrassed about what Madame Vasseur must have viewed as a total lack of interest in her own daughter's abilities. She could feel the woman's critical eyes on her. Cecile looked away, but everything in the claustrophobic room was ballet.

"I mean, I know she's good… but I'm her mother," Cecile mumbled.

"I need your permission," Madame Vasseur said.

"Of course... she can... I mean, I never would hold Viv back..." Cecile's words were as jumbled as her thoughts and feelings at the moment.

"Auditions are in a couple of weeks," Madame Vasseur said. "They will require a lot of work..."

"What does Viv say about this?"

"Why don't you ask her?" Madame Vasseur replied, gazing over Cecile's shoulder. It was if she sensed the uneasiness between mother and daughter.

Cecile turned around. Viv was looking at her with the calm, satisfied smile that seemed so odd for such a young girl.

"I guess we'll be going now," Cecile said, hastily putting her hand on her daughter's shoulder and thanking Madame Vasseur. She didn't want to exchange private words in front of this woman who probably knew Viv better than she did.

Viv followed her quickly through the emptying hallway and onto the street.

"Congratulations," Cecile said, glancing at her daughter out of the corner of her eye. Viv nearly glided along, with the perfect posture that drew the eyes of strangers.

"Thanks."

"If you're chosen, what does this mean for school?"

"Double the work, but I can handle it." She tossed Cecile one of her faraway smiles.

"Does anyone else know about this?"

"Just Joel."

Joel. The only person who seemed able to break into Viv's shell. Her 17-year-old brother who had protected her since the day she started school. Cecile didn't understand how her charming little girl had changed—closing the door to all but Joel and ballet.

"I'm going to see if he's at the café," Viv said, pointing her finger in the direction of a tiny corner spot where Joel studied with friends. Then she took off in a sprint, leaving Cecile in much the same way as always.

"So what new and exciting things happened today?" Manu asked as he poured himself a shot of whisky and loosened the crooked, striped tie the kids had bought him for his birthday. Classes hadn't yet begun, but he already had started spending days in his office at the university.

"What do you mean?" Cecile almost snapped back. He had come so close to the truth.

Cecile had been thinking of the artist all the way home. If she didn't have the drawing in her pocket, she could have easily convinced herself that he had been a figment of her own wistful imagination. But she felt it there, even now as she sat facing Manu.

"You say I'm never interested in what you do during the day, so I'm simply asking," he said.

"Well... nothing."

Cecile felt unusually ornery as she settled back into the plush navy semi-circle couch that had a view of the street below, bustling with activity.

"This apartment is like a fishbowl," she said suddenly.

"What do you mean, Cecile?" Manu asked as he slipped onto the strict armchair across from her.

What she really meant was that she felt trapped in an artificial world, and it seemed as if no exit was available to her.

Instead, she sighed and told Manu that the blues and greens that were supposed to be relaxing were becoming monotonous.

"But we redecorated the place six months ago! You said you liked it, Cecile... You never mentioned anything negative about the colors..."

He took a sip of his drink and shook his head. She studied Manu for a second. He still had the physical charm of his earlier days, with the dark hair—now graying—pushed back from his wide forehead and the almond-shaped eyes inherited by Viv. But one of the most important elements of a relationship had taken a tumble somewhere along the line. The excitement. The passion. It was gone. Cecile had been with Manu for 20 years, and ironically enough, the disappearance of this essential quality didn't take off as part of a seven-year-itch. Only the past two or three years had announced the arrival of the mundane. Slowly and unexpectedly, it had crept up on them.

In the very beginning, life was wonderful. She was a college student, and he was her literature professor. The whole idea of a forbidden romance turned out to be highly overrated two decades later. Sure, it was exhilarating back then when her experienced 30-year-old lover took her out to exotic restaurants, told her about his travels, and seduced her better than any boy could. And that lasted for such a long time. Then life started unraveling. She didn't want to think about it. She didn't want to know why.

The front door flew open just as Cecile was about to tell Manu to forget the whole fishbowl subject. Viv's and Joel's footsteps scampered across the hardwoods and into the living room.

"Hope we're not too late," Joel said, flashing a grin in Cecile's direction as he tossed his backpack onto the floor. "What's for dinner?"

"Don't wait for me," Viv called out. "I have to find something for dance..."

"What's up Viv?" Manu asked.

But she already had hit the stairs two at a time.

"She's auditioning for a new program with a ballet company," Cecile said, following Joel into the kitchen.

"Wait," Manu said. "That's a big deal! Why didn't you tell me right away, Cecile?"

"I was going to let her tell you... but I see she's not in any hurry to let you know about it," she said over her shoulder. Cecile ignored Manu's words, which she couldn't hear from the kitchen. But she could imagine them well enough. "Cecile don't be so petty," or "You take everything so seriously."

She preferred listening to Joel prattle on about his study group. He and three others started hitting the books a month before classes began. Then they were off to boarding school at various parts of the globe, with the hope of earning strategic positions in the government one day. Cecile didn't know how Joel had become so drawn to politics after growing up in a home where conversations never turned in that direction, but she did understand him better than she understood Viv. His cards were always on the table. The only subject they couldn't discuss with intensity was that of Viv, because Joel refused to say anything insightful about his little sister.

Cecile spent most of her quality time with Joel in the kitchen. He would prepare the roast pork while she boiled the rice or vice versa. The shared duties and light conversation had a way of soothing her mind. On this particular night, though, the pickings were slim. A wedge of aging brie that perfumed the refrigerator, a few handfuls of wilting lettuce and a leftover salmon steak wouldn't do the trick for the four of them. Four. Not five. Manu's daughter from a previous marriage rarely joined them at the dinner table.

"I think we're going to end up at the bistro down the street," Cecile said. "I was supposed to run to the store this afternoon, but I ... lost track of time."

She felt heat rise into her face, but Joel didn't seem to notice.

"You mean where the crazy actor has lunch every day and makes a scene the whole neighborhood ends up talking about?" Joel asked with a smile. He had one of those infectious, mischievous grins that reminded Cecile of her own smile a few years ago. She couldn't help but return the expression and run a hand through his wavy dark hair.

"I don't think we'll see him there now—so don't get your hopes up for a scene," she said. "He doesn't like crowds— other than at the theater." Cecile thought most of his skills were highly overrated, but she would never express such a thing out loud. The Rue des Martyrs was a very small world, and word traveled much too quickly for her taste.

Joel smirked and settled onto one of the bar stools at the corner island in the periwinkle blue kitchen—the fishbowl effect again.

"I wonder what's taking Viv so long anyway?" he said.

"What's she looking for?"

"I don't know."

"Well, I'm going to go and nudge her along. It's getting late…"

Cecile trudged up the two flights of creaking wooden stairs to the attic. The heat was beginning to get to her. She felt a dull pounding in her head that only intensified as she opened the door to the stuffiness of the small room.

"Viv?" she called out.

She looked beyond the dust, shadows and ray of sunlight that slipped through the single window and saw her daughter sitting stiffly on the floor, legs crossed, with a cluttered mass of papers around her. Viv turned around abruptly and wiped her eyes.

Cecile felt her heart flip flop. Viv had been crying. The last time she had seen tears fall from her eyes was when Viv was about four and fought with a friend over Ballerina Barbie.

"What is it?" she asked. "What's going on?"

"Nothing." Viv tucked a wad of papers into her dance bag and stood up.

"Viv, I'd like to help…"

"No," Viv said, shaking her head authoritatively. "Everything is perfectly fine."

She approached Cecile and took her hand.

"I'm not coming to dinner," she said. Then she turned and hurried out the door.

Cecile was convinced that something was going on, and she would get to the bottom of it, whether Viv liked it or not.

Chapter 7

Andre

Andre had few clear memories of his son. The first was of Hugo at about age four or five. It was when Andre was traveling back and forth quite frequently between Paris and New York. On a day off from a production of CATS, he took the commuter train out to Westchester County to one of those sleepy little towns where quiet, winding roads, the sea breeze and flower gardens filled with roses were a much-appreciated respite from city life. It was a pause in the mile-a-minute existence of Andre Wren.

Jack was having an outdoor party behind the Tudor-style mansion he bought after years of getting Andre and other actors prime roles. Theater people, carrying glasses of frothy pink cocktails or foaming dark beer, mingled and admired the velvety roses and sculpted shrubbery as they strolled around the property. Everyone Jack invited had some connection to the industry, and that, of course, was why June was there. She was a costume designer for the New York stage. All of the actors knew her and loved her. Hugo was proof that Andre had loved her once too.

Andre remembered walking around the back of the house

with Jack, and then enthusiastically plunging into the admiring crowd of friends and acquaintances. He didn't recall any of the vapid moments spent with these people, whom he no longer saw very often.

Instead, one picture came to mind. June, her big, blue eyes shining, was sitting beside a small boy at the edge of the pool. A towheaded child who smiled timidly at his mother and paddled tiny, flipper-clad feet in the water. Andre's heart filled with panic. And then June caught his eye. She never had wanted him to leave. He could see it in her gaze, beckoning to him. His heart was beating rapidly. June. The June with eyes that danced. And this boy. His boy. No. He shook his head. She was trying to manipulate him once again. She knew how he felt about kids. They were fine—as long as they were someone else's. He turned around and made his way through the crowd that gathered between green hedges and marigolds. He could hardly take care of himself. He had no business being a father.

"What's the matter with you?" Jack yelled after him. "Where are you going?"

But he didn't answer. He just kept on running and never stopped.

෨෴

Andre flipped a few coins into the jar of the same beggar who sat outside of Café Martyrs every night. He kind of felt sorry for the poor bastards wandering up and down these grimy streets. *This whole damn city can be so depressing,* he thought to himself as he pushed open the door and limped into the café.

He lit up a cigarette and sat down at a round table in the back, where he usually could get away with having a smoke. He ordered a scotch on the rocks, took a deep breath and waited. Waited for the boy who likely would spit in his face for being such a son-of-a-bitch. Andre smiled ironically, sadly, as he thought of his own shitty weaknesses. His scotch arrived. He took a sip, feeling it burn a path to his stomach.

Ten minutes passed along with most of the scotch and

two cigarettes. Then he arrived. Right on time.

A tall blond with his mother's dazzling eyes. He was wearing jeans and a white t-shirt that showed off a thin, well-built physique much like Andre's at the same age.

"Might as well get the ball rolling," Andre said under his breath. He lifted his glass in the boy's direction and received a smile back. A brilliant, unexpected smile. Why the hell would this kid he had abandoned look at him with anything other than disdain?

He approached with the same timidity Andre had seen in him so long ago.

"Andre Wren..." he said. "I'm the Hugo you've been sending checks to all of these years."

His voice was smooth, like Andre's own, but with a slightly uneven pitch. He shook his father's hand firmly, and then sat down opposite him.

The anxiety that had been building up within Andre since his conversation with the concierge reached a head as he looked up at the boy who had June's eyes, but his expression. He needed a cigarette. With shaky hands, he reached for his lighter.

"I won't offer you one of these," he said as he lit up. "You're better off without them." He shook his head at his own ridiculous parental words, which felt so inappropriate in his situation. But Hugo didn't seem to notice.

"That's OK. I don't smoke."

The waiter returned to Andre's table.

"What will you have? Do you speak French or should I order for you?"

"A Perrier please," Hugo asked the waiter in French. Then he turned back to Andre. "I learned from Mom. She said I would end up here one day."

"Why would she say such a thing?" Andre asked, taking a long stress-relieving drag on his cigarette.

"Because..." He gazed at the table for a moment, the little boy expression returning. "She said that if I wanted to be an actor, I would be better off starting here, where the world isn't as harsh."

Andre snorted. "You want to be an actor? I wouldn't

recommend it to anyone anywhere. They—the audience, the industry—chew you up, spit you out and start over with someone new."

So that was the reason for Hugo's appearance. He wanted help getting his career started. He probably wanted to use the "Wren" name. Being that his old dad was no longer in tip-top shape, this would be the time to take over. Another Wren would make it to the top, only to eventually fall in one way or another.

Andre didn't want this blood-related stranger to join his world. He didn't want to explain the existence of a son to all of those people who didn't give a shit anyway. But most importantly, he didn't want to draw this boy into the trap of self-admiration that had ruined Andre's chance for personal happiness. Andre told himself this wasn't out of parental concern, but simply a part of wanting to keep any naïve kid from falling on his or her ass. Andre's well-being depended on the stage—not on affection from family. The stage was a drug.

"Mom told me the same," Hugo was saying. "She didn't want this for me, but it just happened. As soon as I took part in one play… I was pushed into the performing arts program. Then the special high school."

"So you've been involved in theater for a while…" Andre's heart pounded. Was that voice anything like his? "Sing a few bars for me," he said suddenly.

Hugo blushed, making those June eyes appear bluer.

"Anything you want," Andre said nervously.

"I don't sing," he said.

The waiter returned with Hugo's Perrier, and the boy took a sip. Then with serious eyes he looked at Andre.

"I didn't come to you to discuss career plans," he said.

"Why else would you want to see me?"

"I wanted to let you know that I'm here in Paris now…" He took another sip of his drink.

Andre lit up a cigarette and gazed into the blue eyes. It was as if this boy was seeking some sort of normal relationship with him. He was half surprised, half frightened.

"You actually want to talk with me after the earfuls June has given you?"

"Mom never has said much of anything, as a matter of fact."

Even worse. That meant the boy would want detailed explanations about why Andre Wren never wanted to accept his own son.

"Look, Hugo," Andre said, for the first time addressing his son by the name June had chosen alone. "You can't expect much from me. One thing I can do is set you up in a decent apartment while you're here so you won't have to struggle."

"I don't want your help," Hugo said firmly. "I have a place already, an acting class and a job."

"Whose class?"

"Tatiana Ricci."

"No, no, no," Andre said, exasperated. "She hasn't made a name for herself yet. I can sign you up with…"

"No—I didn't come here for that. I came for answers. I want to know why you left us."

"Well that is all I have to offer."

Hugo's face went pale, as if he had been slapped. He pushed his drink aside and got up.

"I thought seeing me would make a difference… I thought you would want us to get to know each other. I don't understand you, Andre Wren."

His voice was hollow with disappointment.

Andre felt his heart sink, but he didn't know how to change his attitude and life. And he didn't have the desire to do so anyway. Even at his age, he was terrified at the thought of being a father, of taking responsibility for this younger version of himself.

Hugo dropped a few coins on the table. Andre pushed them away, but Hugo insisted.

"I'm going to be late for work."

Andre watched him go, his heart as empty as that of a broken old man.

Chapter 8

Mira

Arrival at the Anvers subway station. Mira moved forward with the wave of travelers eager to visit Montmartre. The fresh air felt like a blessing as she emerged. Then the five-minute walk and a funicular ride up the hill to the center of Montmartre. The sun baked into Mira's skin and her dress clung to her damp chest, but she wouldn't slow her pace. The wheels of her travel bag bumped along the uneven cobblestone as she headed toward the studio where Tatiana gave acting classes to both well-known actors as well as a handful of carefully selected hopefuls.

And then, in the square known for its galleries and the artists who painted portraits in the street day and night, Mira stopped. A poster caught her eye. A special exhibit of modern art at the Marceau Gallery. She swallowed hard. Septime Galino, seventh child in a family of eight, was in town. Her older brother: the artist who had both inspired and alienated her.

It was because of him that Mira knew Montmartre so well. Septime, who had spent two years living right around the corner, had been her guide. She had visited him once, when she was about 12, and her brother, ten years her senior, was an art student at a well-known school in Paris. Mira had never wrapped her thin fingers around a paintbrush until her visit to Septime's new world.

At home, he had been a mystical and unruly stranger, smoking pot, inviting in friends with purple hair, and rushing in and out at any hour. He was pure excitement. Mira would sit half hidden in the alcove in front of her bedroom and listen to the wailing music seeping out of his room at the end of the hall. Then her father would march up the stairs, order her to her room and make his way toward the source of the commotion.

There were many arguments. She could still remember putting an ear to the door well after midnight and hearing her father screaming at Septime, the front door slamming, and her mother crying. For Mira, Septime had become some sort of renegade hero fighting against such unfair oppression. She wanted to approach him, yet was petrified.

Then he was gone. Off to school in Paris. Months passed without sight or sound of him. But one day, out of the blue, this fabulous person invited her to spend a month with him in a wonderful city that was completely new to her. When her parents refused, she broke her piggy bank and made her escape. Septime said she was a pretty cool little sister.

Mira thought back fondly to those precious days they spent together. She followed him in and out of cafes, around flower gardens in the center of Paris and into the corner of classrooms where he and his fellow students perfected those paintings with violent slashes of reds and blues. They visited the Marceau Gallery together. She still could see the wire sculptures that held Septime's most-critical attention.

Mira took this in with excited, inquisitive eyes, but she didn't ask Septime to show her how to become an artist. Even back then, she realized that would have been silly. She quickly understood that she needed to find the way within herself. And she realized she wanted to paint, but not those obscure images that Septime created with such flair. Mira wanted to tell a story. She wanted to reproduce everyday experiences. She yearned to paint life.

"What are you thinking, Mir?" he asked her as she lingered in front of one of his most radical works. Her packed bag slumped sadly at her feet. "You don't want to leave, do you?"

She shook her head and tried to hide the tears shining in her eyes. She didn't want him to see her vulnerability. He threw an arm around her shoulder, and she glanced timidly into the large light eyes that reflected her own dark ones. No, she didn't want to leave. That was certain. But there was something that bothered Mira much more.

This visit and her days with Septime had stirred up a revolution within her. She had become someone new, and the idea both intrigued and terrified Mira. That was how the dream of becoming an artist was born.

If it weren't for the raucous laughter at the neighboring restaurant, Mira would have passed the Marceau Gallery without noticing its existence. Her thoughts had transported her back in time. Now, she approached the slim storefront with its freshly painted violet trim. There, in the window, was one of his paintings. The modern art that drew interest from around the world. He was exhibiting at one of his favorite small, Parisian galleries.

Mira gazed beyond the darkened glass with disdain. The admiration had tarnished. She hadn't seen Septime since her departure from his Paris apartment so many years ago. He ignored her letters and phone calls, and didn't even respond to the invitation to her gallery's opening. She had looked up to him with such adoration, and in the end, he turned his back on her. Mira's parents and other siblings, who hadn't spoken with Septime since his days in art school, told her she was better off without him. Yet, Mira couldn't budge from her spot in front of the gallery. She wanted to confront her brother. She wanted to confront all those who had hurt and disappointed her. She wanted to take charge of the situation.

A young woman with raspberry cat's-eye glasses and scarlet hair was adjusting the notice in the window. The work of artist Septime Galino would be featured for a month instead of two weeks as previously announced, the paper said. Mira knocked softly on the glass. The woman pointed to the hours on the door. Mira shook her head in desperation and tapped her fingers on the window once again. The woman looked at her with apparent annoyance, but cracked the door a few centimeters.

"Look, we open in ten minutes…"

"I just have a question," Mira said, fumbling for an excuse to say something. "Why is he staying longer?"

"Who?"

"Septime Galino."

"Oh, you're talking about the poster in the window…" Then she narrowed her eyes suspiciously. "What difference does it make to you?"

"I'm a fan," Mira mumbled uncomfortably.

"Well, if you want the answer, you would have to ask him the question. He'll be here soon…"

The woman turned blindly away, her polka-dot skirt swirling around her knees, and flicked on a dim light. Mira's eyes fled to her watch. The gallery would be opening in five minutes. She couldn't face Septime right now. She needed more time.

ço~ợ

Mira arrived at Tatiana's top-floor atelier. She left her bag in the hallway, slipped through the back door and sank onto the hardwood floor. Rays of light baked through the slanted windows overhead, but she hugged her bare legs against herself as if chilled to the bone. She felt completely wilted after her trek across the city.

Tatiana was so absorbed in a demonstration with one of the students that she didn't seem to notice her friend's arrival. But Mira was no longer watching Tatiana's expressive face. Mira, who until that moment could only think of her own miserable situation and a possible confrontation with her estranged brother, found herself distracted all at once as she scanned the faces looking down in meditation. It was that young man over there. The only one with eyes trained attentively on Tatiana. He seemed to be about Mira's age, as did most of the students. But he was different from the others

in the room. He had more of a story to tell. Mira could see it
in his gaze when it rose now and again, as if seeking sanctuary
through the slanted skylights overhead. He was too fragile.
Like the butterflies she never tried to catch.

Laughter and voices suddenly interrupted Mira's thoughts.
Class was breaking. The young man lagged behind the others
as they hurried out of the sun-drenched room. Her eyes
curiously followed his light blue T-shirt out the door.

"What are you doing here, Mira? Admiring my students
like that…"

Her face reddening, Mira jumped to her feet. Tatiana
rushed over and kissed her on both cheeks.

"You didn't tell me you were coming! Is this some kind of
last-minute getaway?"

"It's a getaway, that's for sure," Mira said grimly. "I left
Antonio."

"What?" Tatiana ran a hand through her platinum hair
and wrinkled her brow.

"He was cheating on me with Clara…" And then the
details of the previous afternoon followed in one great torrent
mixed with tears. The pain came rushing forth.

"You don't know how long this has been going on?"
Tatiana asked as Mira wiped her eyes and tried to regain some
sense of composure.

"I don't know how or when it started… and I don't care. I
won't go back to him. I can't. I loved him, we were together
since we were teenagers… and then he did this! Can you
imagine? I never thought it would happen to us, Tatiana.
Things were natural for us. I thought we were meant to be
together… And now that just sounds completely ridiculous!"

Mira held her face in her damp, pink cotton handkerchief.
"I was a fool," she said, her voice drowned in the soft
material.

"No you weren't," Tatiana said. "He's an asshole and a
coward. Only cowards do such things secretly rather than
ending a relationship in an honest manner."

"You can say 'I told you so' because I know you never
liked him…"

"That isn't the point. Look, I'm going to give you the keys

to my place so you can get settled right away...Will you be OK alone?"

"Of course," Mira said, feeling slightly embarrassed by the past few minutes of hysteria. "Don't worry about me."

Tatiana raised an eyebrow skeptically.

"I mean it. Really."

The clock struck the hour, and Tatiana's students began wandering into the room. The one Mira had been watching was the last to enter.

"His name is Hugo," Tatiana said softly. "He's quite an amazing actor... He's deaf, but his lip reading is so close to perfect that you never would guess. He's going to have a great career. I can sense it..."

Mira's eyes widened in surprised fascination as she glanced at Hugo's serene expression. Watching him earlier, she never would have guessed that he faced such a challenge. Before she could say another word, Tatiana had returned to class.

Chapter 9

Rafael

He met her at 120 Rue des Martyrs, the girl with the faraway eyes that were too light to be emeralds. They hardly spoke as she led him to a café down the street, but Rafael felt no discomfort in this silence. She didn't seem to either, as she flicked her cigarette into the gutter and smiled at him.

"Here it is," she said, nodding in the direction of the café, its sidewalk tables packed. Rafael had passed the place earlier that day.

"Why don't we go to the one farther down the street," he suggested. "It seemed less crowded."

She shook her head vigorously.

"The pressed lemon juice here is much better. And we'll sit inside, away from the crowd. I don't like being jammed in the middle of a bunch of people."

"That's the first thing I've learned about you," he said.

They settled down at a small round table in the back. "Other than the fact that you smoke too much," he added.

"We all have to go somehow, now don't we?" she said, using words that seemed to belong to someone much older.

"Why did you want to meet me again tonight?" he asked.

"Do you have any leads whatsoever?"

"It's a very long story…"

The waiter arrived, to Rafael's annoyance. He ordered a pressed lemon juice for Laurel and a beer for himself. When the waiter disappeared around the corner, Laurel leaned forward as if she were about to share the most important of secrets.

"I'm not from around here," she said. "I came from the south a few weeks ago, and I'm staying with my father and his ridiculous wife."

She rolled her eyes.

Rafael smiled at the liveliness that took over her face.

"I'm here for a university project. I'm writing a book… and taking a year off to do it. I'm one of those overachievers," she said with a smirk. Out of anyone else's mouth, this declaration would have been pretentious, but in Laurel's case, it only seemed like a statement of the pure and simple truth.

"What's your book about?"

"It's a secret," she said. "But maybe I'll tell you sometime."

She acted as if it were the most natural thing in the world to assume they would see each other repeatedly.

Rafael couldn't help but feel a sense of excitement building up from within at the idea of knowing more about this girl. But at the same time, his quest for Carmen was most important. He wouldn't let himself forget that.

"Look, I've run into someone named Carmen… in my travels in the neighborhood," she said, as if reading his mind.

"Where is she?"

"Hold on," she said, putting a slim hand on his. "I don't quite know. She's an acquaintance—not a friend or anything."

"So where do we go from here?"

"Let's meet again… in a week."

The waiter delivered their drinks, and Rafael took a refreshing sip.

The late summer heat and the stagnant air were nearly suffocating. In Colombia, at least, he was often outdoors, where rain washed away the grime.

Laurel held her drink between those long, pale fingers and

looked him straight in the eye.

"Tell me who you are," she said. It was almost a command.

He took a deep breath and gazed down at the table. The smooth, round marble top was permanently stained with remnants of someone else's breakfast, lunch or dinner. Then, feeling the warmth of her hand as she touched his again, he told her everything. About Diego and Tina. The night of the last emerald run. And the hasty trip to France.

Her eyes were attentive until his last words. Rafael leaned back in his seat, wondering why he had opened up to her so easily. To this girl, who wasn't ready to share much about her own life except a few vague excerpts.

"Do you want to return?" she asked.

"I don't know," he said, thinking back wistfully to the colorful plants bathed in sunlight and the warmth of his family's home. "But one thing I do know is I can't return to the emeralds. That business makes me sick."

"Did they find out who killed your parents?"

"We all know him!" he said, shaking his head. "A rival. Someone Dad knew for years and never trusted."

"What kind of prison term did this guy get?"

"The only punishment is from Dad's loyal customers, who won't ever buy emeralds from him. I hear he doesn't go to the mines much any more, though. He sends his flunkies instead."

"But what about jail?" Laurel insisted.

"Things don't work that way in the emerald business, Laurel. He's got connections in the justice system. Most guys like him do."

Laurel was silent for a moment.

"So you left everything behind," she finally said.

"My aunt, uncle and little cousins are staying in my parents' home. They said they would look after things for me. I told them I no longer wanted a part of that world."

"What are you going to do here—or anywhere—after finding Carmen?"

"That's a good question," Rafael said, with a melancholy smile. "Build my own dream, I guess." He wasn't sure what that would be, but as he looked into Laurel's confident eyes, he felt a flicker of hope.

"Why did you come to Paris?" he asked her. "You could have written a book back home. I mean it sounds like you're unhappy at your dad's place."

Laurel's spirit seemed to retreat for a moment, and then returned greater than ever.

"Paris is idyllic for writers—at least that is what I'm told. And I have a place to stay here, no matter how annoying the situation can be at times. I figured I'd live with them for the convenience."

"And your stepmother…"

"I don't refer to her as that. Basically, she's this… this bitch who stole my dad away from my mom when I was a baby. Now here she is—poor, little Cecile with her perfect family and miserable as hell."

She grinned ironically, pain and bitterness mixing for an instant in her eyes.

"Cecile thought she was smart back then going after my father, the older man. She didn't care about his wife or baby. She realizes her mistakes today, but it's too late. I bet he doesn't even see her any more and hasn't in years. He seems to look right through her. Dad's cheated on her, and she doesn't have a clue."

"How do you know all of that? I mean that your stepmom is unhappy with her life… She hasn't said anything to you?"

"She doesn't have to," Laurel said. "I'm a good observer. And I have enough experience with unfulfilling relationships… I can recognize them a mile away."

Laurel looked down, as if lost in thought. Rafael could sense that she wasn't ready to offer more than this vague explanation or talk about those who had disappointed her.

"What about your brothers or sisters…" He yearned to learn more about her so didn't want to entirely drop the subject.

"Half-siblings from the second marriage. My sister and I talk sometimes… Oh, but let's not discuss this right now, Rafael!"

"Why not?"

"I didn't realize you were so interested in me," she said

with that flirty smile and wisecracking voice.

Rafael felt the heat rise in his cheeks as it had done very often in the past several hours.

"That's all right, you don't have to answer," she said.

He didn't know what to say or what to think of this girl whose life didn't seem any clearer to him now than earlier that evening.

"Do you like being a mystery?" he asked. "Are you doing this intentionally?"

"Sometimes I'm a mystery to myself."

Rafael took a last sip of his beer and smiled at her. She grinned and leaned across the table. Her lips met his in a gentle flutter, and then she stood up. Rafael still could feel the softness of her mouth on his, but by the time he moved to reach out to her, she had run out the door.

ৎ৵৶

Rafael had rented a room on a quiet street just behind the Place Pigalle, the red-light district. The fishnet-clad legs that sauntered along the main boulevard and the sex shops and girly shows that decorated every corner didn't interest him. Rafael experienced a certain sense of relief each time he walked through the front door of his building. To him, the tiny apartment was a haven from the chaos outside. He felt rather out of place in the Pigalle area and much preferred the neighborhood charm of the Rue des Martyrs. But when he decided to come to Paris so abruptly, he didn't have much time to select accommodations.

He pulled this address out of his father's paperwork. It was a place where Diego had stayed whenever he came to Paris. He had been renting it from the same old woman—who wasn't so old in the beginning—for the past 30 years. Rafael imagined that it must have been different then. More artistic. Now, it seemed the artists had fled to the upper edges of the *butte*, Montmartre's highest point, along the base of the Sacré-Cœur Basilica. And the trendy types with their designer hand bags and vintage shoes had infiltrated the Place des Abbesses, a few blocks away from his place, but oh so unlike it. Rafael had made these observations as he wandered around the area during the past few days.

But now, he only could think of Laurel, kissing him and then dashing off in her simple yet mysterious manner... It was as if she was always in flight, and he only captured her for a few privileged moments. She reminded him of no one.

Suddenly, as he turned the corner onto the street he called his temporary home, voices jarred him from his reflections. Someone was being mugged. Adrenalin surging, Rafael ran forward, his mind racing back in time. With one crazed movement, he wrenched the man with an unshaven face and a knife away from the other. His knuckles landed squarely on the mugger's jaw and the shabby street weapon fell to the ground. The other man grabbed it and watched the scene with widened eyes as the attacker staggered away, hurling unintelligible insults.

Rafael ran a hand nervously through his hair. His own rage frightened him as he thought back to Colombia and the ease of taking someone's life in a split second. He stepped back and leaned heavily against the cold stone of the apartment building.

The man, who seemed to be about his age, approached him.

"You OK?"

Rafael returned to reality and nodded. "Just a drunk... a crazy fucked-up bastard."

"Yeah, I guess there are plenty of those around here. I should be more aware of things, but I guess my head was in the clouds... Anyway, thanks. That guy came out of nowhere."

"They usually do," Rafael said soberly.

The young man glanced at the door to the building and then back at Rafael.

"Do you live here too?"

"I'm renting a room... for a while."

"Me too." Then he held out his hand. "I'm Hugo."

"Rafael."

He handed Rafael the knife.

"You keep it... as a souvenir of bravery."

"No, that's all right... Anyone would have done the same."

Rafael smiled bitterly. If only he had the same courage back when Diego could have used it. He should have been making the trip to the mine by himself that day. But he hadn't yet felt comfortable to go it alone.

"Why don't you let me buy you a beer..." Hugo said. "You did save my neck... And it would be nice to get to know a neighbor."

"I've already had one, but after that experience, I can go for two."

Rafael led the way to the closest café, which was right around the corner. They squeezed their way by the packed tables and found a spot next to two cross dressers wearing glittering Marilyn Monroe-style clothing. Hugo's mouth turned up in a smile.

"A typical scene here," he said.

"You've gotten used to it?" Rafael asked. He wasn't the type of person to judge or criticize others. He simply found the diversity in the city curious, intriguing.

"I'm from a show-business family, and I lived in New York. Nothing shocks me."

Rafael smiled. He wondered what Diego thought about the exhibitionism around here. His old-school ideas were unlikely to have found a place in Montmartre. He couldn't imagine his father in this kind of atmosphere, where liberty of body and mind reigned. Diego was about control.

"What should bother us about this place?" Hugo asked, shrugging. "At least here, you can be yourself."

"I've always been nothing but that."

"Then you're lucky," Hugo said.

But what Rafael said was only half true. He felt a lot less like himself than he once did, because he had lost much of himself on that horrible night. The waiter approached, and Rafael distractedly ordered a house-brewed beer. Hugo asked for the same.

"How long are you planning to stay in this lovely city?" Rafael asked.

"As long as it takes for me to accomplish something: To

prove to my father that I can be a great actor on my own. I don't need his connections for that... or anything else."

So, in a different way, he was on a quest too. Rafael studied Hugo with a steady gaze. His large expressive eyes carried an openness that was foreign to Rafael, who was used to life filled with hidden thoughts and emotions. Hugo evidently was one to share his feelings immediately. For Rafael, what had happened with Laurel was an oddity. Goose bumps ran up and down his spine as he thought about everything that he had revealed to her after her simple request. Her instant power over him both frightened and intrigued him. He had to get her out of his mind. He brought his attention back to Hugo, who wrinkled his eyebrows together as if in deep thought.

"I hope things work out for you," Rafael said.

"You don't have a million questions like everyone else I've spoken with?"

"That isn't necessary. If you want to tell me more, I'll listen."

The waiter delivered their drinks, and Hugo took a long sip.

"I might take you up on that one day," he said.

Chapter 10

Cecile

It was one of those boring breakfasts with Manu's friends. Paul, an art history professor at the university, and his wife Vanessa, a talk-show hostess who no longer had a show. One Sunday a month, the two couples met for croissants, jam and coffee at their favorite sidewalk café. It was wedged into the back corner of the busy square where artists painted portraits day and night—the Place du Tertre. Cecile used the occasion to study those quick hands at work with the paintbrush and the forms that took shape in minutes. She loved watching the tourists gather in excited admiration around the intense faces immersing themselves in their work. That, in fact, was the only thing she enjoyed about these interminable dates with Paul and Vanessa, who were more Manu's friends than hers.

They loved to discuss customs of the Middle Ages or scientific discoveries or even the latest shows on the Paris stage, while Cecile would have preferred talking about the reality around her. They didn't seem to see the young girl with a charcoal-stained face who diligently worked on a drawing like it was her first or her last. And they didn't notice the toddler who just bit his sister on the arm and now was being paid back by the chubby little hand's well-prepared punch. They just blathered on endlessly.

Cecile often was tempted to get up and leave. She was almost certain they wouldn't notice. She glanced at Vanessa's silky blond French twist and elegant profile. She, like Paul, was closer to Manu's age. But she drew more young men's eyes than Cecile ever would. Vanessa knew it too. That's what made her even more annoying than her husband. In any case, the two had known Manu before he had met Cecile, so they came with the package.

Cecile slathered the sticky raspberry jam in great globs on her croissant and took a bite. Suddenly, Vanessa's high-pitched voice climbed a notch higher.

"Well, look who's here, Paul?" she grabbed the edge of his khaki silk shirt.

Then the two of them were standing up and waving. Manu was sipping his coffee in perfect tranquility and Cecile was swallowing hastily as her eyes rose from the messy plate. It was him. The artist. His eyes had captured hers, and they weren't letting go. She was frozen, unable to wipe the butter from her fingers as Paul and Vanessa jumped around like excited puppies. Cecile turned her eyes away.

She couldn't keep staring at him like that. She was certain her face was scarlet. Then Manu stood up. Everyone was standing except for her.

"Oh, our little Cecile," Vanessa was saying as if this woman of 38 was a child. Cecile stood up and wiped her hands against the snug ecru sundress that Joel told her was awesome even if she didn't believe him.

"Don't be shy, Cecile," Vanessa cajoled. "Cecile, Manu, this is Septime Galino, an artist friend of ours."

He leaned forward and kissed Cecile on both cheeks. She closed her eyes slightly, inhaling the clean woodsy scent of his skin. Cecile felt as if all eyes were on them. She stepped back quickly, hoping no one had noticed the heat that had risen to her scalp and now was coursing through her entire body.

She glanced up again at the large hazel eyes and the wavy chestnut hair pushed back from his face as he shook hands with Manu. He wore a blue linen shirt over jeans, and exuded the confidence of one who had places to go and people to see.

"Sit down, please," Paul was saying, pulling a chair next to him from a nearby table.

"I can't stay," Septime said. Cecile noticed a slight Italian accent that made his words dance. "I have an exhibit."

"Oh, come on, we haven't seen each other in ages, and you've just met our charming friends Manu and Cecile."

"All right," Septime said, with a smile in Cecile's direction. "How can I refuse the company of such a couple?"

Cecile took a nervous sip of her tepid-turned-cold coffee.

"So Septime, what kind of exhibit are we talking about?" Manu asked.

"A collection that represents modern art of the past 20 years."

"Ah… interesting. Where are you showing?"

"The Marceau Gallery… right around the corner."

As he talked, his eyes strayed to Cecile. She felt trapped. Her glance fell into her plate, to the scattered crumbs.

"We'll have to swing by soon, won't we Cecile?" Manu was saying.

Cecile swallowed hard. She couldn't stay there like that with four pairs of eyes studying her. She stood up. She had an idea.

"Cecile, what's the matter?" Manu asked, reaching for her hand. But she brushed it away.

"I have to meet Viv at ballet," she said. It wasn't a complete lie. Cecile had promised her daughter that she would meet her after class, but she still had plenty of time.

"On Sunday?" Vanessa said, raising her eyebrows.

"She's training for an important audition, if you have to know." Cecile couldn't help snapping back as she gathered up her sweater and little clutch bag.

Just then, Septime stood up.

"I'll follow you into the square," he said. "I really must be going too."

Cecile hurried away as he was bidding the others goodbye. But moments later she could feel his footsteps close behind. They passed by overcrowded café tables until their feet found the cobblestone street. Cecile darted between tourists who lingered everywhere and hurried toward a narrow street that led out of the square.

"Cecile…"

She heard his voice, imagined his eyes. No, she told herself. Don't stop. She knew she would be the loser in this situation. What could he possibly want with a mother of two who had no sense of direction in life and whose major joy was eating sugar doughnuts and daydreaming?

He caught up with her and touched her hand. She stopped and swiveled around. She felt as if flames were snapping from her eyes. She resented him for bringing any sense of turmoil to her boring, yet comfortable lifestyle.

"Why were you sketching me the other day? Watching me stuff my face? Was it for some sort of comic relief?"

"There's nothing wrong with a woman caught in a moment of peaceful reflection. It's inspiring, Cecile. I do have the right to draw what I choose…"

"Why did you leave it behind?"

"For you."

"What do you mean?"

"I knew you would want it. You needed it to see within yourself."

He smiled, but she refused to return the expression.

"Let's go for a walk," he said.

"What are you trying to accomplish?" she asked. Cecile felt invigorated, as if some strange challenge had been placed before her.

"Come with me," he said. She glanced at the people streaming by them from every direction. No one seemed to notice that they stood frozen to the spot locked in tense conversation. The world continued beyond.

"I have to meet my daughter," Cecile said with determination.

"I'll walk with you."

"Look, I'm a married woman…"

"You think I'm out to seduce you?"

Cecile blushed and looked down. Now would come the big rejection that would make her feel like two cents.

"Well… you're right."

Her eyes widened. He was trying to make a fool of her. That had to be it. He wanted to see how far this would go. She turned around and ran. But he followed. She turned a corner, and he caught up with her at the end of the street. He took her hand. She pulled away.

"I meant what I said."

"You don't even know me!"

"Does your husband really know you?"

Cecile sighed.

"That isn't any of your business.... Why did you come here anyway? What made you decide to pick me for whatever you're trying to do instead of someone a little more your type? That would make more sense."

"What's my type?"

"Younger, prettier… single, for instance."

"I'll answer your questions if you give me a few minutes."

"I'm listening."

"Not here. Follow me."

She hesitated for a moment. But Cecile never won the battle when her curiosity appeared.

"Fine," she said. "But it's going to have to be quick."

He led her back to her secret place. That patch of grass where he had been sitting, just in front of the almost-hidden bench. She sank to the ground beside him, not caring if grass stains ruined her skirt.

"OK, start talking…"

"Your face…something about it. A longing. That inspired me."

"And?"

"You can't expect me to explain away the magic, Cecile. Art doesn't work that way. Inspiration can't be understood."

"So that's why you supposedly want to seduce me?"

He took her hand. Her reasonable self wanted to pull away, but she ignored that little voice.

"I wondered if I would see you again. I told myself that if I did, I wouldn't let you slip away."

"Septime… unusual name for an unusual person."

"The seventh child…"

"… of a large family. I hope the others aren't like you."

"I'm serious about this, Cecile."

Cecile loosened her fingers from his and stood up. She thought of his drawing of her, hidden away in her secret drawer at home. She should have thrown it away.

"Meet me at the gallery tomorrow night. I'm having a cocktail party…"

She shook her head.

"I can't parade around like that. I'm a married woman. I don't do that kind of thing…"

"Does that negate it in the future as well?" he asked with a sparkle in his eyes.

"And what if I don't come? What if I say yes to get away from you and then I change my mind?"

"Then I'll find you and seduce you in another way."

Cecile couldn't help but laugh. She had to leave him while she still had an ounce of self-respect. She waved him away and started the trek toward Viv. She pretended to be one of those strong-minded women who knew exactly what she wanted out of life.

"You'll see, Cecile," he called after her. She could hear his laughter, and in her mind's eye, she saw his smile. A small shiver ran up her spine as she wondered for an instant what life would be like with Septime.

෴

Viv's eyes were bright red. That was the first thing Cecile noticed when she found her daughter sitting on the front steps of the place that for years had been her second home. Her hair, pulled from its usual bun, fell messily around her shoulders, and she twisted the ends with nervous fingers. In a matter of 24 hours, Cecile had witnessed her composed daughter unravel.

"Viv, what happened?"

"It's me… I was awful."

"C'mon," Cecile said, taking her daughter's hand and lifting her from the ground. "It's one class, Viv, one session. Tomorrow will be better. That's how you have to look at it."

But Cecile felt as if her words were useless, empty. She

had nothing motivational to say to her daughter. Viv nodded her head anyway.

"I didn't think you were going to show up," she said, changing the subject too quickly for Cecile's taste. But Cecile knew she never could obtain information from Viv by force. She was convinced that something else was bothering her daughter, but uncovering the truth would be nearly impossible. Cecile knew her children took advantage of this lack of authority, but it had gone on for so long that she was certain it couldn't be corrected.

"Did you actually stay at brunch this whole time?"

"Yes of course! Where else would I be, Vivienne?" Cecile's words ran together nervously as she was questioned by this teenager, who sometimes seemed so much older. Viv shrugged her shoulders.

"I don't know. But I do know how you feel about Paul and Vanessa."

Cecile gave her a wry smile. "What do you mean?"

She never before had shared her feelings about them with the kids or with Manu.

"You think they're a big bore," Viv said.

They were silent for a moment as they passed through the narrow winding cobblestone streets to make their way around the busy square. Avoiding the craziness of that place on a walk home from ballet was an unspoken agreement.

"How do you know that, Viv?"

"Mom," she said, pronouncing the word she said so little, "it's obvious from the look on your face when you're with them or when you get home from the Sunday brunch."

"And you noticed?"

"Yes, that's what I'm saying... And I don't blame you. That Vanessa character drives me nuts when she starts talking about how she used to do ballet... Every time she sees me it's the same thing, the same stories."

Cecile listened to the thing closest to a confidence she ever had extracted from Viv. And for once, with her daughter, she experienced a moment of solidarity.

Chapter 11

Andre

The lights dimmed except for the spots on Andre. He belted out a song about saying goodbye in the hushed theater where the greatest stars had passed their most glorious moments. Andre had been looking forward to this—the best item on his agenda by a long shot—for months. It was a special evening of music featuring a lineup of singers most known for their roles in musicals. He had been asked to choose a song, so he selected one that would bring tears to the many eyes upon him. He would never admit it, but the reason he poured so much energy into those words was because they expressed the sadness he felt within.

The rush that surged through him with each performance was stronger than ever as he stood there, almost steadily in the misty light from above, sweat pouring down his temples. The final note and then applause—joyous applause that made Andre's face light up for the first time in a long while.

A scrim descended before him, masking his less-than-graceful exit from the stage. He made his way through the dingy hallway, accepting the accolades of the technicians and a couple of singers he had known for years, but he didn't linger.

He returned to the dressing room for a touchup on his face powder. There was one more performance and this one would be the most difficult. A duet with Clarisse. They had been booked to do this show a year ago, before the accident and the problems it had unleashed.

How would they ever get through the song filled with passion that they had chosen specifically for what would be their first and only duet? He had seen her outside her dressing room earlier, waiting for something or someone. He could tell by the impatient look in her black eyes outlined in charcoal for the stage. Her long, dark hair was wound into a bun on the top of her head and she wore a silver-beaded gown that reminded him of falling raindrops. It was a vision from the past. A scene from the day they met. Except instead of a warm smile, she looked at him emptily and turned away.

"Clarisse, we have a show to do," Andre had whispered.

"Don't worry, I won't humiliate you by a less than stellar performance," she said coolly. "But I'm not doing it for you, Andre. I'm doing it for the audience who paid to see us singing happily together like the perfect couple."

No one knew of their separation. Andre preferred to keep it quiet. He didn't like being the subject of scandalous press. Clarisse agreed to it, as she never had appreciated her private life being made public either.

Andre slipped out of his blue silk shirt and changed into a gray suit for the next performance. Calmly, he went through his breathing exercises and tried to push thoughts of the day Clarisse left him out of his mind.

But that proved impossible. He had come home from a doctor's appointment that day to find her packing suitcases. She seemed startled to see him as she looked up from the clothing strewn across the bed. He could still see her hair, falling like a glossy curtain across the amethyst sweater he had given her for Valentine's Day.

"What's going on here?" he asked, his voice hardly able to make it out of his throat.

"I'm leaving, Andre," she said simply.

"Wait a minute," he replied, lurching forward as best as he could and grabbing her hand away from the skirts she was folding into her leather overnight bag. She had said those clichéd words that he had heard in God-only-knew how many shitty films. "What are you talking about, Clarisse?"

He knew she had been distant for weeks, but he hadn't expected this.

Clarisse pulled away. She looked up at him in silence for a moment. The longest silence he had ever known.

"It's your whole career, Andre," she finally said. "After being married to you for five years, I finally woke up. I'm now realizing that your career is what's fulfilling you—not us."

"That isn't true!" he had exclaimed, sitting down beside her. But he knew deep inside that he was lying. Clarisse was part of his lifestyle. She was the woman on his arm when he sauntered about town in those pre-accident days. Everyone had admired them as they made their way from one glitzy party to the next. But their relationship never had made it to the next level, to where emotion overtakes the superficial.

"If it isn't true, why can't you accept what's happened? Why can't love be enough?"

"It is, Clarisse!" he pleaded, hating himself for his lies.

"No, it's not."

The conversation went on and on with her insisting and him negating. But in the end, Clarisse still picked up her bags and walked out on him and the fucking museum of an apartment that she had decorated with too many delicate, ornate paintings of 18th century heroes for Andre's taste.

"Andre Wren to stage right..." The words came too quickly, and in a way, they came just in time. He straightened his tie with determination. He had to face Clarisse.

They met at center stage, and she took his hand as the curtain rose. Then she looked at him with tender eyes and began to sing. He joined her, wishing this was his reality, wishing that life was indeed a stage.

෴

It was late when Andre stumbled through the front door. He threw down the blue duffle bag that he had been carrying to shows ever since his first and made his way into the kitchen for a drink. The place really did look bare without Clarisse. She had taken the paintings from the hallway, the 1940s movie photos from the sitting room, the fluted vases that always had held fresh flowers, and half of the volumes from the antique bookshelves. Andre tried to fill the emptiness by leaving papers and open books on the coffee table or wherever he happened to be when he finished reading them. But nothing seemed to fill the void.

He pushed through the swinging wooden door and stepped into the kitchen. He had gone out for a few beers with some of the other singers and avoided questions about Clarisse. He said she had gone home with a headache. After hearing his companions laughing and saying what a great couple Andre and Clarisse Wren were, he was the one with a headache. He wanted nothing but a glass of water and an aspirin.

He chugged the medicine and hit the flashing button on his answering machine. He never left his cell phone on when he was doing a show or immediately following it, so he wasn't surprised that Jack had left a message here. He rattled off a list of auditions—some less interesting than others—and told Andre to call him no matter what the time. Andre flipped up his middle finger at the phone. That bullshit would have to wait until tomorrow. He wasn't in the mood to argue, and he knew this would put him in a vulnerable position with his agent. He wouldn't ever let go of the upper hand.

Andre was about to turn away when a soft voice came across the line. He froze.

"It's June... look, I'm calling because I know Hugo has gotten in touch with you. I hope things are working out all right. There wasn't anything I could do to stop him."

He hadn't heard her voice in years, but it hadn't changed a bit.

"I'm here in Paris... I need to speak with you. I'm staying at the Hotel du Canal. You remember the little café right around the corner facing the water? I'll be there tomorrow at noon."

Andre sank onto one of the black leather stools pushed up against the counter and looked into the phone as if he was gazing into June's eyes. He was afraid to see her, afraid of hearing that she had found a better life without him.

Chapter 12

Mira

"Fancy seeing you here," Mira said, her voice steady and her gaze cool.

Her brother had been chatting with one of the many admirers and art critics attending the cocktail party to kick off his exhibit. Now, he broke away and turned to her with startled eyes.

"Mir... I'm shocked."

"You do recognize me then..."

"You're all grown up! It's been forever and yet... What are you doing here?"

"Just strolling by Paris," she said, shrugging her shoulders haughtily.

He took her by the hand and led her to a little alcove illuminated by red lights.

"Makes the painting, doesn't it?" he said, nodding at the colors flickering across the oil paint.

She gazed at the odd ovals in various shades of yellow and the violent slashes that cut through them. It was simply atrocious.

"I'm not much for modern art, but you do have a way

with it…"

"As you have a way with portraits. I've read some pretty favorable reviews of your work and seen some of it in the papers on trips back home."

"So you did know that I was still alive?" she said, sarcastically. "I guess that's something."

"Mira, I didn't have a choice," Septime said, lowering his voice to a near whisper. She looked away from the painting and into the eyes that seemed to see right inside her mind. It was as if she and Septime were alone in this room filled with paintings, brightly colored dresses and laughter that jingled along with the wine glasses.

"You mean you were forced to turn your back on me? Oh, I see…" She tried unsuccessfully to hide the bitterness in her voice.

"Mira, don't… You have to understand that I was a in a bad situation for a long time. Things have only improved over the past two years."

"I invited you to my gallery last year, Septime! You could have made the effort."

"It was too difficult… I didn't want you to know the truth, Mir. I didn't want anyone to know. And hardly anyone did."

Mira folded her arms across the black beads that covered her dress and glared at Septime. The yellow lights beaming from lamps above emphasized the dark circles under her brother's eyes. He looked tired, worn out. But Mira wouldn't back down.

"Tell me now," she nearly commanded. "I'm tired of lies."

Septime leaned closer to her.

"Drugs, Mira!" he cried out in a hushed voice. "They ruled everything. It wasn't pot any more… far from it… It was the hard stuff. My life was a goddamn mess. I didn't want you to know I had changed and given in… that I was weak. I didn't want you to see me that way…"

Mira looked at him blankly. Sure, he had his problems in the past, but the idea of him relinquishing control of his life to anyone or anything seemed totally out of character.

"But your art," she said in a dull voice. "Didn't you worry

about being able to function, to create? I never would have thought you would take such a risk, Septime!"

"Mira, to create, I felt as if I needed every damn pill and needle I could get my hands on! It took me years to realize that I could live and work without drugs. That's why I stopped seeing Mom and Dad."

"You mean they knew?"

He nodded.

"Why didn't they tell me? Did they actually think I would copy you or something? Because I admired you? As if I'm that easily led…"

"It's not that, Mira. They didn't want you wasting time on me. And I had to get my life together on my own."

"Are you back on speaking terms now?"

"Things are strained. We're better off apart… You're better off without me, as well. I'm not the person you thought I was, Mira. If I had been, I wouldn't have gone down that road, and I never would have turned my back on you. I'm sorry."

"Me too."

Mira didn't know if she wanted to run out the door or stay at Septime's side forever. She hated and loved him all at once. She was fascinated and disgusted by him, by his art. She wanted to understand him.

Mira looked up at her brother strangely, as if seeing him for the first time. And then, the moment of solitude they had shared disappeared. Septime's eyes had caught hold of something in the distance. Something that filled them with awe. It was a face Mira had never seen before.

A woman across the room who looked as if she wanted to be anywhere but here. She wore a colorful, striped Mexican skirt that fell in silky folds to her ankles and a raspberry top that made her cheeks appear flushed. But what interested Mira was her face. A very plain, unlovely one, with the exception of her eyes. They were observant eyes that had stories to tell.

"Who is she?" Mira asked.

"You should stay out of this, Mira."

"Why? Give me one good reason!"

"OK, fine. You want to meet her? Well, then I'll introduce

you. But I don't want any commentary." Septime took Mira by the hand and crossed the room with authoritative steps.

The woman wanted to turn and run. Mira could see it in her eyes. But she remained rooted to the spot. Mira could sense Septime's desire for this woman as she followed him, sidestepping paintings, satiny skirts and trays of drinks swirling by.

"Cecile," Septime said, taking the woman's hand. Right away, Mira noticed the wedding band on the freckly finger. That was it. That's why Septime didn't want Mira to get involved. She looked into the woman's hesitant eyes, and a story began to develop in her mind. Septime was trying to seduce Cecile, and she wasn't yet ready to succumb to his charm. There was something like guilt in her expression.

But what Mira didn't understand was Septime's attraction to this woman so unlike the ravishing beauties he always had dated before. She hadn't seen her brother in years, but she'd heard about the women by his side at exhibit openings and dinners. There seemed to be a constant supply of them at his doorstep.

"This is my sister, Mira," he said.

Mira nodded and smiled, feeling uncomfortable because of Cecile's emotions, blatantly exposed on her face. It was as if Septime enjoyed this uncertainty, this sensation of being on the edge.

"You decided to accept my invitation," he said with a sly smile.

"I wanted to see what this exhibit was about."

"That's all?"

"Yes." She turned, and Septime grabbed her arm.

"Where are you going?"

"Coming here was a mistake."

And then a band of waiters swished by, offering Cecile enough room to break free from Septime. Mira followed her. Before Septime could say another word, she had managed a quick escape through the art lovers who held her brother back. None of them cared about Mira, this rather unknown artist who wasn't publicly recognized as Septime's sister.

Mira ran awkwardly in her silver, high-heeled sandals until

she reached Cecile. They were both outside, lost among crowds lingering in the cool, evening air.

"Hold on, Cecile, it's just me…"

The woman turned around, her skirt floating to a halt in swirls of purples, reds and yellows. She looked at Mira inquisitively with, for the first time, a spark of feistiness in her blue-gray eyes.

"You can tell him I had a moment of weakness—my curiosity," she said. "Now that it's satisfied, he won't see me again!"

The tone of her voice didn't convince Mira.

"I didn't follow you for him," Mira said.

Cecile looked down for a moment, obviously embarrassed.

"Then why did you?" she asked.

"I'm curious too… I don't quite understand my brother…"

Cecile shook her head. "I would be the last person to ask," she said. "I hardly know him, and I certainly don't understand him. I refuse to get involved in his family problems."

Cecile turned around and continued on her way. Mira followed.

"You like him, don't you?" she asked. They were strolling down a narrow cobblestone passage, lined by artist studios and apartments on each side. The two women had walked far enough from the gallery to let down their guard.

Cecile was silent for a moment. "He's interesting, and there hasn't been much to draw my attention in a while."

"Then why won't you see him again?"

Cecile stopped and looked intently at Mira. Her eyes had little silver flecks in them that seemed to pulsate in agitation.

"I don't think it would be a good idea," she said. "I have a marriage to think of…"

Mira hoped that for this woman's sake, her husband had a better sense of loyalty than Antonio.

"Septime likes you a lot," Mira said. "What did you do to put him under such a spell?"

Cecile blushed up to her hairline. "I'm not one of the

usual beauties, I guess."

"No, I didn't mean it that way." Mira's words rushed out. "You just seem to be more intelligent and clear-headed than the usual ones…"

"Me, clear-headed?" she said with a slight laugh. "I certainly haven't felt that way lately!"

"Well, we can't be perfect all of the time…"

"I'm far from it, Mira. If anything, what Septime might like about me is that I showed him a reality. It's not pretty, and it's not exciting, but it's my life. Anything but perfect."

And with that simple statement, she'd hit the nail on the head. Mira was sure of it. Reality: the one element missing in the life of Septime Galino.

Mira curled up on her side and pulled the fluffy comforter over her head. She took several deep breaths, hoping that would calm the nausea. It had gotten worse over the past few days, waking her in the early morning hours. Then by 9 or so, she was exhausted and back under the covers. She was pregnant. That drugstore test she took last night proved it with an electric blue plus sign. A tear slipped out of the corner of her eye as she thought back to the dream that seemed so real. She and Antonio were sitting in the park under blooming chestnut trees as they did when they used to have time for each other. As little white and pink flowers cascaded from the branches above, she told Antonio about the baby. He pulled her into his arms. She could feel the warmth of his skin against hers.

Mira wiped the tears away and continued her deep breaths. She was trying not to panic. She would have to tell Antonio and maybe even return to him. Either that, or go through this pregnancy alone. The thought of solitude terrified her, yet the idea of maintaining a broken relationship seemed much worse.

Of course she could try to convince herself that they had a chance if they really wanted to take it. She and Antonio had been spending less time together than they did a few years ago, but that wasn't by choice. It was simply the fault of work schedules, her gallery exhibits and his corporate cocktail parties. Ever since her departure, Mira kept asking herself how and why their relationship had ended up in shambles. She hadn't seen it coming. It was like she had been anesthetized these past few months. And then, abruptly, she came back to life, to a shocking reality. Mira didn't know how she could possibly see beyond this betrayal and return to him. Then she thought of the baby.

A buzzing sound broke into her thoughts. Throwing the covers aside, she looked around as if expecting to find the source of it. She could hear the steady sound of water flowing at the end of the hall. Tatiana was in the shower. Mira glanced at the clock. 10 a.m. The buzzing sound again. The doorbell. Of course.

Mira stumbled across the room and pulled open the door.

"Hi, I'm here to see Tatiana... It's about a portrait."

"A portrait? ... I don't understand..." Mira rubbed her eyes sleepily, half hidden behind the door as she addressed Hugo for the first time.

"I really didn't feel comfortable refusing her," he said.

At that moment, Tatiana flew out of the bedroom in her purple peignoir.

"You're here—perfect!" She kissed Hugo on both cheeks and led him inside. Mira didn't know if she was more annoyed at her friend's interference or thrilled by the opportunity to paint the calm combination of hope and desperation she had discovered in Hugo's face the first time she saw him. She had told Tatiana later in the day that he would make a good portrait model. Portraits always had been Mira's specialty.

"I think this is the best thing for you," Tatiana now said to her. "While you get dressed, I'll show Hugo to your rooftop studio."

Mira shook her head, but decided to play along. Maybe an interesting new project would do her some good. In any case, she had to get her mind off the pregnancy test, Antonio and Clara.

During the past few days, she had tried painting a few floral scenes in the makeshift studio she had set up on the terrace sprawling along part of the roof, but she wasn't inspired. She never liked those kinds of paintings anyway.

"What should I do?" Hugo asked as Mira arrived under the sun and among the overgrown plants. She had thrown on an old pair of jeans and a smock, and tucked her unruly curls under a scarf.

Mira sat down at her easel, tore up a half-finished still life of yellow roses and looked at Hugo, who was grinning at her.

"I hope that isn't your reaction after you paint my portrait..."

She shook her head vigorously.

"Never... Portraits are different. They're stories about people. I couldn't destroy that."

"How did Tatiana get you to agree to this anyway?" she continued. "She did tell you it would take several sittings, right?"

He sat down facing her. It was amazing how he read her lips so quickly, almost imperceptibly.

"She told me it would be a valuable exercise for me as an actor, so I agreed to it. And by the way, you don't have to speak slowly. I can keep up with you...." He smiled as he said these words. "Don't feel uncomfortable... and I'll try not to feel uncomfortable modeling for you."

She felt the heat in her face reach her scalp. "All right, it's a deal."

Mira glanced from his face to the paper, and for the first time since she arrived, she didn't have a mental block on where to start. "How did you lose your hearing?" she asked.

"I had the mumps when I was seven... and this is the result."

"It must have been difficult, learning a new way of communication."

"I think it was in the very beginning, but I don't remember much from back then. I feel as if I've always been this way. It's normal for me."

"Where are you from? Why did you come here?"

"Are you sure you want to hear an earful?"

Mira had begun to capture the fine lines of his features.

"I don't like working in silence... and I'd rather recreate

the face of someone I know."

"Did you ever feel like the more you've spoken with someone, the more you find it impossible to understand him?"

"Yes, unfortunately."

"Well, that's how I feel about my father—Andre Wren."

Mira hesitated for a moment and squinted her eyes thoughtfully. *The actor!* The pompous guy who always lunched at the café downstairs. Tatiana had told her about him.

"He doesn't even know I'm deaf," Hugo said.

"Why didn't you tell him?"

"It wouldn't change the fact that he never wanted to be a father. I talked to him a few days ago. It was the first time since I was a kid. I don't want to tell him my problems. I don't need sympathy."

"But he'll have to come around at some point... He needs one little thing to make a spark."

"No, he left the only one who could light that spark long ago. Her name is June, and she's my mother."

Chapter 13

Rafael

Rafael sat on the front stoop, the pleasant breeze tousling his hair, and held the envelope between his hands. A first-class letter from Bogotá. It was from his aunt Mariana. He could sense that it was important by the careful handwriting rather than her usual scribbles. But he didn't quite understand why she hadn't simply called him. Money wasn't an issue in the Mendez family even though Rafael pushed away his connection with such riches. The emerald business had left them comfortable, and Rafael had inherited the greatest fortune the family had to offer. But he didn't care. He had traveled to Paris with a simple suitcase and a few belongings that carried only sentimental value. As long as he had enough to live on, money wasn't important to him. He associated it with the danger and greed of the emerald trade. This was what separated him from Diego, whose taste called for 18-karat gold and the priciest champagnes.

"I thought I could bring you into this business by enticing you with a fancy car or a promise of vacations in trendy places," his father had said as the two of them made one of the early trips to the mines together. "But I was wrong. All of these years, Raf, and I don't know you. But you'll learn, kid. You'll have to. Change is good."

Then he laughed roguishly and continued steering through the underbrush. Rafael remained silent by his side. He was following in his father's footsteps out of honor for his family, and this was the closest Diego had ever come to recognizing it.

Rafael's attention returned to the letter. With nervous hands, he pulled open the paper.

My Dear Rafael,

I hope this letter finds you well and undiscouraged in your quest for your birth mother. (Here, Rafael knitted his brow in surprise— He hadn't told Diego's sister why he had come to Paris.) *I've thought this over quite a lot and have decided that I must do everything I can to help you, even if it is simply passing on this address. It seems to be Carmen's, and I hope you will find her there. I came upon it in some of your father's things in the office. The new renter discovered a closet filled with papers. The rest were related to old emerald transactions. This was the only thing of a personal nature.*

Rafael couldn't even finish the rest of the letter. He had no time to lose. He stuffed the paper into his pocket and hurried along the cobblestone street to the main boulevard.

৩৵৻৶

The apartment was across the Seine River, burrowed within the neighborhood that was home to students and young people lingering in cafes. Rafael hadn't yet visited this part of the city. He liked it immediately for its trees, sleepy little storefronts and the laughter he heard in the streets. The building was one of those former bourgeois homes, long ago split into several apartments. Rafael recognized the style, with scalloped edges and balconies. He rang for the concierge, and when she popped her head through the door, he asked for Madame Pantin. She was the owner of several apartments in the building, according to his aunt's letter, and certainly would know where Carmen lived.

"Who should I tell her is calling?" the small, white-haired woman asked.

"She doesn't know me. My name is Rafael Mendez, and I'm looking for someone named Carmen."

The woman repeated the message into a telephone, nodded several times and then hung up.

"She'll see you," she said, directing Rafael up to the fifth floor. Relief and excitement ran through him as he took the stairs two at a time. But deep inside, he knew the search could never be this easy. He refused euphoria.

The woman was waiting for him on the landing.

"Finally," she said. "Finally, someone here to clear up this whole story!"

Rafael raised an eyebrow and studied her for a moment, this 50ish woman with a blond chignon and a flowing tangerine dress.

"I'm looking for Carmen," he said.

"Well, I was hoping you could tell me where I could find her!"

"What do you mean?"

"She disappeared almost a year ago and never returned. And she left her belongings behind—or at least some of them. No note. Nothing."

"Tell me about her."

"So you're like me… You've never met her. I bought my apartments right after she disappeared. The former owner told me that a person named Carmen rented this particular one, but had vanished. I know I should clear out the place and rent it—I have the right to do so—but I can't…" The woman shook her head. "There's something left here… I can't bring myself to disrupt it."

"Can I take a look?"

"Be my guest…" She reached into her pocket, pulled out a ring of keys and unfastened one. "Here you go."

"Thank you," he said. But the woman already had returned to her apartment.

Rafael made his way to the end of the hall, the hardwood floor creaking under his heels. He turned his key in the lock, feeling like an intruder in this abandoned place.

A whiff of dampness mixed with a stale scent of old roses hit him as he entered the one room that had been home to Carmen. His eyes traveled throughout the humble abode: from the single, unmade bed with flowery sheets to the square table with a box of granola cereal on it, to the French windows firmly closed behind silky drapes. He took a step forward as the dressing table in the corner caught his attention. A few bright scarves, a tube of red lipstick and some magazines were scattered along the scratched wood top.

The magazines were what told Rafael a little more about Carmen. She had to be a teenager or maybe in her early 20s, he thought as he flipped through pages with a beauty guide for summer vacation and tips on how to impress college men. He opened the single drawer, but the only thing left was a brush with a couple of long black hairs twisted through its bristles.

The kitchen wasn't a separate room. It was a corner with a hotplate and a mini-refrigerator, which was empty except for a few bottles of water.

Rafael crossed the room in two strides and opened the door to the wardrobe to find empty hangers dangling from a rickety wooden bar. On the floor, covered with dust, there was a photo album. A heavy, leather one with a silver binding. Slowly, he knelt down and opened the cover before his weary conscience could stop him. And he was certain the picture on the very first page was of his birth mother.

He drew in a sharp breath, recognizing his own eyes in hers. He felt dizzy as he drank in every detail. Her hair fell in ringlets to her chin and she looked into the camera with a half-smile that seemed to bring her face to life on paper. Around her neck, she wore a black cord with a piece of Venetian glass dangling from it.

He flipped to the next page, but it was empty, as were the others after it. What was most frustrating was the fact that it hadn't always been empty. The other photos had been torn out. He could tell by the marks left behind. Rafael turned back to the first page. The photo was old, of Marie in her mid-20s perhaps. He wanted so much to take this rare souvenir with him, but he couldn't. He already had intruded. Rafael gingerly placed the album on the floor of the wardrobe and made his way to the front door. His only hope was the return of Carmen.

Madame Pantin was in the hallway making her way toward him as he closed the door.

"There's one thing I brought into my apartment for security reasons," she said. She held out her hand and in it sat an emerald ring. Rafael's breath caught in his throat.

"Here, have a closer look," she said.

He took it in his hands and studied the rare qualities that he immediately had recognized. It was one of their stones. One of their best stones. Diego only sold them to his loyal customers, those highly reputable sellers that counted the rich and famous among their clients. Even Tina wouldn't allow herself to keep a stone like this one. How did this girl end up with such an emerald?

"Are you all right?"

He nodded, but he hardly could hear her words.

"I'm holding onto this until she returns," the woman said in matter-of-fact voice.

"Why didn't you keep it?" Rafael said, surprised by the woman's honesty.

"And have bad luck?"

"I've never heard that one before…"

"Well, I take it seriously. A piece of jewelry is meant for its true owner and no one else."

Rafael smiled numbly at the woman and took one last look at the stone.

"I have to see Carmen," he said. "It's extremely important. When and if she returns, could you please call me?"

He pulled a notepad and pencil out of his shirt pocket and scribbled down his name and number. He knew it was a long shot, but it was all he had.

"What if I never find Carmen?"

"What if you do?" Hugo said.

"Yeah, think positively…" Rafael sighed. He was standing at his door facing this person who quickly had become a friend when he heard rapid footsteps flying up the staircase. Hugo looked down at his feet, where the vibrations made the floor shudder.

"Someone's in a rush," he said. Then he patted Rafael on the shoulder. "Keep the faith... Things will work out. I wanted to tell you about an amazing experience I had today... but it'll have to wait. I've got to run to work. I'm doing the last part of someone's shift."

Hugo hurried in the opposite direction as that taken by the climbing feet. Rafael felt guilty about dominating their short conversation. He wasn't used to leaning on anyone's shoulder. He scolded himself for his own weakness.

Rafael was about to close the door when a familiar voice echoing in the hallway nearly made him jump. Laurel stood at the top of the steps, her red hair tangled around her shoulders and her eyes glistening with unshed tears.

It was the first time he noticed even a hint of vulnerability in this girl. In an instant, he took her hand and pulled her against him. He didn't ask how she knew where he lived or why she had come. He just wanted to feel her skin against his. He wanted to shelter her from whatever woes had overcome her. Laurel carried a sense of sorrow that seemed to perfectly reflect his feelings of the past six months. She let him lead her into the apartment.

He unlaced the cotton straps down her back and watched her red sundress slip to the ground in a heap. A sparkle returned to her eyes as she unbuttoned his shirt and slid with him onto the sheets. Her skin was soft against his, and wore the same musky perfume that had installed itself in his memory when he saw her for the first time.

ি৯৯

Laurel switched the station to a tango and settled into his arms.

"I love this music," she said. "It gets in my head and takes me to faraway places... kind of like the effect you have on me."

Rafael kissed her delicately on the ear and looked into her

eyes as she turned to face him. It was now that his thoughts returned to the desperation he found in her earlier that night.

"What was wrong, Laurel? Why did you come here? How did you know where to find me?"

Her eyes clouded over, and she sat up and twisted the white cotton sheets in her hands.

"I followed you that very first night we met," she said. "I slipped back outside and ran after you. I wanted to make sure that if you never returned, I would at least know that you weren't a figment of my imagination." She grinned and watched her own fingers as if they were of particular interest.

"And then I was supposed to meet someone who could lead us to Carmen," she blurted out. "But I screwed up. I'm sorry. It was my fault, but I had no choice. I was with my sister, and I couldn't leave her... I was sure she was going to do something crazy."

Her hands began to shake, and he took them in his. "What's happened with your sister?"

"My innocent little sister Viv found letters to my dad from some woman he's obviously having an affair with. They were pretty graphic. Anyway, she hasn't told Cecile. I don't pity Cecile or anything because she knew how to break up my parents' marriage. But I'm worried about Viv. She shouldn't have to bear the burden of keeping that secret.

"I stayed with her until everyone got home, and then I remembered that I missed the meeting..."

She held a hand to her temple and shook her head.

"That's OK," he said, drawing her into his arms again. And he meant it.

"Look, it's not like I won't see this woman again... I'll take care of it."

Rafael couldn't help but think that certain parts of Laurel's story were dubious, but he wouldn't push her away. It was too late. She had entangled him in a web of emotions that he couldn't quite understand. He had never wanted a girl as much as he wanted her. He couldn't let her go.

Chapter 14

Cecile

Cecile yearned to forget about that seductive look in Septime's eyes and the way he called out to her as she turned away. She yearned to forget the artwork that she found ugly, yet intriguing. And she wished she could stop thinking about her conversation with Septime's sister, an ethereal young woman with eyes that danced as she spoke. Several days had passed. She hadn't returned to her once-favorite spot in Montmartre. Instead, she had turned her attention to Viv, who didn't seem to appreciate much of it. She was spending more and more of her time with Laurel.

Cecile pretended that she didn't care, but seeing the two of them smiling at one another across the dinner table sickened her. She never had liked her stepdaughter, a rather eccentric girl who seemed to have everyone in the house eating out of her hand. Except for Joel. But he had just left for boarding school so Cecile no longer had him around for moral support.

Behind everyone's back, Laurel would strike out at Cecile. The words she said a day ago rang clear in Cecile's mind. A voice filled with venom: *I don't understand why you ask about my mother's condition, Cecile. You didn't seem to care about her when you broke up her marriage.*

And Cecile was left speechless because Laurel's words were true. But it was unnecessary to bring up that story two decades later. It was over now. It didn't matter any longer. At least that's what she always told herself.

In any case, Laurel had been difficult since she was a child. Then, it was sullen looks and disobedience. Now, it was about words that hit home. Manu wouldn't hear of putting her out— not his precious first-born darling. And Viv thought she was fascinating—or about as fascinating as a delinquent can be, Cecile thought with annoyance as she walked through the front door with a bag of groceries. She was expecting to find silence. Instead, all that she could hear was tango music, which she hated for its reminder of the days when she was free. When she was 18. When she went to clubs and danced the tango with a different man every night. Before she became this woman who witnessed life rather than experienced it. She dropped the thin, plastic bag onto the counter and pushed away the box of chocolate macaroons that fell into her hands. They were part of the stash she secretly kept in the top drawer of her nightstand. With Septime's drawing, folded deep within.

She crossed the kitchen and stood at the foot of the stairs. It was probably Laurel with nothing better to do. Cecile ran up the steps with determination. She would let her have it once and for all. Cecile was tired of the discomfort the girl added to a household already on the rocks. But as she reached the landing, she realized the music wasn't coming from Laurel's room, but from Viv's.

She pushed open the door and it was then that she felt as if her heart and her world stopped. In the midst of those ballet posters, schoolbooks and teddy bears, she saw Viv and a boy half-undressed, writhing in a giggling heap on the bed. He was kissing her neck, touching her breasts. And she was smiling, running her hands through his hair. Cecile was horrified, helpless and confused as she looked at these two strangers. She took a step back. And then Viv saw her. Viv pushed the boy away and grabbed her T-shirt. Silence. Cecile could hear her own heart pounding. The boy's startled eyes caught hers.

Cecile remained paralyzed in the center of the room. Finally, after what seemed like hours, the boy rushed past her and out the door, leaving Viv there, staring back at her mother with pathetic eyes. Cecile swallowed hard. She couldn't think straight. The words poured out.

"What do you think you're doing, Vivienne? Just because Laurel is a goddamn tramp doesn't mean my daughter is going to become one too! Put your clothes on!"

Cecile swiveled around, her hands on her hips. On the back of the door, a poster of a ballerina in first arabesque caught her eye. That was supposed to be Viv. That and nothing more.

She heard Viv sniffling behind her.

"And you're supposed to be at ballet! I trusted you! I thought you were dedicated to dance…"

"I am… My class was cancelled… I never would skip it!"

Cecile looked into those childish eyes filled with dashed exuberance.

"Who is that boy?"

"Seth… He's one level above me in class. In dance… He wants me to be his partner for the audition."

Calm, stay calm, Cecile thought to herself, holding her head in her hands.

Slowly, she approached the bed and sat next to Viv. It was in part her own fault for never addressing the subject of sex with her daughter. But how could they talk about that when they couldn't even seem to have a normal conversation?

"Viv, you're too young to be… getting involved with a boy," Cecile said, hating her own prim voice. "He'll take advantage of you." She could feel the heat rising into her temples. The room was suddenly closing in on her.

Viv's eyes widened, and she glared defiantly at her mother.

"No! You don't understand… He's not like that! He's serious."

"Viv, I've had more experience than you… I know what teenage boys are about. I'm telling you that I want this fooling around to end!"

"You don't understand… you can't understand!" Viv was shaking her head. "If you knew so much, you wouldn't be so miserable! Maybe you should pay more attention to your own relationship with Dad!"

"What is that supposed to mean, young lady?" Cecile snapped back.

Viv caught her breath and looked down. Cecile could tell she was at the breaking point.

"What's going on, Vivienne?" she demanded, her voice trembling. Viv looked away.

"Look at me and tell me exactly what you are hiding." Cecile could feel herself stiffening.

Viv took a deep breath, and then words and tears flew forth in one great jumble.

"I wanted to protect you. I didn't want to say anything… Laurel told me I should, but I couldn't and now…"

"What is it for goodness sake?" Cecile asked in exasperation.

"It's Dad… I found… letters to him from some woman when I was in the attic."

Viv sniffed and gazed at the plush lime carpet under her crooked dancer's toes.

Cecile felt sick. She wanted to throw up. She wanted to scream.

"It can't be true," she finally whispered almost to herself. "Viv, how could you say such things?"

"I'm not lying!" Viv stood up and looked at Cecile with blazing eyes.

"Where are they? These letters…"

"I don't think you should see them."

"That's not for you to decide, Vivienne! Give them to me immediately!"

Viv reached under her mattress and pulled out a small, messy stack.

"Did you read them?"

"Yes." Viv's gaze hardened, and she walked over to the window that overlooked the Rue des Martyrs.

Cecile told herself she wouldn't cry. She bit her lip. She wouldn't show her 14-year-old daughter that she was so damn mentally destructible.

"Are you OK?" Vivienne asked, returning to her mother's

side. She awkwardly put her hand on Cecile's arm.

"Everything is fine," Cecile said calmly. But in her heart, she knew it wasn't.

 co-oc

Septime's eyes undressed her as they tangoed in the darkened gallery. The music for once didn't repulse her. Slow, slow, quick, quick, slow… her feet moved to the rhythm set by his body, pressed against hers. "What made you decide to come here?" he murmured in her ear.

"I wanted to feel the passion again…"

Slow, slow, quick, quick, slow. A spin, a dip. The blue and red lights passed in a blur. She ran her fingers through his soft, dark hair.

His mouth crushed hers hungrily, and she didn't resist. She wanted him as much as he seemed to want her. The music continued as he pushed her against the wall and unbuttoned her dress. Naked against him. His hands on her thighs made her moan with desire. It hadn't been this way in a long time. She could hardly remember anything like this. And then the pleasure that made her scream like she never dared in that quiet apartment on the Rue des Martyrs.

A sharp buzzing noise suddenly burst out of nowhere. Cecile groaned and pushed at the sheets that weren't supposed to be there on the floor of the gallery. Early morning sunlight streamed in. She wiggled around to see Manu heading toward the bathroom.

Cecile felt a few unexpected tears spring into her eyes. She hadn't experienced any kind of adventure at all. She still was the same woman with a life that disappointed her. The idea of Manu cheating on her made it worse. She had cried herself to sleep before he had returned home that night. But it wasn't as if she was still in love with him, she told herself convincingly.

Cecile had spent months and months complaining about him. Yet she couldn't let go of the sick feeling within as she thought of the letters. The letters that she hadn't yet mustered up the courage to read. She hid them deep in her secret drawer and chewed on a macaroon instead. And then she started to cry. She must have fallen asleep and dreamed of what she had wanted since she set eyes on Septime.

Cecile pulled the sheets over her head. She had to break free.

Chapter 15

Andre

The idea of seeing June both terrified and angered Andre, but there would be no avoiding it. She was in town and wanted to see him. His heart leapt for an instant.

Andre was so susceptible to female charm. He was addicted to the idea of impressing one beautiful woman after the next. They had fallen at his feet when he had been in the limelight.

But not any more.

They would be sorry when he made his big comeback. He still was certain that his agent was wrong. Andre had heard those cheers in the theater last night. The fans wanted him back.

He stepped out of the shower and dried his torso. He had started to put on a few pounds. No more heavy workouts at the gym after his accident. Andre looked at the slight, round bubble that used to be a washboard stomach and turned away from the mirror.

He had to avoid thinking of how things were and start living in reality. He pulled on a pair of beige trousers and one of those fluid linen shirts that he had become fond of and made his way into the bedroom.

The phone was ringing.

"Yes?" he said, pushing the speaker-phone button with annoyance.

"I know better than to ask you why you didn't call me back last night," Jack said.

"What is so important? Does this conversation have to be right now? It's fucking 3 a.m. in New York…"

"You know I hardly sleep, Andre," he said with a soft chuckle. "And I knew I could catch you home at this hour. Anyway, Brenda and I were having an interesting lunch with the Linovskas yesterday… You know Stan Linovska, that young director who was up for a Tony last year?"

"Yes, yes… So what is this about?" Andre tried to keep his voice from trembling with excitement.

"Well, Stan was a fan of yours years back."

"What do you mean by 'was'?"

"Andre, you know the business. It's fickle… The next pretty face is the most important thing… Getting back to Stan, well, he wants to offer you a role."

"Just what are we talking about?" Andre asked cautiously. He wasn't naïve. It was obvious that Jack was dancing around something he was certain Andre wouldn't like.

"It's a small role. The father of this young man who…"

"No."

"Andre, damn it… You'll never work again with this attitude! And they're even shooting the film in Paris…"

"What the fuck do you know anyway, Jack? And this guy, all keyed up because he was nominated for a Tony. He didn't win. I have a Tony! I should be the one calling the shots! Now you want me to get involved in this joker's first film? When you know how I feel about film…"

Andre could hear a familiar impatient sigh on the other end of the line.

"I didn't want to approach one of my other actors with the role, Andre, but I'm going to have to. You have two days to change your mind."

"By then, I hope both of you go to hell!"

He slammed his hand down on the speaker button,

grabbed his cane and hurried as best as he could out of the room.

He was already late.

৵৽৶

June always had liked the charming little streets twisting around the Canal Saint-Martin, which ran from the north of the city into the center, where it snaked underground and poured into the Seine River. They had come here together years ago, when the neighborhood was far less chic. They would stroll along the canal, under the chestnut trees that formed a canopy overhead, and watch the barges drift by. He remembered sitting along the water's edge and gazing into those incredible light eyes.

"I love you," he had said to her for the first time.

Her cheeks turned pink, and she threw her arms around him.

"What took you so long?" she whispered in his ear. He touched her long, dark hair, which felt like silk against his cheek.

They remained there, undisturbed, for hours, laughing and talking about how they would have the most exciting life together forever. Nothing would tie them down. No one recognized Andre here, and he relished the freedom. Anywhere else, he was mobbed by crazed fans. It was before the days of his international career.

Now, he could do with a little mobbing. He walked unnoticed to the café where he knew June would be waiting. He hated for her to see him like this, but he resigned himself to the fact that everyone in the business was aware of his condition.

As usual, the café that they used to frequent was buzzing with activity. He hadn't been back here since the last time they were together, yet nothing had changed. The same cluster of round tables on the sidewalk, the same long, zinc countertop beyond the windows marked with today's specials. He stopped a few feet away from the place. He didn't need anyone to point June out to him. In his eyes, she had hardly changed at all. She smiled at him as he approached the table. Her hair was cut in a chin-length bob—a modern Louise Brooks. He leaned over and kissed her on both cheeks, inhaling the familiar sent of wildflowers that made shivers run up and down his spine.

"How is it that everyone changes except you, June?" he asked, slipping onto the chair opposite her. "What's your secret?"

She laughed.

"You still are the king of compliments, aren't you…"

Then she glanced at the cane, which he had leaned against the side of the table.

"How are you doing? After the accident and everything…"

"Fine," he said quickly. He didn't want any sympathy. A sensation of discomfort overwhelmed Andre as he thought of the unwanted looks of pity that had plagued him ever since the accident. "Everything is getting back to normal…"

"You never responded to the cards I sent you when it happened… other than by sending the usual checks for Hugo."

Andre couldn't answer. He didn't want to return to that painful time.

"And Clarisse? How is she?"

Andre shook his head. He hesitated for a moment, and then his gaze returned to those mesmerizing light eyes.

"We've separated," he said, lowering his voice. "We haven't made it public though… We're not interested in being in the tabloids. Whenever something negative happens, they want to broadcast it to the world… Otherwise, they don't give a shit about you."

"I'm sorry…"

"Sorry that old Andre Wren never could keep a relationship on its feet?"

"Andre, don't say that," she said, putting a hand on his arm. "Things sometimes end up… falling apart. It's happened to me too."

"Oh?"

"After you, it was difficult. For so long it was that way… and then the wind changes direction… I'm with someone now, and things finally are going well. That's why I'm here in Paris actually."

Andre felt a twinge in his heart. Of course June's personal life would be perfectly fine. What else could he possibly expect? This beautiful, kind woman couldn't remain available eternally. He swallowed hard and straightened up in his chair. It was time for a cigarette. He pulled one out of his pocket, lit up and inhaled deeply. The waiter arrived with June's apple juice and took Andre's order for vodka on the rocks.

"So why did you want to see me?" Andre asked June. He tapped his cigarette against the rim of the ashtray and watched the cinders dissipate in the breeze.

"It's about Hugo."

"I could have guessed that much."

"Did you tell him to leave?"

"It's not my business whether he leaves or stays."

Andre took another drag and blew smoke out of the corner of his mouth. June sipped her drink and gazed toward the canal. She had that faraway look she used to get whenever she was ready to tell a story.

"I had no idea that he had a role in the play... He was 14 and as shy as could be. He told me to come by the auditorium that afternoon—he had a surprise for me, he said. And so I went. I was in the middle of costuming for '42nd Street,' but I told my assistants that I had to slip out for an hour no matter what... And there he was, Hugo as Romeo taking the hands of the prettiest little brunette on center stage. I felt the tears slipping down my cheeks as his voice rang out perfectly..."

Then she turned to Andre and leaned across the table.

"Don't you see what a victory it is, Andre? That he lost his hearing at such a young age and was able to conquer the challenge..."

Andre swallowed hard on too much smoke and started coughing. He dashed out his cigarette and tried to catch his breath.

"What are you talking about?" he gasped.

"You mean he didn't tell you?" June asked with an odd smile. "It's difficult to guess. He reads lips so well..."

"What the hell is this about, June? You never told me he

was deaf, and now you come and dump it on me like that? Have you gone crazy?"

A spark of fire lit within her eyes.

"What difference would it make to you anyway, Andre, for the kind of father you've been? How dare you accuse me of keeping anything from you! What right did you have to know?"

Her words hit him like a blow. She was right, but he would never admit it. He thought of Hugo and their first conversation. Maybe his eyes did follow Andre's lips more than what would be considered normal, but Andre hadn't really noticed. Maybe it was because he didn't notice much of anything unless it had to do with himself. He brushed away that thought.

"Hugo has too much pride to tell you," June was saying. "He doesn't see himself as different from anyone else. And he's not. Everyone has something to surmount. He's proving that he can follow his dream. What's better than that?"

Hugo had appeared perfect. How could he have such a challenge? It seemed almost surreal…

"Listen, Andre, I can see that you're shocked, but you'll learn to live with it as I have and as Hugo has…"

"You still haven't told me why you wanted to talk with me about Hugo," Andre said, his voice a shadow of its usual self.

"I wanted to find out if you were able to discover any paternal love within yourself for Hugo…"

"I offered to help him out… to find him a place to live, an acting class…"

"I think he could use something more personal than that, Andre, but I'm wondering if you'll ever be ready to offer it." June shook her head and stood up. She placed a few bills on the table. "If you make any progress, you know where to find me."

❧

Andre's deliberate steps arrived at the front door of the building that housed Tatiana Ricci's acting studio as well as dance and music rehearsal rooms. It was a slim, stone three-story building with yellow window frames that set it apart from its more traditional neighbors on the quiet Montmartre street. He had visited the place several times—but that had been 30 years ago, around the time Tatiana must have been born. He had known the studio when an older man named Victor ran the music classes. How he loved coming here, singing under the skylights with sun streaming across his face.

But now as he stood looking up at the mustard-colored windows, his heart only was filled with anguish. He didn't understand how his son could ignore his own problems and plunge ahead into a career that would end up making him miserable. Andre had to warn him. Andre, who had never done a thing for Hugo other than send lifeless checks every month, decided he had to open up the naïve eyes that reflected all that was June.

With a determined flick of the wrist, he pushed open the door. A wide, varnished wooden staircase took up the entire lobby. He had forgotten that there wasn't an elevator in this old place. Andre took a deep breath. He wouldn't let his son see him pathetically waiting at the bottom of the stairs. He didn't care if he had to crawl up them, but he would make it to the third floor. With his cane and the support of the sturdy banister, he climbed stairs for the first time since the accident. He refused to imagine how long it took him when he finally reached the top with aching knees. He had arrived. That was what mattered.

He looked at the schedule to be certain, but found that very little had changed at the studio. Classes still ended for lunch at 1 o'clock. He stood to the side as laughter rose and voices approached the door ahead of hurried footsteps. He watched the young faces rush by, not even noticing him. In an instant, they had disappeared down the stairs.

Tatiana emerged and pulled the door shut behind her. All of the young actors Andre knew fell at her feet. They were taken in by those violet eyes that spelled seduction. But Andre found her too brash. He remembered her firm handshake and her arrogant expression when they met for the first and only time. It was at an industry party in a candlelit garden. This was before the accident, when he walked proudly beside Clarisse and made time for the most exclusive galas.

"So you're Andre Wren..." she had said, languidly perched against a trellis in her long, red velvet dress. "The one who thinks real actors don't need classes... Well you're wrong. Just have a look at some of my students and see how well they do at auditions. What kind of roles have you been offered recently?"

And then she slid away in a cloud of laughter with the tall young man who had been playing in a recent production of "Chicago" at the Carmine Theater.

"Don't start, Andre," Clarisse had said, clutching his arm.

"That little bitch," he hissed.

"I'm sure she resents the fact that you've been criticizing her classes every time you're invited on one of those talk shows, Andre..."

"I refer to all classes."

"Yes, but you keep saying, 'like those classes of Tatiana Ricci.' That hasn't helped your popularity with her."

Tatiana Ricci had crawled out of nowhere, charmed the acting world and set up a business that trained some of the country's top young performers. After that meeting, Andre only saw her one other time, from afar. She was giving a class in the same theater where he was rehearsing. He slipped into the back of the auditorium and watched her at work. He didn't exactly agree with her method, but he realized that she had some talent. She seemed to know how to connect with the students and push them to the edge. She knew how to bring out the rawness of each emotion. But Andre never would admit it.

"Andre Wren, what a surprise..." Tatiana Ricci now said, with one of those smiles that Andre couldn't interpret.

"Where's Hugo?" he asked. "He's supposed to be in your class, isn't he?"

"Usually, yes. He doesn't have the same views as his father apparently."

Andre ignored her comment. She tossed her hair back from her face and leaned against the door.

"Where is he then?"

"He had an audition."

"Oh really? For what show?"

"You can ask him when you see him," she said, looking at Andre firmly. "You must be proud to have such a talented son. And one who is following in your footsteps."

"He has nothing to do with me," Andre said, waving a hand in the air.

"Then what are you here to see him for?"

"Aren't you the curious one, Miss Ricci? You would be better off sticking to your classes…"

"I should have known that a pleasant conversation with you doesn't exist, Mr. Wren," she said stiffly. "If you'll excuse me…"

"Wait a minute… I have to find Hugo. Will he be back here today?"

She shrugged her shoulders.

"I have no idea."

Then she flew down the stairs before Andre could say another word.

Chapter 16

Mira

The phone rang as the clock struck eleven. Tatiana was out for the night, and Mira was on her way to the futon in the little alcove outside of the living room when the sound pierced through the silence of the apartment. In the darkness, Mira hurried to the phone and caught it on the fourth ring. She immediately recognized Clara's high-pitched, dancing voice.

"Mira, wait, please don't hang up, listen to me!"

"We don't have anything to say," Mira's voice was ice cold.

"Yes, I have to talk with you..."

"How did you find my number?"

"I've been looking up the numbers of all of your out-of-town friends," she said. "Mira, I wanted to tell you that I'm sorry! I never thought such a thing would happen."

"You didn't fall into bed with Antonio by accident!"

"No, I mean, it started out as a one-night thing... When you were traveling a few months back, we both had a couple of drinks in the gallery after hours and... and things just happened."

Mira felt nauseated, but this time it was entirely because of the disgusting story that had unfolded so secretly right under her nose. She, like a blind fool, had continued along in her daily life as the loving girlfriend and caring friend while they were betraying her in the worst possible way.

"I don't need to hear any more," Mira said abruptly. "I don't care how it happened or if it's continuing. I don't even care if you move in with him. That part of my life is over. It's dead, do you hear me?"

"Mira, don't say that. Antonio and I had a fling. We don't have what it takes for a real relationship. I don't want to see him again, and he doesn't want to see me."

"You actually think that makes a difference? The point now is that I can't trust either one of you."

"But you can't possibly cancel the wedding! I know it's going to be a small group, but still…"

"That's the least of my worries!" Mira had already asked Tatiana to make the difficult phone calls. She didn't want to speak with her parents or siblings at the moment. She dreaded the comments that meant to help but would only hurt. Tatiana kept a cool head and was removed enough from the situation to be able to deal with it more effectively. Tatiana had even managed to keep her calm when Mira told her about the baby, and promised she wouldn't say a word about the situation to anyone.

"Well, what about the gallery?" Clara was saying. "It was our dream!"

"The gallery can sink or swim. I don't care. Find a new artist if you'd like… Once things settle down a bit for me, I'll talk to our lawyer about dissolving the partnership."

"You can't be serious!"

"But I am… very serious. I have myself to worry about, and soon, I'll have a baby to worry about too!"

Silence. Then a little cough.

"Mira, did I hear you right? You're pregnant?"

"Yes, now you see, I have more important things to handle…"

"Does Antonio know?"

"I only found out myself."

"Oh Mira, I'm sorry…"

"I don't need your apologies," Mira said, an odd sense of calm overcoming her. And then she hung up the phone, lowered the ringer and padded triumphantly over to her futon.

୨⚬୨

Hugo arrived at Mira's rooftop studio at 8 a.m. sharp and sat among the overgrown flowers and ferns in the dewy morning light. He had brought her a bouquet of yellow roses, which she transferred into a vase and placed near the red and pink ones already growing in the garden.

"Why the flowers?" she asked.

"They reminded me of you."

She could feel the heat rise into her cheeks, but she covered her embarrassment with a laugh. Mira scolded herself for being so sensitive to a compliment.

"How's the portrait coming along?" he asked. "When can I actually see it?"

"Patience, patience… I'm happy with it…but you know I won't show it to you until I've finished. That was the agreement."

She dabbed a bit of paint onto the canvas. It was amazing how inspiration returned when Hugo sat there across from her, when she could see the story of his life in his eyes and hear it in his voice.

"What's new?" she asked. She longed to focus on anything but her own problems.

"Well, my father gave me his first parental order—other than that, nothing much."

"Is everything OK?"

"Yeah… I guess. He was waiting for me outside of Tatiana's class when I arrived. I ended up missing the first half hour because we spent that much time arguing out in the hallway. He said it was foolish for me to embark on an acting career. According to him, I'll always be limited by my deafness as he's limited by his limp. He had an argument with my mother about it."

Hugo swallowed hard and looked down for a moment. Mira had glimpsed the pain in his eyes and felt a sudden surge of anger toward that crazy actor, whom she only knew through Tatiana's stories. She didn't understand how he could push Hugo away all of his life and now try to stop him from pursuing a dream. It seemed like a complete contradiction.

"What did you tell him?" Mira asked softly.

"That he was the only one to disappoint me so far in life... And that was it. I blurted it out without thinking. He turned around and left, taking the stairs slowly, one by one. I felt guilty after saying those words, watching him walk away defeated... I should have let him talk. It wouldn't have changed anything...."

Mira set down her brush and approached Hugo.

"Follow me," she said, leading him to the railing that overlooked the Rue des Martyrs.

They stood side-by-side, gazing down at the street.

"You see that bistro down there?" she said, pointing at the little cluster of sidewalk tables occupied by newspapers hiding the sparse breakfast crowd.

He nodded.

"That's where he goes to lunch every day," she said. "And I hear he often makes a big scene, yells at the waiters... the whole show, I guess."

Hugo grinned and shook his head.

"I can't say that I'm surprised..."

"A person like that doesn't need your pity, Hugo. He's used to treating people poorly, and doesn't think twice about it. You shouldn't feel guilty. You were only being honest with him. And there's something to be said for honesty."

They were silent for a moment, and then Mira turned back to Hugo. His eyes moved from her lips to her eyes and then back again. They were close all of a sudden. She could smell his fresh, soapy scent. The noise of traffic below and the sounds of birds singing above seemed suspended. The whole world stopped as he leaned forward and kissed her, a soft fluttery kiss that she wished had gone on forever. And then she remembered reality. At this point, she couldn't get involved with Hugo or anyone else for that matter. Mira's mouth still burned from the touch of Hugo's lips. She wanted to reach out and pull him toward her once again.

"Mira…" he said.

"I can't," she whispered, raising a hand to her mouth as if to preserve the sensation of his lips against hers.

"But I love you."

She froze. She didn't know what to think or what to feel. Before she could say another word, he had grabbed his light jacket and flew down the stairs, through the trap door and into the main stairwell. Her breath caught in her throat. Mira watched from above as he left the building and ran down the street. She could feel tears gathering in the corners of her eyes.

Chapter 17

Rafael

The world went by faster and faster as the 747 sped along the runway and lifted off in one, smooth trajectory that always seemed to make Rafael's heartbeat quicken.

He looked blindly at the tray table securely stored against the back of the seat in front of him and tried to quell the frustration that had been building up since earlier that day. Since that strange phone call had broken into the cloud he had been floating on after a night with Laurel.

The phone rang an hour after she had left, as the sun was rising and tossing its glow across the sheets. He snatched the receiver off the cradle, thinking it would be her wiseass voice, but it wasn't.

"Juan Carlos is innocent!" an old man's shaky voice hissed into the phone in Spanish. "Diego's killer is among us…"

"What? Who is this?" Rafael felt the blood pumping furiously through his veins. Beads of sweat formed along his temples as he gripped the receiver and tried to identify the familiar voice.

"That doesn't matter," the man whispered. "What you need to know is that your father's killer is a danger to you and

Carmen!"

"How do I know you're not lying?"

"Would I put myself in danger—calling you like this—if it wasn't true?"

Rafael was silent for an instant. The urgent desperation on the other end of the line, and the reality that a phone call like this could very easily result in the caller's murder, convinced him that this wasn't simply a joke or a mistake of any kind. Diego told Rafael to never trust the telephone—in the emerald business, the enemy always would be listening.

"Who is he? Where can I find him?" Rafael still couldn't place the voice, but he was certain he knew its owner. "And what do you know about Carmen?"

"I don't have much time," the old man said weakly. "Return to the mines, and you will find him. He has taken Diego's place."

Rafael knew exactly what that meant. This person would be the one courting the miners who brought forth the purest emeralds. They would rush to him first, as if his simple acknowledgement could change their wretched lives.

"Why are you telling me this?" Rafael pleaded. "What do you care…"

But he found himself talking into pure emptiness. Rafael smashed down the receiver. His hands were shaking. With his entire being, he dreaded this trip.

Rafael abandoned Paris in one great rush, telling no one and leaving his room in disarray, still holding the scent of Laurel. He would return as soon as he found that fucking bastard who took down his parents. He would put an end to the never-ending nightmare that had cast its shadow over his existence. Rafael planned to work quickly. He couldn't imagine more than a few days without Laurel.

For the first time in years, Rafael rang the bell at the front gate of a ranch-style house outside of Bogotá. He prayed that he wasn't too late. Nervously, he shifted his weight from one foot to the other until he saw Tigo Garcia's bulky, compact figure appear at the front door. Rafael let out a sigh of relief.

"Raf!" Tigo called out as he jogged toward the rustic wooden gate. "What are you doing here?"

"You recognize me even after all this time?" Rafael said as his friend unlatched the hook that sealed him from the grimy life beyond.

Tigo let Rafael in and threw an arm around his shoulder.

"I could almost sense you a mile away," he said.

That's how it always had been between Rafael and Tigo. Natural communication. Finishing each other's sentences. Two boys born and raised within the closed circle of families that controlled the real activity at the emerald mines. They played soccer together in their earlier years, ignoring the fact that their fathers were rivals. As teenagers, they began making trips to the mines, avoiding each other's gaze, as they represented separate camps and understood the responsibility bestowed upon them. But their friendship never wavered. Even after Tigo retreated from the world of emeralds. He had told Rafael many times that he wanted nothing but to escape this kind of life. But he suffered from the same malady that plagued Rafael: the pressure to please his father. Until the towering, jovial man with a steely gaze was gunned down in a bloody ambush on a trip for emeralds.

"Most stories end this way," Diego had said when the teenager came to him with sadness in his eyes. "He was a fair competitor. But not everyone plays by the rules in this business."

Rafael shuddered as he remembered his father's prophetic words. He glanced at Tigo out of the corner of his eye as they walked through the path of gardenia bushes that perfumed the air and led to a flower garden around the side of the house. He hadn't seen Tigo in two years, when his friend left the country to travel the world. It was all part of adapting to life beyond the emerald mines.

"Sorry about your father, Raf," Tigo said, interrupting his friend's thoughts.

"My father was right about this kind of life, Tigo…"

"I know. It's rotten. But somebody's got to keep going."

"Why did you return to the business?" Rafael asked. "I

heard you've been back for six months or so…"

Tigo offered Rafael a wrought-iron chair amongst the little pebbles and man-made waterfalls that the two boys used to use as a playground. They sat facing one another in the dim, early evening sun. Tigo ran a hand through his closely cropped dark hair, which fell back into place like the bristles of a baby brush.

"Life on the outside wasn't what it seemed," he said, shaking his head. Then he lifted his transparent blue eyes to meet Rafael's gaze. "For me, this was home. You'll feel the same someday, Raf. You'll come back to the mines, and you'll be a champion—just like Diego."

Rafael smiled bitterly.

"No. I don't want any part of it."

"Then why are you here today? I know you want to come on an emerald run with me. Your timing says more than words."

Rafael looked at his watch. It was the hour that their trek to the mines always began.

"There are some final issues I want to deal with," Rafael said. "Nothing more. I don't care about this business the way my father did, Tigo! The desire has to burn from within your soul or else you'll be eaten alive. I can't find those feelings…"

"They'll come back to you. By the end of this trip, they will."

"How can you be sure of that?"

"Because no one before you has been able to resist."

Rafael swallowed hard. He didn't want to argue the point. And he knew he couldn't explain his reasons for being here to Tigo. No matter how difficult it was to lie to his friend, Rafael wanted to handle the situation on his own. Only he could defend his family.

"That's your bag at the front gate?" Tigo said, with that familiar sly smile of his. "You ready to go?"

"Let's hit the road," Rafael said. He and Tigo rose from their seats as a young woman with a long, messy ponytail and large, brown eyes emerged from the French doors with a backpack over her shoulders.

She wrinkled her brow and looked at Rafael suspiciously.

Tigo took her hand.

"Rafael, this is my girlfriend Lea. She'll be making the trip with us."

"Nice to meet you."

"Same," she said gruffly. Then she turned away and walked stiffly toward the 4X4 in the driveway.

"Don't mind her," Tigo said. "It takes Lea a while to trust someone. Especially on a mission like this."

"Does she come to the mines?"

"She's taught me a thing or two."

"Really... She's not from around here though."

"I didn't believe it either at first. But with her, it's natural. One thing though—don't ask her too many questions."

"She'll clam up?"

"Worse—she'll blow. And she packs a pistol... Speaking of which, you do have yours, don't you?"

"It never leaves my side," Rafael said.

He followed Tigo through the slim strip of light hanging on to life and steeled himself for one last voyage to the place he hated most in the world.

Chapter 18

Cecile

Cecile pushed through the doors of the gallery before her inner voice could have anything to say in the matter. All was calm and still at 11 a.m., and her brusque movement jarred the slim redheaded woman who was rearranging the window display. She turned around in a flash and raised one triple-pierced eyebrow well above her glasses.

"You know we're closed, right? The exhibit doesn't open until three."

"The door was open," Cecile said defensively.

She walked into the middle of the room. Dark slashes of blues and fluorescent yellow sprang aggressively from a large canvas in the light of day. Septime's eclectic artwork looked strange in the absence of admirers. But it was beautiful. Everyone said so anyway. She shook her head. Art wasn't what she was here for, and she had to keep her mind on the subject at hand.

"Septime… Where's Septime?" she asked.

"Why should I tell you?" the young woman asked with a strange smile. It was as if she knew about the affair that hadn't yet begun and relished Cecile's discomfort.

"I'm a friend," Cecile said, crossing her arms across her chest. "And I don't have much time for conversation."

The woman rolled her eyes.

"Oh, he has tons of friends…"

"What is that supposed to mean?" Cecile was starting to regret her decision to come to this place, but she refused to be scared away. That was the old Cecile. The woman who never made rash decisions and never took control. She had spent too many years being passive.

"Look, if you want to see him, he'll be in around 4 o'clock today."

"I have to find him now!"

The woman extricated herself from the nearly acrobatic position in the window and approached Cecile.

"The only other thing I can suggest is to try the café right around the corner. The one with the blue awning. He goes there for breakfast a lot. And this is the early morning hour for Septime."

Cecile turned and hurried out of the gallery, letting the door slam with a jingle of the bells on the knob. She knew of that café. It was the one Joel and his friends always stopped at after five. She had never been there. She had only watched her son from afar.

In a moment, she arrived beneath the tattered awning that flew whimsically above a chalkboard listing the specials of the day. Her heart was pounding wildly, and her eyes flew from face to face amid the sidewalk tables. Nothing. Just a young woman writing furiously in a notebook, two old men playing cards and a mother scolding a little girl with braids who had just spilled a glass of apple juice all over herself. The scent of fermented fruit filled the air along with the child's crying. It reminded her too much of Viv when she was a toddler.

Cecile shivered, pushed the thought away, and slipped between the unoccupied chairs and away from the commotion. Once inside, she looked around frantically. Of course he wasn't there. That woman probably only led Cecile here to get rid of her. She most likely double-locked the door behind her.

"Can I help you, Madame?" a young waiter with streaked

blond hair asked.

"No, um, nothing…" She scanned the place in confusion and then her eyes returned to him. "One for tea, please."

She had to sit down, regroup and calm herself. Cecile ordered a cup of green tea and closed her eyes. She kept thinking of those awful letters that she only dared look at this morning after Manu had slipped noiselessly out the front door. Those passionate words signed by someone named Claire in delicate yet hurried script. Her eyes burned with tears as she read about excitement that was so unfamiliar to her. She felt cheated, unloved and pathetic. Had Manu responded to those notes begging him to come over once again and press his naked body against hers?

Herbal-scented steam rose to her cheeks, and her eyes flew open.

The waiter had delivered her tea and disappeared around the corner. Cecile sighed miserably and dropped a sugar cube into the murkiness.

"I heard you were looking for me."

She stiffened, feeling a rush of nervousness and excitement. It was Septime. She recognized his voice as if she had heard it a million times before.

He seemed to come out of nowhere, looking smartly dressed as usual in an ash gray suit. He sat down opposite her and took her hand. Cecile wouldn't let him see the lack of assurance that she desperately tried to hide. She was confident and bold, she told herself over and over in her head.

"Who told you?"

"Claire back at the shop."

"Did you say Claire?" Cecile asked, her stomach flip-flopping.

"Yes. Why?"

Could she be the one? No, no, no, Cecile said to herself. Claire was a common name. Of all the Claires in France, Manu didn't necessarily have an affair with this one. Cecile was being ridiculous and overly sensitive. She couldn't imagine Manu with a girl with eyebrow piercings and black miniskirts. His taste would be more of a classic sort. She shook her head. She had to stop obsessing about this stupid affair. Why did she care anyway? She was tired of Manu. She needed liberation and would find it with Septime. That's what she had been telling herself since daybreak.

"Is everything OK?" Septime asked, squeezing her hand.

"Yes, perfectly," she said. "And I was looking for you."

"What made you change your mind?"

"We all need a little excitement every once in a while, now don't we?"

ೋ∼ಲ

Cecile remembered the first night she spent with Manu. They had both had too much to drink and had danced until two in the morning. She raced up the four flights of stairs behind him in high-heeled shoes that banged out a drunken rhythm. She could still hear his laugher in her ears as he picked her up and they tumbled onto the bed in her one-room apartment. She felt his desire course through her entire body as he pulled off her blue silk dress…

And now Septime lifted the soft, blue cotton over her head and ran his mouth hungrily along her breasts. The images mixed together. Manu's eyes in his. Septime's eyes in Manu's. Their bodies intertwining as they moved roughly against hers until she screamed for the first time in years.

She fell back listlessly, and Septime rested his cheek on her chest. She felt desired again. She still was able to seduce. Even if Manu didn't realize it, she was as sexy as she had been that very first night. Feelings of relief and elation ran through Cecile as she lay there wordlessly entangled with the person who had been able to revive her.

Chapter 19

Andre

Andre looked out at the Rue des Martyrs in annoyance as he chewed on a morsel of undercooked beef. Those silly people hurrying around at this hour, running to buy flowers across the street or balancing several loaves of bread as they made their way out of the bakery. He was glad that they didn't recognize him as often as they used to. He was happy to find tranquility at noon in the same lunch place where everyone knew him, yet treated him with quiet discretion.

This was especially important today as he was thinking about the argument he had with Hugo. He shook his head. He didn't even know why he had bothered trying to give the boy some good advice. Hugo was dead set on doing exactly what he wanted. Nothing could stop the determination in those June eyes.

And why should I care? Andre thought to himself. *I was right to reject any kind of parenthood long ago...* But every time he tried to convince himself of the idea that long had been central in his mind, he could hear June's voice whispering just the opposite in his ear.

The only way to stop it would be to confront June and let

her know that father and son were incompatible. Hugo would be better off working out his life alone.

He took a sip of Beaujolais and sank back into the stiff chair. It was only then that he felt the eyes on him. He turned to the right and found himself staring into the pupils of the young woman at the next table who was intently sipping a bubbly drink and doodling on a notepad. She was rather attractive, with tousled dark hair and slim hands that moved gracefully along the paper. Yet those eyes that now moved away bothered him.

"Are you one of those tabloid writers here to bug the hell out of me?" he spat out in her direction.

"Why are you asking me that?" She held her pencil poised above the paper and now looked at him with startled eyes.

"Because you were staring at me and noting something on that paper! You have no right to!"

The girl closed the notebook and stuffed it into her backpack as Andre reached across the tables to grab it.

"Hey," she said, yanking her bag away. "What do you think you're doing? That's my sketchbook!" Then she stood up and looked at him angrily. "I've heard awful things about you, Andre Wren, and now I see that they're more than true."

Another crazed critic, he thought to himself. All eyes were on them, which annoyed him even further. "Waiter!" he called out, waving his hand in the air. "Please remove this woman."

"I don't want to spend one more minute here next to someone as crazy as you," she said, spinning around and marching toward the door. She pushed a few coins into the waiter's hand as she passed.

Andre looked down at her half-finished drink and then up at the fellow diners who continued to look his way. "OK everyone, show's over," he said harshly. Slowly, the buzz of voices returned, and the attention turned once again away from Andre Wren.

Andre looked down at his food in distaste. He had completely lost his appetite. He shoved away the plate, grabbed his jacket and made his way out the door.

"What do you mean she's checked out?" Andre asked the receptionist as he leaned against the counter and tapped his fingers with impatience. "Look again: June Adler in room 12. She has to be there! She wasn't supposed to leave until Friday."

The girl with a sleek blond chignon turned back to the reservation book and bit her lip. Andre's eyes scanned the emerald-colored tapestry that covered the walls and watched the comings and goings of the fancy people who gave him a second glance before turning to their companions and nodding in his direction.

"Did you see Andre Wren? The actor! He's right over there!"

He could hear the whispers half in his mind and half in his ears. He tried to hide the hideous cane between his leg and the counter. In this position, with it just tucked against the marble, he was at his best angle. He looked over the rim of his dark glasses and made eye contact with a lovely brunette standing near the elevator. She smiled blankly and turned away. For Andre, this was like a slap in the face.

"I think I might have something for you, Mr. Wren," the blonde said, breaking into his unpleasant thoughts.

"Well, what is it? Don't keep me standing here like a fool!"

"It's a note from Ms. Adler. And she did indeed check out."

"Fine. Thank you."

Andre turned away from the counter, hobbled over to one of the plush red couches in the lobby and tore open the envelope.

Dear Andre,

If you're trying to see me, I suppose you've made progress and do care somewhat about your son. So that is why I'm telling you he has an audition on Wednesday. I hope you receive this note on time... You'll find the details below. If you don't believe that he has enough talent for this business, then go and see him at work. Deville is the casting director. I'm sure he'll let you sit in the auditorium.

June

Andre looked at the time and location. It was starting in 30 minutes. He hailed the taxi parked in front of the hotel and was on his way across town. His eyes gazed through the dirty windows at the historic apartment buildings with their finely sculpted balconies and elegant window frames. Their splendor was marred only by soot from a century of pollution. But Andre didn't care about the scenery. A million thoughts at once collided in his head, and they all had to do with Hugo. *What was the boy trying to prove? He never would make it in this rough business. And what about his deafness? He couldn't possibly think that wouldn't grind his career to a sudden, painful halt more likely sooner than later.* The list went on and on, but Andre shook his head violently as if to eliminate the thoughts that tormented him, twisting his spirit into knots.

The cab flew around a corner, nearly tossing him across the rotting, leather seat. They were making their way up a shabby, cobblestone street leading to Montmartre. Andre remained blind to the city's beauty and homeliness as he thought only of what he was about to witness from the back row of the theater. He went through two cigarettes on that ride.

Andre sat in the dark for an hour in the musty-smelling velvet seats. His eyes didn't leave the circle of light that fell on the young men who took the stage and read the part of Stanley in "A Streetcar Named Desire." How many times had Andre heard those lines? Maybe ten thousand. He even had pronounced them himself a few times. He listened to each voice turn itself into a new Stanley and watched the character emerge differently from countless faces. But nothing gripped him.

Until Hugo.

It was only then, as he watched his son's timidity evaporate beneath the rage of a passionate and crazed Stanley that he felt goose bumps run up and down his spine. He wasn't watching his son on the stage. He was watching a true actor. A professional. Andre swallowed hard. No matter how difficult and rotten a road, he couldn't block Hugo from it. *Hugo is already on that goddamn road,* he thought to himself. There would be no changing that.

With longing eyes, he watched his son leave the stage. This son who didn't need Andre for anything—not even for his name.

Chapter 20

Mira

In exactly 24 hours, Hugo would be returning for his next sitting. Mira should have nearly completed the portrait by now, but her hands and mind were frozen. His declaration frightened her because it awakened the instant attraction that she immediately had pushed away. She tried to ignore the crazy magnetism that drew her to him at the very worst possible time. If she didn't, she would get hurt yet again. Hugo couldn't possibly be interested in sharing the kind of life that lay before her. He was too young to tie himself down with a woman who was pregnant with another man's child. Mira had to face reality.

She forced herself to focus on the portrait and that alone. Lacking inspiration, she had taken a trip downstairs to observe Andre Wren at the café with the hope of gaining more insight into the pain in Hugo's eyes. She thought that might put her back on track. But she only ended up rattled by a confrontation with the actor.

Mira closed her eyes and rested her head in her lap. A soft breeze brushed her hair back from her face. She didn't know how she would ever face Hugo or complete his portrait. Her entire body suddenly felt heavy. She inhaled and exhaled slowly and tried to forget everything.

"Who's the young man?"

Mira looked up, startled, at the sound of Septime's voice. It had been so easy to doze off in the warmth of the sun.

"Snoozing in the breeze?" he asked.

Mira stiffly stretched her back and looked around the familiar rooftop garden in confusion. She didn't understand what Septime was doing here. His eyes studied the portrait as well as a few failed still-life paintings featuring flowers and plants.

"How did you find me?"

"I have my sources…"

Tatiana, of course, Mira thought to herself in annoyance. First, she had to bring Hugo into Mira's life. Then she had to invite Septime here. She would say it was for Mira's own good. What would be the point of arguing with her? Mira sighed and shook her head.

"Decent work," he said a moment later, nodding at Hugo's portrait. "I'm sorry I couldn't have been there when it mattered."

Septime sat down on the folding chair across from her. He ran a hand through his disheveled hair and leaned forward thoughtfully. She sensed the question he was about to ask.

"Why did you come to Paris, Mira?"

"Why do you care? I thought we were better off apart."

"I don't want to turn my back on you again." His eyes softened and he reached for her hand. "My drug problem is a thing of the past. It's over. I can't use it as an excuse to distort the future. So I figured I might as well try to pick up the pieces of what used to be a pretty good brother-sister relationship."

Mira bit her lip. She didn't want to let down her guard.

"I'm here to see Tatiana," she said.

"There's more to it than that. I can feel it, Mira."

Mira swallowed hard and closed her eyes. Could she hide everything that had happened from Septime? No. Years ago, they had a way of knowing what the other was thinking, and it seemed as if this strange element that drew them together was still intact. She thought back to Hugo. She told him that

honesty was important. Wasn't it the same in her own
situation?

"I caught my fiancé cheating on me… with my business
partner, who I thought was a friend." She said this matter-of-
factly, by now used to the sound of these words. Mira had
shed so many tears these past few days and gone over the
situation so many times that all emotions had drained from
her. Her broken heart had gone numb.

"Do I know him?"

"My high school sweetheart Antonio," Mira said. "I'd sent
you a couple of pictures…"

Septime, his face red with anger, jumped up.

"Yes, I remember him… Fucking bastard! Where can I
find him?"

"No, no, no!" Mira put an arm around her brother and led
him back to the chair. "I don't want any part in that. It's over.
I don't want to see him again, and I don't want to see her
again. I'm starting over right here. You have to promise me
you won't get involved, Septime!"

"Mira, how can you say that after what they both did?"

"Because I'd rather turn my back on them entirely! They
don't exist for me. That's the best solution. Now are you with
me or not?"

"You can trust me."

"Do I have your word on that?"

"Absolutely."

"Then there's one more thing." Mira closed her eyes and
took a deep breath. She had to tell him. It would be apparent
in a few weeks anyway.

"I'm pregnant."

He clutched her hands and pulled her closer.

"Oh shit…" There was confusion and sadness in his eyes.

"I'm OK with it, Septime. I was doing well with my art
back home, selling more and more paintings. I can do the
same here, and I'll do it on my own." Mira said those words
not only to convince her brother, but also to convince herself.
She swallowed hard and continued.

"I don't need Antonio's help. Really. He doesn't know.
But Clara will probably tell him. She called here the other day,

and I told her."

Mira smiled smugly. "Now, we'll see how he feels…"

"Mir, are you completely sure about this? I don't agree with what the guy did, but you probably should talk things over with him… This changes the picture."

They remained silent for a moment, and Septime, furrowing his brow, returned to the easel. As he studied Hugo's half-completed face, Mira turned away.

"You never did answer my question," Septime said. "Who is your model?"

"His name is Hugo," she said softly. "He's an actor… Well, he's studying to be one, actually."

"He has a powerful gaze…"

"I tried to capture it as best as I could."

"But now you're stuck?"

"How did you guess?"

"Why else would you be dozing off in the sun with a tense look on your face?"

"So does that ever happen to you?"

"Of course."

"What do you do to get back on track?"

"I make sure my personal feelings are separated from my work."

"What are you suggesting?" Mira asked, her heart skipping a beat. She stood up as nonchalantly as possible and walked over to him. They both gazed into Hugo's eyes.

"Did something happen between the two of you?"

"Of course not! I'm not like you, Septime, driven by desires for every attractive or inspirational person I see…" Mira could feel heat rise into her face.

"If the feelings are mutual, which I'm guessing they are, I can see your dilemma."

Mira didn't answer. She didn't have to. She was certain that her brother could read the turmoil in her eyes and she hated the fact that she couldn't seem to hide her emotions from him—that she couldn't put up a stoic front.

"I'm returning to Naples tomorrow," Septime said.

"But I thought your show here was running longer…"

"It is. I'll only be home for three or four days… It's a

small showing, and the university has asked me to give a talk while I'm there as well... Now that I've seen your work, I'd like to ask you a favor."

"What's that?"

"Meet me there."

"Why?" Mira asked, confused by the intensity in his eyes.

"I want you to discuss the portrait with some of the students. You would be perfect for the job—much better than me, Mir."

"Are you crazy? It's not finished!"

"That's exactly the point. Don't you realize how interesting this discussion could be? Talk about your inspiration, your difficulties... And as a result, finishing it would become less of a challenge. This would feed your mind. Believe me, Mira."

"You expect me to take off like that?" But Mira couldn't help feeling a bit of excitement bubbling up from within as she thought of the opportunity.

"It's good for the spirit, Mira... and at the same time, you might want to have a chat with Antonio." Those last few words deflated her bubble.

"No," she said firmly, shooting her brother an annoyed glance.

"About the discussion at the university or about Antonio?"

"I don't want to talk about either subject."

Mira walked to the edge of the roof and gazed down at the Rue des Martyrs. To carry her thoughts away for an instant. Life went on as usual. She wished that she could be one of those people with places to go and people to see. They looked busy and determined—all, except one. Cecile. Mira squinted. Yes, she was certain that was Cecile arguing with a teenager, most likely her daughter, as they walked up the street. The girl's long ponytail swung back and forth violently as she shook her head and marched defiantly ahead of her mother.

Mira took a step back and turned to her brother.

"Have you seen Cecile lately?" she asked, turning her back to the scene below and returning to the sunny spot where

Septime was sitting.

"Why do you ask?"

"You're curious and opinionated enough about my life…"

"If you want to know whether I've slept with her, the answer is yes."

"You do know that you could end up breaking up her marriage and family, right? And then you criticize Antonio…"

"Mira, this is different! Her husband has neglected her for ages. She doesn't have a thing to lose, only something to gain… a real relationship."

"And you're ready for a real relationship?" Mira said, almost mockingly.

"I don't know," he said, his eyes darkening. "After what I've put myself through, I've had a lot of trouble committing to anyone and anything… but Cecile intrigues me. There's something about her, something different. I can't identify it. This sounds silly and imprecise…"

Mira sank onto the stool opposite Septime and looked him in the eye.

"Some things haven't changed," Mira said with a sigh. "I hope you don't hurt her…"

She knew he wouldn't answer.

Chapter 21

Rafael

They reached the depths of the forest in the dead of night. Side by side, in rough territory that was sadly familiar to Rafael. He placed his hand gently over the 9-millimeter. It was the one Diego carried on every emerald trip. It only had failed him on his last. Rafael closed his eyes for a moment. He could still see the bloody scene as the 4X4 took to the underbrush. The sounds brought him back in time. Leaves crunching under the tires, nocturnal birds calling, and faraway gunshots every now and again. He stiffened at the first loud popping noise.

"It's getting worse and worse around here," Tigo said. "It's not only us any more."

"What do you mean?"

"The emeralds aren't as good as they used to be, and the real beauties get snatched up by these goddamn bastards who take them by force…"

"Which means there've been more ambushes, I suppose."

Tigo nodded. "The Ramirez family is wiping everyone out."

"Why do you want to continue, Tigo?"

Tigo glanced at Rafael with shining eyes that reflected the sliver of moonlight from above.

"It's our life, Rafael! The question is how could you leave?"

"You should know the answer to that," Rafael said.

"But it's part of the game. Diego knew the risks. My father did. Everyone does. And these greedy bastards accept them because they want to have their shot at the jackpot. Diego had a monopoly for long enough. He used his gun plenty of times too. You only see the good... You always were like that."

Rafael swallowed hard and looked away. He saw the girl's reflection in the little mirror that lit up when he lowered the sun visor. She sat sullenly against the black velour seat, with eyes gazing at the nothingness beyond.

"How did you get involved in this business, Lea?" Rafael asked.

Her eyes went to violent from blank as she caught his glance in the mirror.

"Family connections," she said sharply.

"See," Tigo said under his breath. "I told you she didn't like to talk about it."

Rafael glanced at Lea's reflection one last time before pushing the visor back into its place. She had a tomboy look about her, with that bulky sweatshirt and sweatpants as dark as night. Only her face was soft in spite of the fiery expression that had illuminated her brown eyes moments earlier.

Rafael saw nothing through the side window, fogged up with humidity, except for Tigo's twisted reflection. He wore the T-shirt that reminded Rafael of better days. Only five years ago. The two of them kicking the soccer ball around the square. He was dribbling and heading toward Tigo, who played goalie on their makeshift cement field. Right and left, left to right. They were both serious and laughing all at once. They were in their own world, and they didn't give a damn about emeralds.

"Goal!!!" Rafael shouted as he got the ball past Tigo.

"You son-of-a-bitch!" Tigo said, punching him playfully on the shoulder.

Rafael grabbed the ball and tucked it under his arm.

"That means you get the shirt," Tigo said. Rafael could see the disappointment flash in his eyes for a split second.

The two boys stood against the tree trunk where they had thrown their backpacks and the T-shirt they had caught simultaneously at the match last week.

"You keep it," Rafael said suddenly.

"No, no, you won, Raf."

Rafael shook his head.

"You're more of a loyal fan than I am, Tigo. I want you to have it…"

Tigo smiled and threw his arm around Rafael's shoulders.

"Get down!" Tigo shouted, bringing Rafael back to the forest, the dead of night, and the lust for emeralds. The 4X4 screeched around a hairpin turn, spun and came to a halt in the blinding light. Lea flew out of her seat and nearly landed between the two men, but she didn't make a sound. They were surrounded. Rafael slipped out his 9-millimeter.

"It's them," Tigo hissed. "Ramirez wants me dead, Raf." His voice was a reminder of the past.

"Stay here," Rafael said. "I'm going to talk to him."

Tigo grabbed his arm. "Are you crazy? Use the fucking gun! That's the only way out!"

"He'll let us by," Rafael said. And he didn't doubt it. His heartbeat quickened as he thought of Diego. He never let anyone intimidate him. He had his hand on his gun and was ready for anything. He had won many battles before being brought down. Rafael wouldn't let his last images of his father tarnish the strength he had lived by for so many years. He took a deep breath.

"I'm going with you," Lea said.

"What?" Tigo hissed. "Have you lost your fucking mind, Lea?"

"Stay here!" Rafael said to her.

"No one has ever told me what to do," she said, crawling into the back seat and kicking the back door open.

"Have it your way, but you'll see!" Tigo said to her. Rafael squeezed his friend's arm and then turned away. He refused to be afraid.

"This is for Diego," he whispered as he pushed open the door and stepped into the glow of what had seemed to be a thousand headlights. Lea was at his side, with a hand resting on her holster. He took a step forward.

"Ric, it's Rafael Mendez," he shouted out. He heard the scuffling of feet, a few hushed whispers. Then a figure approached him. A group of three or four shadows remained in the background.

Ric Ramirez, a pot-bellied emerald king who had known Diego since they played ball together at the age of five, smiled raucously. Rafael lowered his gun. The men shook hands.

"Well, well, well... I never expected to see you around here again, Rafael. I thought you were finished with this business."

"I wanted to be."

"Couldn't stay away?"

"I figured one more run wouldn't hurt."

Ric nodded in the direction of the 4X4 as Tigo emerged and made his way into the light. "You're traveling with that bastard?"

"He has the right to get through to the mines and try to make deals like any of us..."

Ric shook his head. He lifted his gun and aimed it at them. They froze as if in a lineup at the county jail. Then Ric smiled crazily. Rafael could feel his heart pounding. He could sense Lea's grip strengthen on her weapon. In a split second, Rafael thought back to the times when his father and Ric shared the territory in a rather amicable way. They shook hands when they arrived at the mines and again before leaving. That had been their sole communication. But it was enough to avoid violence and enough to make Ric send flowers for Diego's funeral.

All of a sudden, Ric lowered his gun and howled with laughter.

"You're not a rough type like your father, you know that don't you, kid?" he said. "Diego fired first, then asked questions. That's what we all did, and that's what they're still doing. And there you are, standing next to that little girl, who is trying to look tough. She probably is tougher than you."

"Don't," Rafael whispered, directing the order to Lea. He knew she was close to firing. They stood there in silence for a moment. Rafael could feel his cotton shirt sticking to him in the musty, humid air. The crisp greenery was closing in on him. He took in another deep breath and thought of his father's strength.

Ric waved his hand in the air.

"I'm wasting too much time here with you goddamn kids," he said. "The only thing you might have at the mines is beginner's luck. That doesn't impress me. Now get the hell out of here!"

He laughed and shook his head once again.

"If this is the new *comisionista*, I'll be the king of this place forever!" Ric yelled out. Then he fired one shot that slashed through the car's already bent side mirror. Rafael lifted his gun with a shaking hand, but Ric had turned away.

"Get him!" Tigo hissed.

But Rafael remained motionless as visions of his father spun out of control before his glassy eyes. Tigo grabbed him by the arms and shook him.

"Raf, get with it! What the fuck's wrong with you?"

"Look, let's get back to the truck, all right?" Lea was saying.

Rafael took a deep breath. He couldn't show such weakness. Slowly, they made their way to the shiny chrome that almost beckoned to them, an ounce of security in this frightening place. Rafael's hand never left his gun as he walked backwards, his eyes trained on Ric's shadow now in the distance. And then, in what seemed like an instant, Ric and his faceless companions were gone.

Tigo started the engine. He looked at Rafael out of the corner of his eye.

"I knew Ramirez had a decent amount of respect for Diego, but I guess I underestimated it…"

"Drive," Rafael nearly commanded. "Let's get this fucking mission over with."

Chapter 22

Cecile

Cecile couldn't remember the last time she had sat in the dark corner of a restaurant waiting for the arrival of the man who made her heart pound with desire. This was their fifth secret meeting. She counted the seconds until their passionate encounters. The world seemed to stop when she looked into Septime's eyes. She blocked thoughts of Manu and the kids from her mind during those moments of freedom, when Septime caressed her with his gaze. If she let them in, even for a second, this new life would be over.

He asked her to meet him here in this grotto-like restaurant way too close to home for her comfort. But she couldn't resist. This place spelled romance. Dim, yellow candlelight was the only illumination against the glossy, dark blue walls and ceiling. Round tables made of crushed shells populated the asymmetric room tucked into the back of a trendy wine bar. Cecile glanced around timidly. It seemed as if everyone here was seeking refuge from the real world.

His hand touched her cheek gently, and his lips crushed hers. Her lover had arrived, his dark hair windblown and his jacket left half-unbuttoned. Septime slipped into the chair opposite Cecile and reached across the table for her hand.

"I hope I didn't keep you waiting too long," he whispered. "I had to stop by the gallery…"

"I've only been here five minutes," she said. Cecile felt the same rush of adrenalin she experienced each time they met. "It gave me time to think of you…"

"You look gorgeous as usual."

Cecile smiled. She hardly believed such an exaggeration, but it felt good hearing those unfamiliar words anyway. And she did her best to please him. She wore a silky black dress that hid those chubby parts of her body that defied any kind of weight-loss program. He told her she was sexy, and she tried to force herself to believe it. But she still wasn't the most free-spirited woman on the planet. Cecile, who couldn't accept her body in the much-hated harshness of light, made sure that the most passionate of encounters with Septime happened in the safety of darkness.

"Did you order drinks?" Septime asked.

She nodded. "Martinis. I remember you saying they're a favorite of yours…"

"Wonderful. A perfect way to celebrate…"

"Ahh… What are we celebrating?"

Cecile's stomach flip-flopped like that of her 10-year-old self on a surprise outing to the zoo.

The waiter delivered their drinks. She nervously held the cool glass between her palms for a moment.

"Well, tell me," she insisted, a wide smile spreading across her face.

"Now, now… patience, please."

Cecile shook her head. "Fine, but this had better be good…"

"Let's toast… to us and Italy!"

"Why Italy?" she asked, touching her glass to his.

"That's where we're going, my dear Cecile!"

Excitement bubbling up from within, Cecile leaned across the table. "Septime, what are you talking about?"

"I have to go there for a few days… I keep a cottage outside of Naples, which could make quite a fabulous place for us."

Cecile placed her glass on the table and sank back into her chair. All of a sudden those thoughts she wasn't supposed to think came rushing into her head. She rubbed her eyes and inhaled slowly. But nothing would push away Manu and the kids, whose images clung tenaciously to her mind.

"I can't," she whispered.

"Cecile, what do you mean 'you can't'?" He took her hand and brought it to his smoothly shaven cheek. "My love... it won't change anything. If we're here for a few days or there, we'll be doing the same thing..."

She felt the heat rise into her face.

"It's different, Septime... I can't drop everything and leave my family. I have responsibilities. What am I supposed to say to them?"

"Tell them you're taking a little trip with a girlfriend," he said. "It's as simple as that."

Cecile was ashamed to tell him that she didn't have any friends. She would chat mundanely from time to time with a neighbor, or play the role of a sociable wife in front of Manu's colleagues. That was the extent of her social relations.

"Nothing is simple about this situation, Septime. At least not for me."

He looked down and pulled a small notepad and pencil out of his pocket. He scribbled something and tore off the piece of paper for her.

"This is the address," he said, sliding it across the table. "I'm leaving in two days, and won't have time to see you before I go."

Then he took her hands again, warming her cold fingertips.

"Please change your mind, Cecile."

Her eyes escaped his.

She pulled away from him and stuffed the address into the little black satin clutch he had given her two days ago. "I have to go," she said in a hushed voice.

"But I thought you had the whole evening, Cecile."

"No, I can't." She rose clumsily from her seat, kissed him and then ran through the dimness and into the street. Tears had begun to fall as she hurried toward the gray clouds of night. Cecile hated herself for refusing happiness, but she was afraid of leaving with Septime. She was afraid that she would never return.

જ્જ

The apartment was in darkness. Cecile couldn't let them see her like that, with puffy eyes and mascara running down her face. By eleven o'clock, Manu would be in bed and the kids would be in their rooms. She told them not to stay up for her. They thought she was at some drippy romantic film that none of them would want to see.

Cecile slipped off her black Mary Jane's and walked easily through the main hall. It was only when she approached the kitchen that she saw a dim light. She took a deep breath. She had to pass through to access the staircase. Slowly, she approached the light. Her eyes squinted as she stepped noiselessly onto the cool tile. Laurel was sitting cross-legged on a stool with her head in her hands. She looked at Cecile through reddened eyes. She had been crying, but Cecile knew she never would admit it.

"What are you doing here at this hour?" Cecile asked.

"I can ask you why the hell you're so dressed up for the movies…" she said, flipping that thick mane over one shoulder.

Cecile ignored her remark. Laurel had become increasingly difficult during the past few days. She had this odd, empty look in her eyes and would strike out every time Cecile crossed her path. Manu refused to confront her about her behavior, and Vivienne had become her true confidante.

"I thought you worked until 11:30," Cecile said. She opened the refrigerator, pulled out a half-empty bottle of ruby red grapefruit juice and poured herself a glass. The martini was the only thing floating around in her stomach since lunchtime. And it nauseated her.

"I wasn't feeling well, so I came home early," Laurel said. She stood up and shoved the stool under the table. Then without another word, she headed for the staircase.

Cecile   leaned   against   the   countertop.   She   didn't understand why Laurel had to move out of her mother's house in the south and come to Paris just to work as a waitress and make their lives miserable. She had no ambition or direction in spite of Manu's overwhelming support. He was ready to throw money into any kind of course his little girl's heart desired. But no. She had a high school diploma and wanted nothing but to work part time, hang out in the city and mooch off them. And in the meantime, she also most likely loved the fact that she had become the biggest influence in her innocent half-sister's life. Cecile finished her drink, turned off the light and headed upstairs.

Light shined from under the door to their bedroom. Manu wasn't asleep. He was sitting in the red Voltaire-style chair in the corner reading a biography of some obscure writer whose name Cecile could never remember.

He lowered the book and glanced up at her.

"How was the movie?"

"Oh, fine…" she said nervously. She stepped out of her dress and pulled a well-worn blue cotton nightshirt over her head.

"What are you doing up?" she asked.

"You really think I wouldn't wait to make sure you got home safely…"

"Manu, I'm not five years old."

"It has nothing to do with that, Cecile."

He placed his book on the nightstand and approached her.

"Are you all right?" he asked.

"Why are you asking me that?" Cecile looked at him strangely, and then remembered her tear-stained face.

"This is about Laurel, isn't it?" he asked. Cecile breathed a sigh of relief.

He took her hands in his. She pulled away, guiltily thinking of her hands in Septime's only an hour earlier.

"I don't understand how you let her get away with everything, Manu. That's nothing new."

He sighed. "She's had a difficult time, Cecile. She spent her childhood moving around the country with her mother and the series of boyfriends… I think she needs some time to find herself."

His eyes were distant, filled with sadness as he said those words. Cecile felt a shiver run through her body. It was the first moment of raw emotion she had observed in his eyes in years. But it had nothing to do with her. His concern only was for Laurel.

Chapter 23

Andre

"I was looking for you." The familiar, musical voice was as if from a dream. But it solidified itself through the warm hand that touched his arm in the back of the café where no one else in the world would expect to find Andre Wren. No one except Clarisse.

Andre didn't know how long he had been there, nursing a whisky and illegally smoking one cigarette after the next. The last thing he could remember was receiving a phone call from Jack who was on his way to Paris from New York with Stan Linovska, whose mission was to convince Andre to take the role in his film. While this sort of occurrence normally would have been welcomed, Andre this time found himself dreading an encounter with the director. He didn't want a bit part, five minutes in a role that would typecast him at this delicate stage in his career.

He had taken a peek at the script that Jack had e-mailed to him before tossing it out. Max was an alcoholic father who would show his face twice on the screen. Once to argue with his son and once to reconcile with him. He didn't want to play the part of a broken-down old man. Andre always had been

the handsome, virile one, whether playing the good guy or the
bad guy. He would rather turn his back on what he loved than
put his pride in jeopardy.

So after Andre Wren listened to Jack's message, muffled
by the background chattering and announcements at the
airport, he grabbed the cane that he had just leaned against the
kitchen counter and made his way back to the front door. He
didn't know where he was going, but he had to get out of this
place with its memories of Clarisse and the imminent pressure
from Jack. He would soon be arriving and chances were his
first destination would be Andre's apartment, no matter what
the hour.

Clarisse sat down beside him. She looked beautiful, as
always. But this time, she appeared calmer, kinder than she
had been in a long while. She wore jeans and a sweatshirt, and
her tousled hair half covered her face. It was rare to see
Clarisse without her makeup and perfectly styled chignon.
This was the Clarisse Andre preferred, but she wasn't available
very often.

Clarisse studied him for a moment.

"What's bothering you?" she asked.

"It's nothing… Why were you looking for me anyway?"
He didn't want her sympathy.

"I had left behind some jewelry," she said. "But of course
you weren't home, so I figured I would come back another
time. And then I ran into the concierge who told me you had
left rather abruptly earlier… I was concerned."

"Why would you care?" he asked in annoyance. "And
beyond that, I'm tired of that woman spreading stories
around…"

"Andre, stop, she didn't mean any harm," Clarisse said
firmly.

"What did you come here expecting to accomplish,
Clarisse?"

"I wanted to find out if everything was all right with your
son."

"And why wouldn't it be?"

"Andre, word has a way of traveling, you know?"

"You mean Tatiana Ricci has a way of spreading gossip,"

Andre said. The two women took the same yoga class every Monday evening, or at least they did until Clarisse had moved out of Andre's life.

"He didn't get the part in Deville's 'Streetcar,'" she said.

Andre straightened up and leaned across the table.

"What do you mean? He was the best one there!"

Clarisse's cupid's-bow lips turned up at the edges.

"I don't think I've ever heard you sound that naïve, Andre. This must be love. You really do care about Hugo no matter what you go around telling everyone—including yourself. So instead of living a lie, why don't you do something to help him out?"

"Yeah, like what, Clarisse? He won't talk to me…"

"Oh, something indirect, maybe. You know plenty of people."

And then, with those words, it hit him. The starring role in Linovska's film. Now that was an interesting part. That's what had made him hang onto the script for an extra ten seconds before tossing it. *If only I were younger,* he'd said to himself.

Andre swallowed hard. He would have to face Jack and Linovska if he were to push them in Hugo's direction. And he would have to put his pride in his pocket as well. Andre wasn't used to asking for favors. But the thought of his son struggling in this fucked-up business had been eating at him no matter how much he tried to say otherwise. His mind was made up. He would do the right thing.

Andre looked up at Clarisse.

"You're right," he said. "I'm going to do something, but if I want it to work, I have to hurry…"

An amazed smile lit Clarisse's face.

"Maybe you have made some progress…"

But for once, Andre's priority wasn't the admiration of a beautiful woman.

ೕഛೕ

They were waiting for him outside his apartment. It was 11 p.m., but it didn't matter to Jack. When he wanted

something, nothing got in his way. Jack, a silver-haired man
with a perfectly pressed dark suit, looked out of place next to
the disheveled Stan with his jeans and backpack, Andre
thought to himself.

The men shook hands, and Andre showed them into his
apartment.

"Nice place," Stan said, gazing at the small part of the art
collection that Clarisse had left behind.

"It's my wife's taste, not mine," Andre said, pushing away
the pang of sadness that arose when he thought of the time
she had spent decorating each room. "Now why don't you
both sit down while I pour the drinks? I have this wonderful
German beer…"

"Can't say no to that," Jack said.

Andre pushed his cane into a corner and limped
unabashedly into the kitchen. What difference did it make at
this point? His career was shot anyway. He might as well
accept the view that Linovska and all of the others had
developed ever since they heard about his accident.

"Why are you arriving so late anyway?" Andre called out
over his shoulder.

"Problems at JFK," Jack said. "Our flight was cancelled…
then they re-routed us through Amsterdam, and we had a
layover there. The usual airline bullshit."

Andre teetered back to the room, delicately balancing a
serving tray in his hands.

"You don't do this often, do you?" Jack commented with
a sly smile. "I don't think I've ever seen you serving before…"

"What business would I have entertaining?" he grumbled
as he pushed the drinks in their direction.

Moments later they were sitting around the oak coffee
table, sipping beer and chatting about nonsense that annoyed
Andre to no end. Meaningless chitchat blocked everything that
was important in life from happening.

"Let's get down to business," he finally said, trying to hide
his exasperation. "I read your screenplay, Stan, and I know an
actor who would make an excellent candidate for the leading
role."

Stan raised an eyebrow, and Jack glared at Andre. He

hated when his actors took control of the situation, but that never had stopped Andre from saying what was on his mind.

"His name is Hugo Adler," Andre said. "I've seen him at work and have been quite impressed."

"Never heard of him," Stan said quietly. "I want someone who has a confirmed presence."

Jack's eyes hadn't left Andre's face.

"There's one thing that might make a difference," Andre said with a sly smile. "He's my son. I think he's pretty talented and deserves a fair shot in this goddamn game."

Stan squinted at Andre and studied him for a moment. Andre held his breath and counted to ten to keep himself from showing his annoyance at this stupid man's reticence.

"I didn't know you had a son..." Stan said.

"Well, I do. Now you know!" Andre crossed his arms across his chest and leaned back in his chair. He wasn't going to beg. This was about as close as he ever came to it, and he hated the feeling.

"I'd like to see him," Stan said in his low voice.

"All right, fine," Jack broke in. "But what we really came for was a conversation with you, Andre. You've had the chance to read through the script..."

"I don't want it," he said.

Stan's nervous, light eyes blinked rapidly. "Andre, you're the one I need for this. I want a cameo. I want a star for this role... Jack told me you were interested."

Andre turned blazing eyes on Jack. This wasn't the first time his agent had manipulated him and a director.

"Look, why don't we settle down for a minute," Jack said. "I have a fair proposal. Andre, Stan will hire Hugo for the lead, and you'll take the cameo. Can you imagine the publicity? Father and son."

Andre could almost see the wheels churning in his head.

Stan looked at him thoughtfully.

"I'd like to at least see Hugo audition first," he said.

"Fine," Jack said. "In any case, you won't be disappointed. I've heard plenty about him. He's getting quite a reputation..."

Andre was boiling mad at the control that Jack continued to exercise over his life. At other times, he fought to at least modify the situation somewhat to his liking. But he knew that he had no leverage this time. If he wanted to help his son, he would have to bend to his agent's will.

"All right," Stan said decisively shaking his blond head. "Let's go for it…"

He turned to Andre. "Most of the filming won't start for three months, but I'd like to shoot some key scenes involving these two characters over the next few weeks right here in Paris… Can you ask him to come here early tomorrow morning for an audition?"

"No, no," Jack said. "I'll take care of this. If I'm guessing correctly, I would say Andre doesn't want any part of it."

Andre nodded. This wasn't exactly what he had bargained for, but if it could catapult Hugo to success, maybe he wouldn't be such a failure as a father after all.

Chapter 24

Mira

Mira dropped her bag onto the flower-printed rug. She walked through the three large rooms separated by French doors until she reached the sliding one leading to the patio, her former sanctuary. Her supplies were scattered about as if she had never left. Even her pink, porcelain cup, half-filled with murky earl gray, and an opened box of amaretto cookies remained on the metal card table near her easel.

She collapsed onto the rickety, wooden stool and burst into tears. The early-afternoon sun baked down, warming her cheek, but she couldn't accept its consolation. She closed her eyes, but the tears squeezed their way out anyway, leaving behind hot streaks of mascara. Mira didn't want to think about why she was crying. She didn't want to admit to herself that Hugo's image hadn't left her mind for a second. She didn't want to accept her sadness after Antonio's betrayal or her fears about being a single mother.

It seemed to Mira as if hours passed before she was able to take a deep breath, wipe her eyes and scold herself for being mentally fragile. Finally, she walked inside with determination. She had come here to talk with Antonio. Maybe they could work things out somehow, Septime had said. Mira played her brother's words over and over in her head, but remained unconvinced. She decided she would return, face Antonio and then... And then what? Mira didn't know.

Automatically, she made her way to the appointment book that Antonio kept on the kitchen counter. He would return by early evening. In any case, Mira planned on packing up the rest of her clothing and art supplies, and shipping them to Paris. She couldn't count on reconciliation.

Hours seemed to pass as quickly as minutes. Clearing personal items from the bedroom and living room were easy tasks, but packing easels and paint supplies were much more time consuming. Mira attacked the job with gusto as it helped her push the unpleasant memories from her mind. She loaded box after box in the rental car that she would then drive to the nearby mailing center. Everything was going smoothly until she made her way to the front door with the very last crate and found herself face-to-face with Antonio and Clara. They were laughing and holding hands.

Mira swallowed hard and dropped the box to the floor. Brushes of various sizes spilled out and rolled around Clara's red espadrilles. Mira felt her heartbeat accelerate.

"I see you both are doing well..."

"Mira..." Antonio took her hand, but she pulled away.

"It's not what I think, right? Don't try saying that."

"You walked out, Mira. You said it was over."

"And I made a very good decision it seems..."

"Look, I'd better leave you two alone," Clara said, taking a step back and avoiding her former friend's eyes. She flipped her long dark hair over one shoulder and hurried out the door before Mira could say a word.

"Mira, I know," Antonio said.

"Know what?" she asked calmly.

"Why didn't you tell me that you were pregnant? Damn it, Mira! What were you waiting for? Clara had to be the one to break the news! That isn't fair... You should have been the one to share that with me. I want to make things work..."

"You have a strange way of showing it."

"I'm not in love with Clara! It was just a fling, and it's

over now. We only got together this afternoon because she said she had something to tell me. That's how I learned about the baby… and I was asking her where I could find you."

"So it's perfectly normal that you were holding hands?" Mira asked sarcastically.

Antonio looked away in silence.

"You like her enough to sleep with her. I can't deal with that. I refuse to!"

He reached for her hand, but she pushed him away. She looked into the eyes that once melted her heart. They had little effect on her now. All was broken beyond repair. This almost surprised her. She had been telling herself that their relationship had ended, yet she had this fear deep within that seeing him again would weaken her resolve. And right at this moment, she realized that wasn't the case. She wasn't in love with him. In a matter of days, those old emotions had self-destructed. She would miss the person she once knew, or thought she knew. But the man standing inches away from her seemed like a complete stranger.

"Well, I've got news for you," Mira said. "You've lost me. You lost me the day you started screwing around with someone else."

"Think of the baby!"

Mira felt as if she'd been struck. She looked at him through wild eyes.

"Me? You're asking me to think of the baby? I've been constantly thinking of the baby while you've been thinking of your own satisfaction! Even after I left, you apparently continued on with Clara. If you think that argument is going to work, you're way off."

"Mira, I thought you wanted me back, that we had a chance. Didn't you tell Clara about your pregnancy for a reason?"

She shook her head and looked at him bitterly.

"I figured it would be best if she broke the news. It certainly wasn't going to come directly from me. That's why I told her. So you would really understand what you lost. And then I had second thoughts. I came back here today to see how I would feel seeing you again. There's nothing left,

Antonio!"

Mira pushed past him in a fury, forgetting about the final box of brushes and blank paper, and hurried out to the car. He called after her, but the sound of the engine muffled his final words.

Chapter 25

Rafael

Sleep wouldn't come as Rafael squeezed his eyes shut against the moonlight sifting through the narrow bedroom window. It was the same room where he had stayed with his parents. He could still smell the spicy scent of his father's cigars and see his mother counting their money over and over at the wooden desk pushed into one corner. Anita Santini, who had lodged the family for years, would always stop by—right after their 2 a.m. arrival as if it were the most commonplace hour to drag one's bags into a motel—and welcome them to the inn she had run for decades. But this evening was different. She passed away a few months ago, a brusque young woman told them as she coldly escorted the men to one room and Lea to another.

Rafael felt as if he were in a third dimension. The yellowed, smoke-stained walls were the same, as were the sounds of heavy footsteps moving through the dim hallway. The physical characteristics of the place had remained. Yet the atmosphere had transformed itself into something foreign. There was no longer that feeling of eagerness about a mission to be accomplished. There wasn't the raucous camaraderie between them and the regulars who arrived at the same time to claim a room and later the best emeralds. Rafael had seen a few unfamiliar faces sneering in their direction.

The only thing to disturb Tigo's even breathing from the twin bed across from Rafael's was an occasional snore that turned into a grunt. Then he would roll over and slip back into the soundest of sleeps. Rafael pushed away the sheets, sat up and looked at the fluorescent arms on his watch that pointed to 3:30 a.m.

In Paris, what could Laurel be doing? His heart ached as he thought of his flight from the city, from her. He had been foolish to hold back from contacting the woman he loved. He could finally admit it to himself. He wasn't just infatuated with Laurel. Suddenly, more than anything else, he wanted to be with her. Rafael still could feel her delicate fingers running through his hair as his lips met hers. But he was helpless and stuck here in Colombia on this fake quest for a stone that he had grown to hate. Beads of sweat trickled along his hairline. It was damn hot in this musty room. He had to get some air. He didn't care about sleep.

Rafael tiptoed to the door, released the latch and slipped out. He made his way down the hallway, out the side door and into the overgrown flower garden where his mother would have her breakfast before heading out to meet with those who had been trolling the mines for emeralds. He sat down on the same marble bench and looked at the wilting, pink flowers that she would have been able to identify in an instant.

"Haven't seen you around in a while, young man." The familiar voice startled Rafael. He leaped to his feet and found himself facing Anita's husband Hector. The old man shook his hand and then sat down to roll a cigarette with shaky, twisted fingers. Rafael sat down beside him.

"I'm sorry to hear about your wife's passing," Rafael said. His heart pounding with anticipation, he waited for the man to speak once again.

Hector shook his head. "The good Lord took her." He made the sign of the cross and his hands returned to their busywork. Then his murky blue eyes, hidden by cataracts, settled on Rafael's face.

"You called me here, didn't you?" Rafael asked softly.

Hector was silent for a moment. Then he nodded.

"Why?" Rafael whispered, as if a thousand ears were listening from the flowerbeds. "What does it matter to you if Diego's killer is still on the loose?"

"Our house always welcomed the *comisionistas*," the old man said. "And there never was violence here. Until now. Two murders here last time we had a full house. I knew that Diego's killer had to be involved in this. There has been too much tension about who would take over his superior position at the mines…"

"It's Ric Ramirez isn't it?"

Hector shook his head.

"Ramirez's only power is up here," he said, pointing to his temple. "He thinks he's the best… he doesn't have the need to battle it out with the others."

"So who killed Diego?"

"That's one thing I can't tell you."

"Why not?"

"Because I don't know."

"But on the phone you said it was the one who got the best stones…" Rafael said desperately. His T-shirt stuck to his damp skin, but he was shivering inside.

"It is, my boy, but I don't know exactly who that person is—I don't go to the mines. I simply overhear conversations around here. He is among us. He is in this house! Only you can identify him. You will sense it. You will know."

Hector had finished rolling his cigarette and was looking at it complacently. A sense of disappointed confusion overcame Rafael. Nothing was clear. Things only seemed to be getting foggier, as a matter of fact. How was he supposed to figure out whether what Hector said was true or merely a horrible rumor that scared the old man so much that he felt the need to call on someone for help? In any case, Rafael was certain that he would find out no more in the moonlit garden. His unique chance would be the trip to the emerald mines.

☙❧

All began at the crack of dawn. Rugged vehicles pulled out of the little dirt lot in front of the Santini's house and made their way the short distance to the marketplace, a parking area surrounded by mountains on one side and the main road on the other. Tigo, Rafael and Lea slipped out of the 4X4. The two men dressed casually in jeans and T-shirts, while Lea had taken on the guise of a glamorous emerald trader. Her hot pink lipstick reflected her mini dress and sandals. She would be making the deals.

They weren't the first to arrive, but it didn't seem to matter, as they immediately became the center of attention. Eager hands forced stones into Lea's hands for consideration. They were miners, who stuffed their pockets with handfuls of dirt and later sifted out the treasure. It would become their fortune. The same people used to mob Diego and Tina. The miners knew who would pay the best price.

Lea held stones up to the almost iridescent sunlight and quickly made her decisions. She directed an unfamiliar gracious smile at the miners who brought her the best stones. Tigo and Rafael each doled out cash in thousands to sooty hands that would caress the bills gratefully as they thanked "Miss Lea."

Rafael's quick eye scanned the rest of the marketplace, where others made deals between jeeps and near the rinky-dink concession trucks that sold sandwiches and sodas like at a county fair. The air carried that same spicy-sausage scent mixed with the dampness of the deep earth. A sick feeling was rising from within Rafael's stomach. Lea. This girl with the intense eyes and incredible ability to choose a stone. *She was the one! She had to be!*

Rafael swallowed hard. He glanced at Tigo, his childhood friend, who was re-examining the newly acquired emeralds with satisfaction. He didn't want to believe—he couldn't believe—that Tigo was involved in Diego's murder. After all, Tigo hadn't even returned to the emerald mines at that point. He still was traveling the world. Lea had to be the one in charge. Her knowledge of the emeralds was proof in and of itself. Just then, her eyes met those of Rafael. That silent, powerful gaze. His blood ran cold.

Chapter 26

Cecile

She thought he still would be there, at the apartment where she had learned to see herself as a woman again. But she arrived hours too late, as had often been the case in her life. Cecile stood helplessly in the cozy lobby adorned with copies of Van Gogh's "Sunflowers" and remembrances of Arles. The artist supposedly stayed at this old place at one time in his miserable life. It was a modest hotel that offered a good night's sleep to many flamboyant characters before being gutted in the 1960s and split up into apartments. That was what Septime had told her. Its history was what attracted him to it from the start. She turned away from Van Gogh's self-portrait, which she found too depressing, and walked stiffly out the door and away from those haunted eyes.

Cecile tried to contain her disappointment. Even one day without Septime turned her mood sour. Especially with what had been going on at home. She felt as if they had been watching her strangely. She was surrounded. What were they thinking as they looked at her with accusing eyes? Was Manu imagining her in the arms of another man? She shook her head. Of course not, the voice of reason said. But was that morning's conversation some kind of psychological game? And if it was, could it be one that would eventually defeat her?

Cecile had found him staring vapidly at his computer screen. He didn't seem to be aware of her footsteps as they shifted from the hardwood floor to the dense, green carpet in the study. The room was lined with heavy, over-stuffed bookshelves. Volumes of Racine and Voltaire, Shakespeare and Joyce were nearly squeezed out of place with each new book Manu would force into their abode.

Cecile sat down opposite him. His eyes latched onto hers. In the pink terry bathrobe, she felt like a psychiatric patient visiting the resident doctor.

"What is it?" she asked. "Why are you looking at me like that?"

"Nothing," he said with a sigh. "I'm just preparing some material for classes."

"Yeah, school starts in two weeks, doesn't it? Funny how summer slips by and nothing much changes in our lives."

"I never cheated on you," he said suddenly, with a half-grin that rendered his true feelings unreadable.

Cecile's heartbeat accelerated in one, great burst.

"What are you talking about?" she asked sharply. "I never accused you of such a thing." She could hear the panic in her own voice.

"No, but you've been acting distant recently, as if you've lost faith in our relationship."

"What do you mean by that, Manu?" She breathed slowly, trying to keep her cool. She was confused, thrown off balance by his blunt statement.

"You spend your days wandering about the city, Cecile. And when you return, you have a faraway look in your eyes."

"I don't understand what you expect from me, Manu. It's not easy walking on eggshells in your own home... The problem is Laurel. She's disrupted our lives, and the only thing you do is defend her. I'm tired of it!"

"So you do realize that my attention has been drawn away by my daughter—and not by another woman."

"That still puts an obstacle between us," Cecile said, rising from her chair. She didn't want to pin him down on the subject of affairs as she was struggling with her own guilt and desires.

"What do you want me to do?" he asked. "Throw my daughter out?"

He got up, rounded the corner of the desk and took her hands. She pulled away.

"I'd like you to show some authority over this out-of-control 21-year-old," she said.

"She's fragile, Cecile."

"That's an excuse!"

"No it's not," he said, grabbing her hands once again. This time he wouldn't let her go, and she froze as she saw real sorrow in his eyes. "Do you know what it's like visiting your daughter in a mental hospital because her mother screwed up her teen-age years? And then listening to this girl defend her mother no matter what... because I left them. Because I chose you. Don't you understand how responsible I feel?"

Then he lowered his voice and pulled Cecile closer to him. Her heart was pounding as if it was ready to beat its way out of her chest. Yet her body remained stiff, in a state of shock. She knew Laurel had a few rough years, but she had no idea the girl had been hospitalized. Manu had been very vague each time he took a train south to visit Laurel, and Cecile had so little interest in his daughter that she never bothered to ask questions.

"Laurel was raped by her mother's boyfriend when she was 14," Manu hissed. "Do you understand what that can do to a girl?"

Cecile drew in a sharp breath. She tried to speak, but words escaped her.

Manu's eyes were glistening with unshed tears. He released Cecile's hands, turned around and leaned against the desk.

"I didn't realize..." Cecile finally found her voice. "I thought things were difficult but... Why didn't you tell me everything, Manu? Why did you keep this from me?" She approached him timidly and placed a hand on his arm. "Don't you trust me?"

"Of course I do! But this was different. It was for Laurel's sake. She didn't want anyone to know. I made her a promise. And now I've broken her trust… but I didn't think it was fair of you to be so rough on her. I thought this would put things into perspective for you."

"Manu, you're acting as if this was somehow your fault… It wasn't."

"In many ways it was, Cecile! I knew her mother had problems, that she wasn't responsible, that she cared more about men than about her daughter."

"What do we do now?" Cecile asked. "This is difficult for Laurel, but letting her abusive behavior continue isn't going to help matters, Manu! There has to be a specialized center…"

"Laurel is staying here, Cecile. She sees a therapist once a week, and she's getting her life back together at her own pace. She is my priority. For once, she has to be someone's priority."

The words echoed in Cecile's ears as her legs carried her farther and farther from memories of her tryst with Septime. She glanced at the gold arms telling time against a mother-of-pearl background. Viv's rehearsal was coming to an end, and the studio was right around the corner. All of a sudden, she wanted nothing more than to surprise her daughter and show her that she certainly wasn't having an affair or doing anything inappropriate. That intense gaze she had received a few times across the dinner table flustered her. What was this odd, quiet girl thinking? Did she suspect something? But how? Cecile had been careful, yet she felt as if the whole world could read the lies stenciled across her face.

Cecile smoothed her buttercup-colored sundress and hurried as quickly as she could in her skinny-heeled sandals. But before she could approach the little building, she stopped. Manu emerged, arm-in-arm with Viv. How does he even know where this place is? Cecile thought to herself. Viv smiled up at her father with more openness than she ever had shown Cecile. How could she after discovering those letters? Cecile rubbed her aching brow. Manu wasn't the only one to betray her. Now, her own daughter was doing much the same. Cecile turned around. She didn't want to see them. She pushed away feelings of sympathy for Manu as she thought of all he had gone through with his daughter and remembered images of him with another woman. He still refused to be honest about the affair.

Cecile didn't want to return home and face Laurel's tough, sad eyes either. What could she say to this girl whose traumatic past never could be erased? This girl who needed to lash out and had chosen her stepmother as the person she most despised. Cecile had to get away.

Chapter 27

Andre

A small boy of ten, shoulders bent under the weight of a bright blue, shiny plastic backpack, emerged from the brick school building in Brooklyn Heights. Burgundy and mustard-colored leaves caught in his hair as a gust of wind ushered in fall and the chill that Andre already felt running up and down his spine as he lingered several steps behind. He swallowed hard. He hadn't been this close to his son since the backyard party at Jack's house several years ago. Andre didn't know what had possessed him to take a taxi down to Brooklyn on his one day off from *Les Miserables*, which had brought him to New York for the first time in two years.

It was funny how he recognized Hugo in an instant without really meeting the boy face-to-face after the age of one or two. Sure, June had sent pictures, but a still image was never the same as a living person. He would study them, of course, each one documenting the evolution of this child who wasn't a part of his life, yet in some ways consumed it. And now, here he was, this boy, unlatching his scarlet mountain bike from the rack, swinging a leg over the seat and setting off along the sidewalk to the two-family home that June had bought the day Andre walked out of her life. Andre never had been inside the place, and he was certain that June had no idea he had passed by, memorizing its appearance, every time he came to New York.

Hugo waved a hand in the air at a classmate and then pedaled hard, forcing the bike up the slight hill just ahead. Andre didn't understand what had come over him, but suddenly he was running and calling out to his son.

"Hugo! Wait!" he yelled out. His voice seemed to echo well beyond the noise of traffic and street conversation.

But the boy continued pedaling, and the bike made it over the slope and picked up a speed that left Andre far behind, too far to ever catch up.

Andre knew better than to call out now as Hugo emerged from his acting class. This time, the late-summer sun reflected gold in his light hair. Andre didn't speak. Instead, he reached out his hand and touched Hugo on the arm.

"What are you doing here?" Hugo asked with widened eyes. "I already told you that I didn't need anything from you."

"Listen," Andre said, for the first time holding onto his son with a firm grip. "I wanted to congratulate you."

"For what?" Hugo asked. He scrunched his brows together in much the same way June did when she was contemplating something. Andre looked away, his gaze settling on the long row of 19th century apartments lining the street. It was strange how his acting abilities failed him when he was about to hide a certain part of the truth from his son. He refused to use the word "lie"—even to himself. After all, this was for the good of Hugo. Yet, this too-honorable, naïve young man never would accept being given a role because his father had done some bargaining for him. Hugo would be furious. But he wouldn't find out. Andre would make sure of that.

"I heard about your role in Stan Linovska's film," he said.

"I guess word travels fast."

Andre nodded.

"I wanted to tell you something else as well… so you'll be prepared. My agent told me I've got a call back, and he thinks it's likely that I'll be offered a role in the film as well."

"Which role?" Hugo asked. "There aren't any of your usual characters in the script... the big stars... the heroes."

"I'm no longer a hero, Hugo," Andre said with a sarcastic laugh. "I'm in line for the part of the father who fucked up his life... and sometimes, that seems to be not too far from the truth."

"You have regrets then?"

"The fact that this damn accident ruined what was a perfectly satisfactory life." Andre still couldn't open up to his son. He couldn't talk about the pain inside that started when Hugo was born and never really subsided. He wanted to tell Hugo that he was sorry for never accepting him, yet those words somehow wouldn't form in his mouth.

Hugo seemed to take this reply like a slap in the face. He stepped back and gazed at his father with cool eyes.

"No regrets then that you left Mom... and me. I shouldn't be surprised, but every time I see you, I think maybe there will be an ounce of feeling that will slip out... And it doesn't happen. If I have to work opposite you, Andre Wren, I will, because as actors we can't choose our partners..."

Before Andre could reply, Hugo turned around and hurried away, half running until he was out of sight.

"Hugo!" he called out. Then he remembered that his words went unheard.

ॐ

"I tried, June," he said on her voicemail. "But this whole situation is fucked up, and there's no changing it! Hugo doesn't want to talk to me unless I put on a big, drippy act saying I should have been a normal dad who was always around. Well, I can't turn back the clock, so what's the use in crying over spilled milk? I got him a role in this film Stan Linovska is shooting in Paris. I made a deal with him. He gives the part to Hugo, and I take the cameo of the alcoholic father. I never would have accepted this role of a loser otherwise! I'm burying my career—which already has been suffering enough—for this kid... and I can't even tell him. Because he's so honorable that he only would be angry at me for rigging such a plot. So there you go. That's my latest parenting effort. And you're not around to hear about it…"

He slammed down the phone just in time to hear a soft voice behind him.

"You've always loved her."

He turned around.

"Clarisse… you still have your key…"

"This time I brought it with me. I thought you wouldn't be home."

She leaned against the wall and studied him with curious eyes.

"You would have been better off if you admitted to yourself that she was the love of your life. It might have saved us some pain. But I'm glad you at least did something for your son… even if he doesn't realize it."

"I look pretty pathetic, don't I?" he asked, lighting a cigarette and walking toward the couch. He sat down, took a drag and gazed out at the city lights twinkling beyond the window.

Clarisse sat down opposite him. He reached out and took her hand.

"Less pathetic than when you turned your back on me after the accident."

"So what's new with you, Clarisse?" he asked, hoping to steer the conversation away from himself. He was tired of thinking about his own life.

"I'm singing at the Olympia theater next month," she said. "And I'm moving into a new apartment. Across town. Away from here. I need a change of scenery."

"You mean you don't want to go to the same restaurants and shops we always went to together? Well, you're right. It's best to wipe those old stories out of your mind… I wish I could."

"Andre, don't…"

"You were the one who left me, Clarisse. I have the right to say I still love you."

"That isn't true… You're just lonely, Andre. If anything, you're regretting the fact that you left June. I lived in the shadow of her image. I realize that."

"June and I never could have stayed together, Clarisse…
It was different between us."

"It's that way with the love of one's life."

"That's bullshit."

Clarisse pulled away and stood up.

"I don't have a lot of time tonight, Andre. I came by to
pick up a few things, that's all."

"You're going out with someone?"

She nodded.

Andre stood up.

"Take your time," he said, walking toward the door. "And
lock up after you leave."

"Where are you going?"

"To take care of my bike."

"You haven't sold that old thing?"

But Andre ignored the bitter words about the object
Clarisse had hated from the start. His only thought was to
make it downstairs to the garage and spend the next few hours
polishing the Harley that he never would ride again. It brought
him a sense of regret, but at the same time, simply seeing it
carried him far from the Rue des Martyrs.

Chapter 28

Mira

The sun was setting as Mira arrived at the little cottage that Septime kept in the countryside outside of Naples. She unlatched the wrought-iron gate, ran through the wildflowers that prospered in the front yard, and impatiently rang the bell. She was tired of this endless day spent hurrying from place to place. At least her belongings were on their way to Paris. She leaned against the outside wall and deeply inhaled the scent of a nearby gardenia bush as muffled footsteps in the hallway made their way closer and closer. Mira was exhausted, but otherwise felt perfectly fine. The nausea that had made her stomach quake these past few days seemed to have departed as quickly as it had arrived. The door creaked open.

"Septime, finally…" she said, swiveling around. Then she drew in a sharp breath.

"You're his sister, aren't you?" said a slim brunette wrapped in a sky-blue peignoir that matched her eyes. She couldn't have been much older than Mira, but she had a rather assertive expression that often adds years to the face.

"Where is he?" Mira asked, her mood turning to anger from surprise as she thought of her brother's recent conquest of the vulnerable Cecile. "And who… are you?"

"I'm Lenore, a friend of his…" She took a step back, and Mira marched in with an authoritative air.

"He'll be out in a minute," Lenore continued. "He was showering. Please come in and make yourself at home."

But Mira no longer was listening. She walked slowly down the long, tile hallway until she reached the bedroom that looked out on the neighbor's perfect flower garden. The door was closed, and she heard her brother moving about just beyond it.

"Septime, it's me," she said in a controlled voice. "Let me in."

The door flew open and her brother, already dressed in jeans and a T-shirt, reached for her hand. But she pushed him away and entered the room filled with shower mist and obscure paintings. The sheets were tangled, half draped onto the floor with Lenore's clothing. Mira dropped her bag, crossed her arms and glared at Septime. Faintly, she could hear the television murmuring at the far end of the house.

"Mira, what's going on?" Septime asked, approaching her.

"Stop," she said. "I arrived here this morning, and I've already had enough!"

"What's that supposed to mean?"

"Forget about my crazy day. What's going on here with you? You're cheating on Cecile… after seducing her, putting her marriage in jeopardy… you're throwing her away like all of the others! I thought that was over. I thought you had discovered something real."

"Mira, I can't understand what difference it makes to you," Septime said with a half grin that annoyed his sister more than anything else. She hated this blasé attitude about fidelity. "My affairs shouldn't concern you. Cecile is old enough to make her own decisions."

"Your affairs do concern me when you're cheating on an innocent woman who could lose everything because of you! Don't you know how it feels, Septime? She doesn't deserve that."

"Mira, this isn't about you and Antonio!"

"I never said it was," she said sharply. But she was lying.

Her brother's behavior suddenly was a mirror image of Antonio's.

"You need time to deal with your own pain, Mira. Saving the world isn't going to solve your problems. This is a completely different situation! Cecile and I both went into this with our eyes open. Her husband had turned his back on her long ago. Their children are older…"

"This is a game for you, isn't it? She's one of many conquests and nothing more." Mira could feel tears burning in the corners of her eyes. Antonio, Clara and her brother crossed paths in her tortured mind. She felt as if she was reliving the betrayal over and over again.

"Mira, I'm crazy about Cecile!" he whispered. "She's intriguing… but she doesn't have any kind of commitment to me. She didn't accept my invitation here for a few days, so what are you expecting from me? I can't give up everything for nothing…"

"I don't believe you would give up your women for her in any circumstance," Mira hissed. "Not even if she left her family!"

Tears streamed furiously down her cheeks. Again, she saw Antonio and Clara, smiling, looking into each other's eyes.

"Mira, what's wrong with you?" Septime asked. He pulled her down beside him on the purple loveseat in the corner of the room. "You're mixing up everything. That's ridiculous, you know. My life is my business and not yours!"

"Then don't get involved in mine," she said, standing up and marching to the bedroom door. "My artwork, my relationships, the baby. Keep away from them!"

"No, wait… don't leave like this, Mira! Stay here in the guest room tonight."

"I'm getting out of here, and at this point I don't know if I'll ever come back!"

He tried to hold onto her, to convince her to stay calm for the sake of the baby, but she refused his arguments and headed toward the front door with one thought on her mind: returning to Paris.

Mira sat rigidly on a bench at the station where she would wait for the early morning train to Rome. She hastily booked a flight from there to Paris and then jammed her cell phone into her bag. Her last-minute travel plans meant she didn't have much of a choice regarding means of transportation or schedule. She didn't bother trying to find a hotel. The night would pass quickly this way as her eyes wandered dully from voyager to voyager. She had cried all of her tears. She was empty.

The electronic voice rang in her ears now and again as it announced an arrival or a departure. The scent of stale and fresh cigarette smoke clouded the air, turning everything blue-gray. But nothing roused Mira from her state of distracted meditation until a familiar figure emerged from a train that had just arrived.

Cecile stepped onto the platform. She looked around uncertainly and advanced with the mass that nearly blocked her from view. Mira kept her eye trained on the long, white linen skirt that swished back and forth with each footstep. Then she rose from her seat and waved a hand in Cecile's direction.

"Cecile!" she called out.

The woman looked around curiously until her eyes found Mira's. Recognition and then a smile. Almost timidly, she approached Mira.

"What are you doing here?" they both asked at once, their words running over each other.

"I had some business to take care of," Mira said quickly. "You're here to see Septime, aren't you?"

Cecile nodded.

"This is a surprise, isn't it? The last time I spoke with him, he said you weren't coming." A feeling of panic rose within as Mira thought of what Cecile surely would discover if she knocked on Septime's door.

"I changed my mind." Cecile's fingers nervously twisted the straps of her designer handbag.

"Before you go, do you have time for a drink?" Mira asked. She nodded her head in the direction of the little café sandwiched between a newsstand and a flower shop in the musty station.

Cecile hesitated for a second and then smiled.

"Sure," she said. "It's not as if anyone is expecting me…"

They settled down at a table with a view of the tracks and departing trains. The other places around them were sparsely occupied, and the few travelers who were having a drink at this hour looked so glassy eyed that Mira was certain they weren't aware of the women's presence. One weary looking waiter approached, and Mira ordered two herbal teas and stared into Cecile's almost scared, yet eager eyes.

"Are you sure my brother is worth the trouble?" Mira asked.

Cecile looked down for a moment, bit her lip and then leaned closer to Mira.

"Do you know what it's like to be emotionally void for years?" she asked gingerly. "That was my life for too long— until I met Septime. He brought back the excitement that I couldn't remember existed."

"You're set to leave your family for that?"

"I'm not sure what I'm going to do… I have responsibilities that I can't neglect, yet when I'm away from Septime, I feel that emptiness settling in. It's frightening. My husband is obsessed with the well-being of his daughter from a first marriage. I'll never be able to compete with that. And my own daughter lives a life that seems to be in another dimension, far away from mine. This doesn't bother her. She's very independent. Too independent for her age. The only one I see eye-to-eye with is my son, but we send him to boarding school. Manu wouldn't do otherwise. So I'm stuck in a house of strangers. I don't work, because I don't quite know what I would do… I married Manu right out of school and never had to make a living. Now, I'm half regretting everything, regretting the life I missed…"

She was silent for a moment and then blushed as she glanced at Mira.

"I don't know why I'm telling you this. I never pour out my problems… not to anyone."

Mira touched her arm. "That's probably part of the problem. We all need to be heard… I just had a big argument with my brother…"

"I hope everything is all right…"

"I don't agree with his point of view on certain things," Mira said carefully. She ached to tell Cecile to avoid him at all costs, but she knew her words would only be ignored. She saw the sparkle in the woman's eyes when she mentioned Septime's name. It was too late. Cecile already had fallen under Septime's spell. She was on her own, and Mira, who longed to help, realized the situation was well beyond her control.

The waiter arrived with tiny white cups and saucers, and Mira lifted one slowly to her lips. For her, it would be a long night. And if Cecile ended up running into Lenore, for her, it would be much longer.

Chapter 29

Rafael

"Do you always do that well?" Rafael asked Tigo as they sped out of the parking lot.

"You're impressed?" Tigo said with a half-smile. "We've done better."

"Looks like you've taken over my father's position."

"No one could ever do that," Lea piped up from the back seat. "We all look for something different in an emerald."

"Funny how I recognized a lot of the same miners who worked with my parents…"

The short ride back to the inn was a silent, uncomfortable one. Rafael felt out of place with this friend-turned-stranger and the young woman who had so much hidden within her solemn eyes.

"We're leaving in an hour," Tigo said when they pulled into the dirt lot. "I have an appointment first, but I'll be back in time." He dropped Lea and Rafael off at the iron gate that led into the flower garden where Rafael had spent most of his night. It was the back entrance to the inn, and few people knew it existed.

Rafael grabbed Lea by the arm and pulled her into the

overgrown shrubbery.

"What are you doing?" she whispered, looking at him with vicious eyes. Her hand went for her gun, but Rafael had already slipped it out of her handbag.

"You did it, didn't you?" he hissed under his breath. "You killed Diego! And now you're taking over with your own talent…"

"That's not true!" she hurled the words at him and pulled away. All of a sudden, tears were streaming down her face and the cement bench encrusted with seashells caught her as she collapsed. She held her head in her hands for a moment and then looked back at Rafael, who sat down at her side.

"I didn't want him to do it," she mumbled.

"What are you talking about?" Rafael's voice had become gruff.

"It's Tigo! Don't you see? He had just returned from his travels. We met at a little café in Bogotá. We both wanted to sell emeralds so we decided to team up." Lea's words started running together in a frenzied stream. "But I didn't think it would involve murder… And then it was too late. If I ran away, he said I would be next. He needed me to choose the emeralds, to work with him. Only I knew how to identify the best ones, he said. That's true. He wouldn't know a valuable emerald if it bit him. He hadn't learned a thing from his father. And he regretted that."

Rafael felt as if the world was spinning out of control around him. His mind returned to that horrible night and the glass mixed with blood spattering on his shirt as a round of bullets punctured the windshield. Rafael could still see the bitter disappointment on Diego's face at a destiny that shouldn't have been his as he closed his eyes for the last time.

"What proof do you have that it's Tigo?" Rafael asked, trying to push the haunting thoughts from his mind.

"Go into the room and look in his suitcase," she said defiantly. "You'll find Diego's medallion there. Tigo carries it with him, as if that will bring him the luck he needs. You'll see."

"And then you'll get away…"

"Yeah, only to be back again for another emerald run…

there's no escaping in this business. I don't have to tell you that…"

Rafael didn't say another word. He raced through the garden, down the hall and unlocked the door to the room he was sharing with Tigo. He only had a few minutes, but he knew exactly where to go: the small overnight bag that Tigo had tucked under the bed. Rafael lifted the blue gauze blanket and reached for the nylon sack. But it was gone. He reached further under the bed, and found only dust.

"Maybe I can help you with something?"

Rafael froze. It was Tigo. He hadn't heard the door open as he searched so intently in the corner of the room. Slowly, Rafael turned around. Tigo was standing behind him, holding Diego's medallion cockily in one hand and his gun in the other. The medallion, an antique gold sun with an emerald twinkling in its center swung from left to right like a tool used to hypnotize.

"Why did you do it?" Rafael asked, as he stood up.

"For the same reason as the others who tried to take him down all of those years. For the emeralds. Who else even had a chance to get the best stones when the miners only wanted to bargain with Diego and Tina?"

Rafael swallowed hard. He remembered the ambushes. Diego was hospitalized twice with gunshot wounds, but each time the attacker had paid with his life. He could still see his father's bullet piercing one attacker's chest. The man's dark blue plaid shirt drinking up the river of blood that oozed from within. Tina and Rafael helping Diego back to their truck. Tina taking the wheel.

"None of them were able to do the job," Tigo continued. "Then I came along. And I made killing him my mission before anything else. That's why I was successful."

"Why did you return in the first place?" Rafael asked in disgust. "You always said you wanted no part of the emerald business!"

"That was before I ran out of my father's money. I spent two years traveling the world first class, Rafael, and I realized I was used to that kind of living. And it wasn't going to continue unless I came back to the emeralds. It was the only thing I could do! You would do the same if I let you out of here alive… but I don't think that will happen."

Rafael knew it was time. He couldn't think or be afraid. He lunged forward. Tigo's gun went off, but the bullet just grazed Rafael's shoulder as he dove to the side and grabbed his 9-millimeter. Tigo was back on his feet, lifting his gun as Rafael fired, thinking only of Diego and Tina.

He watched, half in victory and half in horror, as Tigo fell backwards like the man in the blue plaid shirt so many years ago. Dead. In only a matter of seconds, everything had changed. Rafael touched Tigo's pulse points, empty of any sign of life.

"I didn't want it to be this way," he whispered.

Tears poured down his cheeks as he grabbed his bag, Diego's medallion and the keys to the 4X4. Rafael wiped them away. Diego never shed a tear when he shot the enemy. But Rafael couldn't look back at that limp figure on the floor. His story with Tigo was humanity at its worst.

Chapter 30

Cecile

Cecile took one deep breath of the fresh, rose-scented air that wafted in from the open window and swiveled around in Septime's arms. The dreary tediousness and tension of the past few days with Manu disappeared in her lover's eyes as she pressed her naked body against his in what seemed like paradise.

He ran his hands through her hair and kissed her fervently as she led him back to the bed. They had spent the morning in this warm place, their bodies entwined.

Time was meaningless. Seconds and minutes ran together. Goose bumps ran up and down Cecile's spine as they never had done with the calm intimacy she shared with Manu. She drew in a breath. The whole room seemed to tremble. Cecile had discovered a new life that made her forget the one she left behind.

Day faded into night, and Cecile prepared herself for their first big outing together. She slipped on the long, black silk dress that she had purchased before leaving Paris and twisted her hair into a perfect coil held up with a pearl clip. Then they ran out the front door laughing like 16-year-olds and made their way into the taxi, where they would spend the whole ride into the city locked in each other's arms.

This time, Cecile entered the gallery holding Septime's hand. His exhibit here was much like the one in Paris, at least to Cecile's untrained eye. But the atmosphere in Naples was warmer, jovial, as old friends approached him and laughed heartily in the blue-green light that for Cecile was the one negative factor. It reminded her of the hideous color scheme that Manu had chosen for their apartment.

"Why don't you like the lights, love?" Septime whispered in her ear.

But she couldn't tell him the real reason. She didn't want to talk about home. She wanted to immerse herself in this freedom and happiness that escaped her back there. It never was too late.

She pushed away any twinge of guilt by telling herself that the kids didn't need her. Joel was independent and away at school, and Viv obviously preferred her father.

Cecile touched Septime on the cheek.

"I find blue and green kind of cold…"

"That's the point, Cecile. It captures the mood of this collection…"

"But in Paris you had red lights…"

"The pieces are different if you look closely."

"Ah, I see," she said, pretending to examine a wiry clocklike figure that she found atrocious.

She still didn't see any kind of difference, but it didn't matter much to her. As long as she satisfied Septime and he satisfied her, life was wonderful.

And apparently she did satisfy him. Especially when she peeled off her clothes after midnight.

She finally had been able to forget about the few pounds that she needed to eliminate from her tummy and bottom as he told her she already was perfect. Desire burned within and she forgot about the headache she had developed from too much champagne earlier in the evening.

"I never would have guessed that you would break free from your strict, orderly life," he said as she curled up next to him. "Are you catching up for lost time with a husband who neglected you?"

"What makes you say that?" she asked breathlessly.

"You have all of the symptoms."

The passion only subsided when Septime had to return to his work, and Cecile prepared to travel back to Paris. She packed her simple overnight bag and took a taxi into town to see him one last time. Cecile had asked him to come with her, but he said they would have to endure two unbearable days apart because of Mira's hurried and unexpected departure.

"What do you mean?" Cecile had asked him. She stuffed her anti-wrinkle creams and other lotions and potions into her toiletry bag as Septime finished dressing.

"We have problems seeing eye-to-eye on certain things— that's all. And because of our differences, she left. She was supposed to speak with some of the local art students about portraits, so now that she's gone, I'll have to be here to replace her. I don't have any other option." He shook his head in annoyance.

Her mind returned to the present as the cab came to a halt. Cecile stuffed some bills into the driver's hand, and slipped out of the car and onto the busy sidewalk. She had an hour before she would catch her train. Septime thought they already had said their goodbyes earlier that morning, but she had to see him one more time before returning to the sad reality that seemed so difficult to escape. She ignored the countless messages that Manu had left on her cell phone over the past 24 hours, and pretended that he and life's monotony no longer existed. Cecile was afraid of hearing his voice. It would soften her heart, and she would return to the comfort of family life that would only make her miserable. Cecile was returning to Paris, but not to the place that always had been home to Manu and her. She would tell Septime that she was all his when he returned. She had made her decision.

Cecile darted across the street with the mass of tourists crossing against the light and laughed out loud with delight as she approached the gallery, illuminated in gold even at midday.

He would be there, talking with his admirers before setting out to speak with those students who were expecting Mira instead. Cecile swung her bubble-shaped black bag along her side as if it was weightless and pushed open the door to happiness. The room was filled with art lovers at this early hour, but her eyes only settled on one person.

He was sitting on a stool at the back of the room in intense conversation with a young woman who pressed her cheek against his as he ran his hands through her long, silky hair. Cecile took a step back and then another, bumping into a jolly older man who smiled and asked her if she was all right. She nodded dully, but she could no longer see or hear anything. The whole room was fuzzy, spinning around, as the music seemed unbearably loud, pounding in her ears. She had to get out before the whole place closed in on her. Before he saw her. She turned around and ran.

Cecile didn't look as she crossed the street, pushing her way through the mass of people unaware of her pain. She yanked open the door of the first taxi in the long line parked crookedly along the sidewalk.

"I'm going to the train station," she said, doing everything in her power to avoid the tears that wanted so desperately to burst forth. She held them in for the bumpy five-minute ride that took her through narrow side streets in a part of town not designed for tourism. Her eyes took in young couples pushing baby carriages, old women pinching fruit at little outdoor stands and kids playing hopscotch on the sidewalks. Everyday life that reminded her of her own. She closed her eyes until the taxi stopped.

Minutes later she had run through the station and secured her seat on the train, where she let the tears fall slowly into her handkerchief. She was grateful for the isolation offered by this single seat near the window. Cecile's heart ached over the betrayal and her own naïveté. How could she have been silly enough to believe that Septime would give up his life of freedom to be tied down with her? She scolded herself for thinking that these past few weeks could result in anything other than an adventure. She was one of how many for Septime? And she actually dared to give Viv advice on love after her failures.

She wiped her eyes and gazed out the window as the train rolled away from the station, picking up speed almost instantly. But her eyes only saw those of Septime, staring intensely into hers. She wanted to scream. She wanted to push those feelings of anger, annoyance and foolishness from her soul.

Where am I going anyway? she asked herself.

Cecile, defeated after the one spark of excitement extinguished itself, still couldn't return to Manu. She didn't know what to say to him. She didn't know whether she loved or hated him. Cecile buried her head in her hands. She remained motionless until the buzzing of her cell phone pulled her back to life.

Cecile felt for it in her purse and looked at the name flashing on the screen. It was Manu. Again. She swallowed hard and stuffed the phone into the depths of her bag. Why couldn't he leave her alone? Tears were welling up again behind her eyes. This time, she let them fall in torrents.

Chapter 31

Andre

"I still don't understand how you could do this to Mom… to our family," Hugo said, with those wide childlike eyes. But he wasn't Hugo. He was Christopher, looking imploringly at his downtrodden, alcoholic father Max.

"Life took me in this direction, Christopher," said Andre-turned-Max, sitting on a rickety chair in the squalor of a poor man's kitchen. "I didn't want your mother to suffer! And now we all are…"

He winced with true pain that he felt from deep within his heart.

"Well I don't want your goddamn excuses!" Hugo-turned-Christopher yelled, violently throwing Max's precious box of photographs across the room, where they would fan out into an amalgam of joy and sadness.

"Those are memories of the times you weren't here…" Hugo said through tears. He crossed the room and grabbed Andre roughly by the shoulders. "All you could think about was the next drink! You didn't care about our suffering! And now, you've come back as if everything could work out… Well, it's too late!"

Hugo pushed him away, turned around and ran for the door.

Andre limped pathetically after him.

"No, my boy, don't go... Don't leave me like this!" Tears streamed down his face.

"Cut! That's a take! Everyone take ten..."

Technicians swarmed across the floor, lowering the boom pole, straightening cords before heading outside for cigarettes and snacks.

Hugo looked back. His eyes caught those of his father and they softened for a moment. Andre took a step forward.

"Takes a lot out of you to be vicious, doesn't it?" Andre said with a smirk. "I can also say that it's not easy for me to play a softie. We're the opposite, the two of us."

He lit a cigarette and settled down on a stool that one of the techs had left in the corner of the small, dim studio. The other actors had dispersed, eager to take any break. But Hugo, studying his father's face, lingered.

"Why did you take this role if it isn't what you wanted?" he asked. "It can't be the money..."

"It hasn't been about money for years. I'm here because I can't turn my back on this business. It's my life, Hugo! But I'm no longer the same actor I was before my accident."

"I thought you were tough as nails, never giving in..."

Andre flicked a bit of ash onto the ground and watched it burn into nothing.

"There are times when you have to accept things as they are, Hugo," he said. "I suppose I've learned that recently."

Hugo remained silent.

"This role brings out your talent," Andre said.

"I thought you were against the whole idea of me being an actor," Hugo said, leaning against the doorframe. He looked down at his father with inquisitive eyes. "You thought I couldn't do it."

"No, I never said that, Hugo. It had nothing to do with your talent... I wanted you to have an easier life. That's all. Living on the stage is the most thrilling experience on earth, but at the same time, it can destroy you."

"But you wouldn't trade it for the world, now would

you?"

"I couldn't. It became an addiction."

The actors began trickling in, and Andre turned around at the sound of his name. He threw his cigarette to the ground and stamped it out.

"I guess we should be getting back," he said. But Hugo didn't seem to see his father's lips move. He was lost in thought.

An urgent, rapid knocking on his door woke Andre just as he began to slip into a calm sleep. He had returned from the set at midnight and didn't even try to think how long he had been tossing and turning in bed before dozing off. He was tempted to ignore the sound at the other end of the apartment, but it continued, louder and louder.

"Damn it!" he said, stiffly swinging his legs over the side of the bed and grabbing his cane. He pressed it into the plush, royal blue rug under his feet and stood up. "Just a minute," he called out as he approached the door.

He felt around for the light switch, turned his key in the lock and found himself face-to-face with June. He swallowed hard. She stood there with those round expressive eyes in a way that brought him back years.

"What are you doing here?" he said. "You've ignored my messages... I thought I would never see you again. I didn't think you would return to Paris."

Her eyes escaped his as she walked through the door and into the living room.

"Sit down... please," Andre said, awkwardly running a hand through his hair and making his way over to his favorite high-backed armchair.

"Andre, why did you have to do it?" she asked, wrapping her oversized sweater tighter around her slim figure.

"Do what?"

"Why did you set up this ridiculous plot to get our son a role as if he were incapable of doing it on his own? And then, even worse, you decided to keep it a secret from him. Can you imagine how he'll feel when he finds out? He will, you know... Word travels in these circles. You know that Andre!"

But Andre was hardly listening at this point. He remained fixed on her initial question.

"June, you were the one who told me to show my feelings for Hugo! For once, to go out of my way and prove some form of fatherly concern."

"But don't you see, Andre, that this isn't what being a father is all about?" Her blue eyes, reflecting the gray tones of her tunic, reached out to him imploringly. "Hugo needs your time and attention—not the benefits of a dirty deal you pulled with some up-and-coming director! I thought that one day you would be ready...that you would recognize Hugo, that you would realize what a wonderful son he is. When you were young, I dismissed your attitude as immaturity. For some silly reason, I thought you would wake up one day and come knocking on our door!"

Then she stopped and bit her lip. Andre could see the tears in the corners of her eyes.

"You mean you would have taken me back?" he whispered. He limped over to the couch and sat at her side, but she turned away.

"I shouldn't be saying all of this," she said, wiping her eyes. "It's the past anyway. What does it matter?"

"It does matter when love is involved," Andre said, his heartbeat accelerating. He touched June's cheek and turned her face to his.

"Do you know how many times I thought of you and Hugo?" he said softly. "I would follow him home from school sometimes when I was in New York. I wanted to approach him more than anything in the world during those moments... but somehow it never worked out. I remember seeing you one time, waiting for him on the front porch. It was Halloween, and he must have been about ten. You were dressed as a rabbit, and he came running toward you."

Andre stopped and chuckled. "I bet he thought you were the coolest mom on earth. That makes up for having the shittiest dad, don't you think?"

"Why didn't you tell me?" she asked between gritted teeth.

"Because I was afraid."

"Of what? Of being trapped in a commitment. Don't say 'no' because I know that's the reason."

Andre swallowed hard, uncomfortably feeling the lump in his throat. Of course June was right, but he couldn't say those hurtful words. He couldn't tell her that he was afraid of being trapped in family life with her and their son.

"Can't you accept Hugo now?" June asked.

"That's a story between him and me," Andre said. "We're both adults."

"So now, you'll finally make amends, in your own strange way that includes getting him parts in shows and other impersonal sorts of things that don't take much effort when you're in Andre Wren's position…"

"I'll do things my way as I always have," he said. "And that includes telling you how I feel."

He brought her face to his and gently touched his lips to hers. It was as if the clock had turned back two decades in an instant. He felt the burst of joy and excitement that only she could bring to him. No one else had ever been able to mimic the effect. June pulled away and squeezed his hand.

"It's too late for us, Andre."

"Why?" he asked imploringly. "A new beginning can take place any time…"

"I'm in love with someone else, Andre," she said, looking down at her fingers enlaced in his. "I'm getting married in a month."

Andre felt as if he had been punched in the stomach. He knew that June had experienced romances now and again, but the idea of her getting married hurt like nothing he had ever imagined.

June got up, and he followed.

"I should be going," she said. "I didn't want to get into all of this… I just wanted to talk about Hugo. I've got to catch a plane out of here tomorrow morning…It's been a quick trip for me this time around."

"I guess this is goodbye then," Andre said, with a death grip on the brass doorknob. And this time, he knew it would be forever.

Chapter 32

Mira

Mira's pace quickened. She lowered her gaze and hurried along the Rue des Martyrs to her building, which basked in the late Sunday morning light. She had seen Hugo out of the corner of her eye at the market where she filled her basket with enough nectarines and peaches for the week. He was at the next stand, paging through worn, leather-bound books that belonged to someone a century ago. Mira had thrown her change onto the table, turned around, and pushed her way through the masses with their bags and baskets.

Her heart was pounding. *Had he seen her?* She couldn't face him right now. She didn't want to fall out of one relationship and into another. And the problem was she couldn't trust herself around Hugo. If she looked into those eyes, she would see the passionate feelings that she didn't want to exist. The simple act of putting the finishing touches on Hugo's portrait proved to be a challenge for her. She kept thinking of the moment of revelation. The moment when he kissed her and those forbidden emotions burst forth. *How could she possibly consider a new life with him at this point?* She would only be setting herself up for rejection.

He was following her. She could feel it. Mira wouldn't let herself turn around. She was approaching the flower shop, with its displays of roses and geraniums in brightly colored pots that decorated the sidewalk. Then there was that café across the way. And finally, a few steps farther, she would reach the apartment.

"Mira!" that familiar voice called out.

She shuddered and took a deep breath. She had to stop. But she wouldn't move until she felt his hand on her arm, swiveling her around to face him. He was slightly out of breath and his hair was blown in every direction from the light breeze that chilled the sun-soaked air.

"I have to talk to you," he said. "I didn't want you to run away... but I couldn't have lied about my feelings either."

"I understand," Mira said. The warmth in his eyes seemed to draw her into the lovely place that frightened her. He took her hand, and she didn't want to pull away.

"Let's have a cup of coffee at the café across the street..." he said. "You can't turn around and leave, Mira."

"OK," she said. She had to face him here and now.

He took her fruit basket, and they silently crossed the street to Andre Wren's favorite lunch spot. Mira remembered the time she saw him in there a few days earlier and how he, thinking she was some kind of tabloid journalist, had yelled at her. She hadn't told Hugo about it and didn't plan on doing so. She felt ashamed of herself for the crazy episode that now seemed to her like a secret intrusion into Hugo's past.

"Is a spot in the corner OK?" Hugo asked her as the waiter led them across the nearly empty dining area. It was too late for breakfast and too early for lunch in this little neighborhood place that was unlike Paris' larger cafes, which attracted mobs of diners at any hour.

She nodded.

They sat opposite one another at a round table. Mira had a view of the street, but her eyes could focus on nothing but Hugo.

"I'm almost done with your portrait," she said, trying to be businesslike but failing miserably.

"You don't need me for any final sittings then?"

"No," she said. "I can see you in my mind's eye."

The waiter approached and took their orders for tea and *café au lait*.

"Who's the other guy?" Hugo asked after the tall, thin man with a perfectly starched white apron hurried back to the bar.

Mira held her head in her hands and gazed down at the table. She had to tell Hugo the truth. She returned her eyes to him.

"I was engaged," she said.

"And now you're not?"

"Oh, it's a long story, Hugo," she said with a sigh.

"I have time to listen."

He reached across the table and took her hand. The softness of his fingers in hers sent a jolt of electricity up her spine. She closed her eyes.

"His name is Antonio," she said, again raising her gaze to meet Hugo's. "I left him and came to Paris because I found out he was cheating on me. And I might as well tell you everything. I'm three months pregnant."

The waiter—arriving at the wrong moment—swiftly set hot cups in front of them and disappeared as quickly as he had appeared. Mira felt her face redden, as if everyone in the café had heard her words. She gazed down at her own sad reflection in the yellow-green liquid.

"Are you still in love with him?" Hugo asked.

She took a sip of tea and leaned her elbows on the table.

"No… for some strange reason I was so hurt, that now, it's like there's nothing left," she said contemplatively. "There's just my artwork, me and soon, there will be the baby too. That's how it's going to stay for a while."

"I meant it when I said I love you…" he whispered.

"Hugo, you don't want to waste your time on me! Do you realize the kind of responsibilities a baby involves? This is something I have to deal with on my own…"

"No it's not," he said. His lips were only inches from hers. She didn't want to let it happen again. One of those kisses that would leave her weak in the knees and one-hundred percent vulnerable. But she couldn't turn away. Again, she felt the softness of his mouth against hers for an instant. And then his eyes seemed to absorb her in their profound depths.

"So how do you feel about this?" he murmured into her ear.

"I need time," she said, breaking out of his spell. "Hugo, don't you see that for you this might seem like the perfect romance… but I'm not ready for that! I don't want to be swept off my feet. I was only looking for friendship…"

"And is that all our relationship is to you?" he asked. "Can you honestly say there's nothing more?"

"I don't know how I'm feeling right now," she said, lying to him and to herself. "Why can't we talk about something else, Hugo? Why can't we be friends at least for a little while? I really could use one, you know…"

He was silent for a moment. Mira could read the disappointment in his eyes, and it made her heart ache.

"OK," he said. "Just friends."

He took a sip of his coffee and then placed some change on the table.

"I'd better be on my way… I'll be in touch with Tatiana about the portrait…"

Mira nodded and watched him make his way to the door. More than anything, she wanted to run after him. But for a second time in the past several days, she did nothing.

୨୦୧

Mira returned to the portrait that needed only a few more dabs of paint. She had to finish it as quickly as possible so that she could get Hugo's image out of her mind. The afternoon sun warmed her back, half-bared by a strapless top, as she turned away from the light and toward Hugo's fine features. She worked diligently without checking the hour, not even paying attention to the chill that had returned to the late-summer air as the day reached its end.

"You're back!" Tatiana's voice startled her.

"You too… Where have you been?"

"Out of town at a conference," Tatiana said. "I would have left you a note, but I thought I would be returning before you. What happened?"

Mira drew her knees up to her chest and looked at her friend, who was her usual glamorous self in a gold mini skirt and sweater.

"It's over with Antonio. Really over."

"You saw him?"

"Yes. I actually feel good about myself. But I hate saying you were right about him back in those days when you said he was selfish and didn't care enough about me."

"I know you hate admitting it," Tatiana said with a sly smile. "But it feels good to hear anyway."

Mira smirked.

"Seriously, Mira, this is the best thing... Now you can get on with your life. You and the baby are better off on your own than with someone you can't trust. But of course, you would be even better off with Hugo..."

"Hold on a second. It's not so easy."

"What's that supposed to mean?"

"Who says I want to get involved in another serious relationship right away?" Mira tucked a few unruly curls behind her ears and stubbornly crossed her arms.

"You do, Mira. Or at least your eyes do when you look at Hugo or at his portrait for that matter. You can't fool me."

"I'm not denying that I have feelings for him... but this isn't the best time. You know that, Tatiana. I don't want to make a huge mistake. It wouldn't be fair to him either."

"We usually don't get to choose timing, Mira. We have to consider ourselves lucky if and when we find true love no matter what the situation. You can't be too analytic about it!"

"But I'm scared of getting involved right now! What if I'm not in love with Hugo, but think I am because it makes accepting the situation with Antonio much easier?"

"Mira, we're not in psychology class here. You can't let Antonio and Clara's horrible behavior poison your life! It's finished. You have to start over. There isn't a formula that says you have to wait five years before falling in love again... And if you start playing the game that way, you're going to end up a loser. Hugo won't wait around forever. So what are you going to do?"

"Well, the portrait is nearly done," Mira said, leaning back and looking at Hugo's perfect image. "I gave it a few touch ups."

Tatiana rose from the chair where Mira's model would usually sit and took a look at the other side of the canvas.

"Has he seen any of this yet?"

"No."

"It's incredible. He's going to love it."

Mira couldn't help but look at her creation through satisfied eyes. Hugo came to life across the canvas. The effect was better than she had imagined. Without going any farther than this rooftop studio, the portrait was one of her biggest successes. It put much of the work displayed at her studio to shame.

"I suppose I'll have to see him, to tell him that this is done," Mira said.

Tatiana smiled at her knowingly, but Mira looked away. She didn't want to answer any more questions.

Chapter 33

Rafael

Rafael slipped down the narrow hallway to Lea's room and knocked desperately. He pressed his cheek against the wood and closed his eyes. She was gone. He could feel it. He glanced around. Not a sound in that dim, abandoned place. The other *comisionistas* were out at the afternoon emerald marketplace or already on their way back to the city with treasures-in-the-rough. Rafael pushed open the door into a room left hastily behind. His eyes traveled from the unmade bed to the little desk in the corner, empty except for a piece of paper and a telephone.

His eyes settled on the scene. He pushed the door closed behind him and crossed the room. His heart pounded double-time as he grasped the paper.

"You have to leave before they get you!" The sharp slashes were written in French, signed at the bottom with a voluptuous "C." He followed the sinuous shape of the initial that had held a vice grip on his mind for months. In a flash it came to him. Carmen. He swallowed hard. *Lea didn't exist!* There only was Carmen. Of course! That was why she was such an emerald expert. Marie must have trained her. No one outside of the

mines had such skill except for the French jewelry designer who had learned all about the precious stones from Diego. "Lea's" apparent knowledge otherwise seemed impossible and hadn't set right with Rafael from the start. But he had let Tigo's words assuage his concern. Now he shook his head bitterly. Who was Carmen? And whose side was she on anyway? She warned him to leave. But she also had been involved with Tigo.

He still had to find her, even if he died trying. Rafael picked up the phone and hit redial. Just as he thought. She had called the airport. She was on her way out of Colombia. And Rafael had a feeling he finally knew where she was going to land.

Rafael sped back to Bogotá as if in a trance. He saw nothing but Tigo's body losing blood on the wooden floor. He had to get out of the country before it was too late. He knew about the "they" Carmen referred to in her note. "They" were the others who were partners in Tigo's lucrative business. And they would find him in no time at all. Rafael looked at his watch as Tigo's 4X4 rolled into the outskirts of Bogotá. He would drive home first. He had to see the place one more time. In his heart, he knew he never would return to this world that no longer seemed real to him. He parked along the side of the road and looked up at the beautiful, ecru hacienda sprawled out amongst the flowers that Tina had planted and cared for so tenderly. The life of violence and apprehension still existed, but it wouldn't be his any longer. It was for those who didn't realize the pain that can't be avoided when one entwines his or her life with a precious stone.

His footsteps fell softly on the pebbles that cut through the grass and flower garden, leading to the big wrought-iron gate. He unlocked it and made his way past the sculptures and birdbaths to the front door. He rang the bell even though he held the key in his hand. Rafael was expecting to hear his little cousin Lola's laugh or the sound of her brother's soccer ball bouncing down the hallway. But there was only silence. He twisted the key in the lock and pushed open the door.

No one was there. *It's probably better that way*, Rafael thought to himself. Otherwise, leaving would be more difficult. He would invite his family to visit him once he settled into some kind of normal lifestyle. They would understand his reasons for avoiding the country that evoked such haunting memories.

Rafael walked through the living room, unchanged with its bright blues and yellows enhanced by the afternoon sun. One large bay window looked out upon the garden. Pure tranquility. This was Tina's favorite room. Rafael felt hot tears building up behind his eyes. He quickly walked across the large, cool tiles and into his father's study. It still held the scent of his cigars and that musky cologne. Rafael sat down at his desk and laid his cheek against the wood. He let his tears spill out in this place where he always maintained his self-control. For once, Rafael was defiant in Diego's territory.

"Why don't you want to be a *comisionista*?" his father had asked.

"I don't know, Papa... It's just that you and Mom have lots of worries."

Rafael tucked his legs under himself on the stiff-backed chair and looked into his father's stern, deep eyes that softened a little when addressing Rafael.

"But life is all about worries, my son. No matter what you do, there will be enemies and you will have to fight... At least, we've been in this business long enough to have an advantage. We've built this through three generations, Rafael. I want to pass that to you, so that you will offer the heritage to your son..."

"What if I don't have a son?"

"Things will come naturally." Diego stood up and walked around the desk to approach Rafael.

"What do you say? How about giving it a try?"

Rafael looked up at the painting of his grandfather, a frightening man with a long black moustache and small beady eyes, and then moved his gaze quickly to the more appealing view of the vegetable garden that flourished outside the French doors. Tina had shed her silk suit for a long, cotton tunic and was watering the row of carrots. Rafael swallowed hard and blinked back the tears that wanted to fall from his eyes. Tears of confusion that never were allowed in front of Diego. Tina had told him that a million times. He absolutely couldn't let them out.

"OK," he whispered. Then Diego took his hand and led him out to the living room.

"Go outside and play for a while," Diego said. "Sunshine doesn't last forever, you know. Not even in Colombia."

A creaking sound from the front of the house broke Rafael out of his trance. Slowly, he rose from Diego's seat and felt for his gun. Self-defense was a natural reflex for him. Diego always said it was necessary for survival at any time and in any place. Rafael crept forward. The sound of his own heartbeat and even breathing made his head spin. He recognized the burly young man who stood in the middle of the living room with a gun in his holster. Rafael had seen him at the mines for years and more importantly he saw Tigo speaking with him that very morning. So he was one of Tigo's men. Rafael took a step forward. He was no longer afraid.

Silently, he took a step into the room and lifted his 9-millimeter. The man turned around. His eyes widened, and he took a step back when he saw Rafael.

"Were you here to find me or to pillage?" Rafael asked. "You're Jose something-or-other aren't you?"

The man nodded gruffly.

"Get the hell out of here!" Rafael yelled.

"Why don't you kill me?" Jose said. "Too fucking scared?"

"I don't want to soil my family's home with your blood…"

Rafael walked steadily toward him. One step at a time, they moved from the living room to the front porch to the lawn. And there, just when Jose most likely thought he would turn around and escape, Rafael fired. The man collapsed into the overgrown grass.

"There, now," Rafael said under his breath. "The Mendez family will have one less thing to worry about."

Hands shaking, he stepped over the man's body and hurried to the 4X4. He had a plane to catch.

Chapter 34

Cecile

After three days spent in bed feeling sorry for herself, Cecile got up and faced her pathetic-looking reflection in the mirror. Her eyes looked tired, with those little wrinkles fanning out from the side. And her hair was tangled and dull from hours spent tossing and turning in a strange bed.

Cecile was staying at a little hotel close to home, but she felt as if she were on another planet. Somewhere safe. For years, this place had fascinated her with its lovely balconies draped in flowers and the diaphanous curtains that seemed to protect it from the outside world. She chose it as her hideaway until she decided exactly what she was going to do to pull herself out of a rather humiliating situation.

And more importantly, she needed the time to think. Cecile felt that, slowly, as the years went by, she had lost hold of her identity, and this was what had driven her into Septime's arms. She had sought solace as well as the delirious happiness that comes with a new romance. She told herself she was over him. Cecile de Champigny didn't need someone like Septime in her life. She didn't need anyone. She swallowed hard as she gazed into the mirror and ordered herself to believe those words that she whispered to herself in a weakened voice.

Her cell phone rang, startling her from this self-observation. It sat there rattling on the dresser, inches from her fingertips among the piles of teardrop-filled tissues.

She picked up the phone. This time it wasn't Manu. It was Viv. Her daughter's name flashed across the screen. Cecile's heart pounded. She didn't know what she would say, but she couldn't stop herself from answering the call.

"Mom… finally! I've been trying forever! I… I … Where have you been anyway?" The hysterical tone of that usually calm voice alarmed Cecile.

"Viv, are you all right?" Cecile asked, trembling as she sat at the edge of the bed.

"Mom, I didn't make it." Cecile could tell she was crying. "I didn't make the cut."

"Honey, what do you mean?" Cecile nervously gripped the phone. It seemed impossible to her that Viv actually could have failed at anything.

"I'm not going to be able to go forward in the auditions," she said, sobbing now.

"Viv, where are you?"

"Outside class," she mumbled.

"Don't move," Cecile said. "Give me 20 minutes, and I'll be there."

Silence.

"Viv, do you hear me?" Cecile almost yelled into the phone.

"Yes," she said softly.

"Just stay put… I want to be there with you."

Cecile hung up the phone and dashed into the shower. For once, her thoughts were only for her daughter.

ॐ

Viv was waiting for Cecile in the little alcove between two apartment buildings that faced the dance school. She emerged slowly and carefully, like a trapped animal, as Cecile, out of breath after dashing up the hundreds of steps leading to Paris' highest point, approached her. Cecile knew that her daughter wouldn't remain near the school stoop for very long. She wouldn't want to have to explain anything to the others.

Cecile met Viv in the middle of the road and drew her close. Viv's arms tightened around her mother.

Cecile remained silent. She felt as if, at that moment, words were simply unnecessary.

Time seemed to stand still for a while, and then Viv took a step back. Tears were floating in the corners of her eyes, but she wouldn't cry.

"Are you coming home?" she asked.

"This is about you—not me," Cecile said. "C'mon, let's sit down at that café across the street and have something to drink."

Viv looked down at the frayed bellbottoms that half-covered her beat up running shoes and played with the strap of her pink dance bag. Cecile was scared of what the girl's next question might be. She couldn't tell her about the folly of the past few days even though she was sure that her daughter probably suspected it.

"So what do you say?" Cecile asked.

"OK," Viv murmured, wiping her damp eyelids.

Silently, they crossed the passage and pushed open the grimy glass door.

The atmosphere was quite unremarkable, but even if it were extraordinary, Cecile wouldn't have paid more attention to it. They sat down at a simple table near the window, and Cecile quickly ordered drinks from the waiter who swooped by before disappearing into the kitchen. She leaned forward and looked into her daughter's eyes.

"When did this happen?" Cecile asked.

"You mean when did the dream die?"

"Viv, don't say that! Your whole life as a person or as a dancer can't depend on one audition… Don't be so dramatic!"

"That's easy for you to say, Mom… You didn't see how I screwed up the *pas de deux*. I couldn't concentrate. I was scared. I'd never freaked out like that before. I don't understand…" Viv rubbed her eyes and then rested her chin in cupped hands.

"Was the audition this morning?"

"No, it was on Friday afternoon…I knew right away that I'd screwed up. I got the official word today, though."

"What did your dad have to say?"

"I didn't tell him, or anyone else."

Cecile swallowed hard.

"But you're telling me…"

"You're my mother! It's different, don't you see? Dad wouldn't get it. He doesn't understand how important this is to me. It's not his fault or anything. It's just that way."

"You've been trying to reach me since…"

"Since Friday! That's why I was so worried! Why didn't you answer, Mom?"

Viv looked at her mother with a combination of anger and sadness.

"I was having some problems with the phone," Cecile replied guiltily. She hoped her daughter wouldn't see through this awful lie, meant only to protect her from further disappointment.

The waiter approached the table and set down a frothy cup of hot chocolate for Viv and herbal tea for Cecile. Viv took a tentative sip. Her eyes looked emptily out the window at a cobblestone alleyway shaded by an apartment building on each side. Only residents probably wandered through the dim passage, and on this day, not too many of them were out and about.

"How did this whole thing happen?" Cecile asked. "I mean, you said you couldn't concentrate… I don't think I ever remember hearing you say such a thing."

"I never have, Mom."

"What was different about this time?"

"You weren't there," she said.

Cecile felt as if this delicate voice had slapped her. She took a deep breath and reached across the table for Viv's hand. But her daughter angrily pushed it away.

"I'm sorry," Cecile whispered. "I didn't realize, Vivienne! I didn't think you needed me for support… or for much of anything for that matter."

"That's not true! Why can't you see it? Why are you blind

to everything?"

Cecile nervously took a sip of lukewarm chamomile and looked down at the scratched wooden tabletop. There were so many names carved into it that she couldn't discern one of them.

"Viv, since you were little, you've always been the independent sort—too independent. I didn't want to step on your toes, to alienate you. Especially since everything that you did was right! You were the adult… and I've often felt like the child…"

She glanced up and her eyes locked with those of Viv. And all of a sudden, Cecile understood.

"I've grown up," Cecile continued. "I'm seeing my responsibilities in your eyes. No matter how independent you might be, you are young, and you do need support… from me. I'm sorry I was the reason for this whole mess… I was convinced you would sail through those auditions!"

Cecile felt uncomfortable, unmasked by her own daughter, but she refused to regret being honest about her failures as a mother.

"Sometimes that isn't enough, Mom! I didn't expect you to take off like that, you know! No one did… And what for? Because of your problems with Dad? You could have kept it between the two of you instead of making my life miserable too! Maybe for Joel it doesn't matter because he's off at school—and that was why it was fine for you. He's your favorite anyway! So if he wasn't going to be hurt, no big deal."

"I've never had a favorite, Viv!" Cecile said almost desperately. Her life was unraveling, with everything that she had assumed for so many years proving false. "I've spent more time with Joel because he's had more time to spend with me…"

Viv shook her head vigorously.

"Didn't you get it when I kept those notes from Dad's girlfriend away from you?"

"What do you mean?" Cecile asked. A sick feeling rose from within as she thought of those horrible love letters that described a relationship she had longed for with Manu.

"I did it because I didn't want you to be hurt! I didn't

want you to find them. They would break your heart... And then I could have kicked myself when I let it slip out because I was angry, and I had to turn those things over to you. I didn't want to do it!"

Cecile swallowed hard. As it was, the idea of her daughter finding those letters nauseated her. And on top of that, she had lived with the secret to protect the mother who didn't seem to understand her children, husband or herself.

"Viv, I wouldn't have wanted you to keep such a secret... Damn him, leaving those things in the house!"

Then she took a deep breath.

"You shouldn't have had that responsibility in the first place," Cecile continued, her voice softening. "But I'm touched that you wanted to protect me." Viv truly did care about her mother. The proof was right there. Cecile felt like a fool for not seeing or understanding what had been unfolding right before her own eyes in her own home.

Viv pushed her half-empty cup away and grabbed her dance bag off the floor.

"Where are you going?" Cecile asked, panicking as she saw the disappointment in her daughter's eyes.

"Home..."

"Wait," Cecile said, touching Viv's arm as the girl stood up. "Let me give you the address of the place I'm staying... until I work things out." She slipped a card from the hotel out of her bag and pressed it into Viv's hands.

"I don't want our conversation to end this way... in anger," Cecile said.

"What am I supposed to do, Mom?" Viv said in her little adult voice. "Should I say that I understand that you've overlooked my entire existence for I don't know how many years? Should I say that it didn't bother me that you left without a trace last week when I needed you the most? I thought maybe today I would get some kind of good reason... but there doesn't seem to be anything!"

Viv turned around, hurried between tables, and managed to knock a few place settings to the floor on her way out the door. Cecile buried her face in her hands and forgot that anyone who passed that grimy window could see her tears.

Chapter 35

Andre

Andre strolled into his lunch place three hours earlier than usual. After June's late-night visit, he hadn't been able to get back to sleep. Good and bad memories from the past 20 years tangled like cobwebs in his mind, putting their sticky touch on any clear idea that attempted to reach the surface. He spent hours trying to read "Hamlet," in spite of the fact that he knew the text by heart. It was his first starring role on the stage in what seemed like a lifetime ago. The familiar words had a way of bringing him back to that exciting time when he loved life and life loved him. But on this occasion, even Hamlet was powerless.

Andre dozed off on the couch as the sun rose, only to awake with a cramp in his back and a pounding headache a couple of hours later. He popped a few pills and forced himself into a cool shower. He decided that only a calm morning spent sipping coffee in the café would transport him far from the emptiness he felt following June's departure.

So that is how Andre found himself facing Hugo and a pretty young woman with glowing eyes. She kissed Hugo tenderly on the mouth, and he gazed at her as if she were the only person on earth. They were laughing and sharing romantic words. A beautiful couple. Like Andre and June. Andre swallowed hard. He saw his own once-amorous self as he looked at Hugo. That way of wrinkling his brow as he whispered something in her ear. And the way he squeezed her hand and held it against his cheek. It was like watching a film of himself and the love of his life. He had tried for many years to block out the happiness and only think of the inconvenience of married life. And now, as he caught a glimpse of this budding romance, disillusionment with all that he had loved for so long hit him like a medicine ball in the stomach. He could hardly catch his breath.

"Mr. Wren, are you OK?" a waiter came rushing over to Andre, who still was standing between the bar and dining area. "You look flushed."

The girl turned around sharply, and Hugo followed.

"I'm fine," Andre said. "It's the change of weather…"

He pointed vaguely to leaves that flew by the window, pushed by a gust of early autumn wind. Hugo stood up and took a step toward Andre, who remained frozen to the spot.

"My father will sit with us," Hugo said to the waiter. "Could you bring him a cup of coffee please?"

Andre saw the quick look of astonishment in the waiter's eyes before he hurried off. Everyone must have been shocked that someone as disagreeable as Andre Wren could have such a kind and charming son. He smirked and shook his head as he followed Hugo back to the table.

"I would like you to meet Mira… Mira, this is my father Andre."

Andre couldn't read anything in particular in Mira's expression. He had no idea whether or not she had ever heard of Andre Wren the actor, but he was convinced he had seen her before. She had to have recognized him as well.

"You look very familiar," Andre said, taking her hand. "Have we met?"

Mira shook her head vigorously. "Not officially, but I live in the neighborhood. We could have passed each other on the street dozens of times."

She smiled and turned back to Hugo, who was studying

Andre with a wary eye.

"This is a little early for you, isn't it?" he asked his father.

"What do you mean?" Andre asked. He slipped a cigarette out of his pocket and lit up. It had a much-welcomed calming effect.

"You know you're not supposed to smoke in here?"

"They let me get away with it," Andre said with a smirk.

Hugo furrowed his brow. "I thought you came here for lunch," he said.

"Well, today, I felt like breakfast."

Hugo didn't buy it. Andre could tell by looking at his son's face.

"What's really going on?"

Mira suddenly took Hugo's hand.

"I'd better leave," she said, rising from her seat and smoothing her long, billowy skirt.

"Mira, you don't have to go," Hugo said.

"Certainly not," Andre echoed.

"No, I should… I have things to do before noon… And this way, you both can talk."

She turned to Andre and shook his hand once again.

"It was a pleasure," she said politely. Then she quickly kissed Hugo on the cheek and slipped away.

"Lovely girl," Andre said, stabbing out his half-finished cigarette as the waiter placed a cup of coffee in front of him. Andre reached for a croissant in the basket at the center of the table.

"May I?"

"Of course," Hugo said. He took a sip of some kind of hot, yellowish drink that smelled like grass. Andre was sure it was the same type of hideous herbal tea that June used to drink every afternoon.

"I see you got that from your mother," Andre said with distaste, nodding at the porcelain cup. He pulled off the crusty ends of the croissant and chewed on them. "This is the best part."

"You're trying to change the subject."

"What's the subject?" Andre asked.

"Something is going on. You wouldn't break your routine

to come here earlier otherwise."

"You think you know me pretty well, don't you?" Andre said with an ironic smile.

Hugo gazed at him with those large, serious June eyes and didn't say a word.

"All right," Andre said. He reached into his pocket for another cigarette and lit it. "If you must know, your mother stopped by late last night. I suppose you're aware of the fact that she returned to town... She just so happened to mention that she's getting married."

"I know."

"Who's the guy?" Andre asked, his heart racing.

"He's not in the business," Hugo said. "They met a few years ago when Mom and I went on a trip to the islands. His name is Eric Daley... He's a jewelry designer and has his own shop here in the city."

"In Paris?"

Hugo nodded.

"So that means your mother is moving to Paris?"

"Not right to the city, actually. Eric has a big house in the countryside. He commutes in for business a couple of times a week."

"But what about the theater? Her career? And the house in Brooklyn... Doesn't she realize she'll have to sell the house you grew up in?"

"She says she's not putting her career ahead of love," Hugo said.

Andre swallowed hard. He knew that those words were referring directly to him. He put out his cigarette and leaned across the table.

"How do you feel about this, Hugo?"

"I know what you want me to say."

"And what is that?"

"That I hate him, and that Mom is making a big mistake."

"And that isn't the case?"

Hugo shook his head.

"Why should she be alone? She deserves to have someone wonderful in her life. Mom is the kind of person who needs companionship... No, I'm wrong. We all need it."

Hugo glanced down and took a deep breath.

"I would have preferred a happy ending, Dad."

Andre's heart skipped a beat. It was the first time his son had called him "Dad." That word he never wanted to hear had transformed itself into something almost magical.

"But you never returned to us," Hugo said. "For years, Mom thought you would. When there was an unexpected knock at the door, you could see her tremble. But you never came, Dad!"

Hugo's eyes, holding unshed tears, bore into Andre's.

"Hugo, I didn't do everything right... No, let's put it this way: I was wrong. I treated June miserably..." Andre could hear his own voice catching in his throat.

"And she waited when she shouldn't have. I told her that when I was about 12 or so and could understand the situation."

"You hated me didn't you? You still do..."

"A little bit at first. Then I was curious. I wondered how you could have done it. How you left us like that and never came back..."

"But I did return, Hugo!" Andre said, taking his son's hands in his. "I watched you from afar as you rode your bike home from school. That bright red bike with the silver stripe. You always carried the blue backpack with a little shamrock hanging off the zipper. I remember everything."

Hugo looked at him in confusion.

"Then why did you stay away?"

"You know about my fears, Hugo... The fear of commitment that ruined every relationship I've ever had. But one afternoon, I broke out of it. I called out to you as you rode up the hill... but you didn't turn around. I thought you didn't want to know me. I imagined all of the hideous things June could have said about me. And she would have been right. I didn't know that you were deaf..."

Andre released his son's hands and reached for another cigarette.

Hugo sat back in his chair and shook his head.

"You know this whole situation... It didn't have to be this way. In an instant—at the right instant—it could have worked out. But we lost our chance. And now nothing can be done to rewrite the past. It's too late for you and Mom! She really is in love with Eric, and I'm happy for her. She finally can break free from the world that tied her to you."

"But June loves the theater!"

"She did at one time, but ever since you left, it carried with it that memory of you. I could see it in her eyes. It marked her whole existence. She wanted a change, but never found the right opportunity. And she needed stability. She had to raise me, after all."

Andre took a drag on his cigarette and tapped the ash away.

"You're right, Hugo... For your young age, you have a lot of sense. It's too late to start analyzing the past and to try changing the outcomes of everything. June deserves happiness. I won't interfere. I've done enough harm."

Hugo was silent for a moment as he stirred his now-cold tea. Then he caught his father's eye.

"Why did she come to see you in the first place?"

"Last night?"

"Yeah."

"She wanted to make sure I was treating you right."

Hugo laughed ironically.

"She can't help herself.... What did you tell her? About us, I mean."

"I said that we worked well together and that you're a very talented actor. The rest, I said, was between father and son."

Hugo smiled.

Andre felt as if he had reached a reconciliation of sorts with this son he never wanted and now only wanted to please. It was as if his appearance had turned upside down the misery that Andre Wren had been feeling since his accident. He was grateful for that. He knew he had to focus on the positive rather than his ruined relationships of the past.

"I guess we'll see each other on the set," Hugo said tentatively.

"I suppose you have to rush out now to one appointment or another," Andre said. "That's good. Keep yourself busy. Nothing better than that."

"I'm glad we had this chance to talk," Hugo said. "I wanted to understand you for so long, Dad."

"That might be impossible. I don't understand myself."

"At least I feel as if I'm getting there."

And with those words, he rose from the table, smiled at Andre and headed to the door. The conversation, a catharsis for Andre, assuaged the feelings of disappointment and sadness that June had left in his heart. Andre Wren was able to face the day.

Chapter 36

Mira

Mira smiled as she thought back to the morning's events.

"I have something for you," Mira had said when Hugo answered his door with bleary eyes. She gripped the portrait, covered with a sheet, between her hands and took a step into the dreary little room with only a streak of sunlight to break through the harshness. It was her first visit to Hugo's apartment, a place that days ago would have fascinated her. But today, with her heart racing, she could hardly think of her surroundings.

Hugo ran a hand through his tousled hair and straightened his plaid pajama bottoms. She looked away, feeling uncomfortable all of a sudden.

"I'm sorry for coming this early… I didn't think." She wanted to turn around and run. She wasn't ready for this.

"No, don't say that," he said, leading her toward a round table near the window. "Have a seat."

Mira bit her lip and placed the canvas on one of the two cotton placemats. In one swift movement, she unwrapped it before she had a moment to lose her nerve. She felt silly for being nervous. She reminded herself that she was a professional.

Dewy natural light touched Hugo's actual features as well as the ones Mira had carefully reproduced. He smiled and turned to her.

"You're very talented, Mira," he said.

He examined her work once again and then looked back at her.

"This is amazing…" he said, his eyes drinking her in as they had done when his lips surprised hers in that rooftop garden.

"I'm guessing you like it?"

He nodded.

"It's strange, looking at myself through your eyes," he said.

"What do you see?"

"I see my feelings for you."

"Me too."

He blinked, as if startled by her words. Mira took a deep breath. It was now or never. She leaned forward and kissed him. Gently, he held her cheek against his for a moment. Then she took a step back and returned her gaze to his.

"What made you change your mind?" he asked.

"Finishing up this portrait… I couldn't help looking into your eyes constantly. I couldn't escape you… and I realized I didn't want to."

He pulled her into his arms, and she remained there for quite a long time until finally they both decided to go out for breakfast to celebrate their newfound happiness.

Hugo gently placed his fingertips on Mira's not-quite-flat stomach as they walked outside to meet one of the first crisp days of the season. She cupped her hand over his and looked up at him.

"Have you been feeling OK?" he asked.

"As fit as a fiddle, as a matter of fact… the morning sickness didn't last for long."

Mira squeezed his hand and turned to him once again.

"Are you sure you're ready for this kind of challenge?" she asked.

"I'm awaiting it with open arms."

"Hugo, I still don't understand how you can accept this whole situation so easily…"

"Let's say family experience taught me a few things. And most importantly: Never let the one you love get away."

He told her to keep the portrait as their first souvenir together. She couldn't help but smile at the thought of seeing it the first moment of every day. That was until the encounter with Andre Wren, which took place as they were finishing their leisurely tête-à-tête over tea and croissants. And that was why Mira knocked on his door a few hours later.

Andre seemed surprised to see her.

"May I come in?" Mira asked.

"Of course," he said. "I hope nothing is wrong…"

"No, Hugo is fine… all is well."

She stepped inside and followed Andre as he led her into the living room. It was obvious that he tried covering the extent of his injury by shuffling his feet in such a way as to minimize his limp. But she could see him wince with pain as he tried to put more pressure on his bad leg. Mira lowered her gaze. He would only hate her for noticing his weakness.

"Please have a seat."

Mira sat down and placed the covered painting against her legs. She was so nervous about what she was about to do that she didn't notice a thing about the apartment that fans would have done anything to visit.

"First of all, I want to tell you something," she said, hoping he didn't hear her voice quiver. "I'm the girl you yelled at the other day at the café."

Andre hesitated for a moment, and then a look of recognition came into his eyes.

"You?" he said, knitting his brows together. "That's why you looked familiar to me… What on earth were you doing anyway?"

"I didn't tell Hugo about our little encounter. And I also want to say that I do know who you are. I went to the café that day because I needed to find out more about you… to see if you were really as everyone says."

"You mean a rotten bastard?" he asked with an ironic grin. "You must have been convinced after that experience."

"Oh, maybe a little bit," she said, allowing herself to look him in the eyes. His gaze had softened. "But today, when I saw you and Hugo together, things changed. That's why I wanted to bring you something."

"That's quite a big package," he said, nodding in its direction.

"I'm an artist, and this is the portrait I'm most proud of."

With a flick of the wrist, she unveiled it and handed the canvas to Andre.

His eyes widened and that movie-hero smile spread across his face. Mira could feel beads of sweat forming along her temples, and she kneaded her hands in her lap. Sharing something so personal was a major step for Mira, whose thoughts and dreams always had remained hidden from the outside world. Her work for the gallery was simply business. This portrait of Hugo was a way of exposing part of herself.

Andre finally pulled away from the reproduction of his son's face and directed his attention to Mira's flushed one.

"This is beautiful," he said. "Where have you been exhibiting?"

"Oh, I'm getting started in Paris," she said. "I had a gallery back in Naples, but I decided to try something new."

"How much do I owe you?"

"Nothing! It's a gift."

"No, no I can't accept it for free…"

"I insist."

"You'll find a check in the mail," he said gruffly. "No one ever wins a fight with Andre Wren."

She smiled and a sense of relief filled her heart as she thought of Hugo and his father. Hugo was on his way to having the kind of relationship he had wanted all of his life. And she, Mira, had done a tiny bit to help.

Mira left Andre Wren's apartment with a spring in her step. The early autumn air tossed her hair about, and rhythmically inflated and deflated her long skirt as she made her way down the Rue des Martyrs. It was one of those

September days that still held the sunshine of summer, while welcoming the brisk, chestnut-scented air of fall. Mira felt as if nothing possibly could mar her good mood until she heard the voice she knew better than any other in the world call out to her. He was waiting at the door in front of her building. Septime, the seventh child of the Galino family, approached her with eager steps.

"Mira," he said, rushing over and taking her hands in his. "Look, I'm sorry about everything that happened... I was stressed out about the whole project that I shouldn't have gotten involved with in the first place."

Mira looked at her brother with steady eyes. Septime Galino was someone who appeared marvelous on the outside, but once Mira scratched the surface, she realized that her brother had a lot to learn. She hoped that Cecile had made the same discovery.

"What happened with Cecile?" Mira asked.

"You want to talk about that right here on the street?"

Mira glanced at her watch. Tatiana wouldn't be home, so the apartment would be as good a place as any for a conversation with her brother.

"Come on up," she said.

They climbed the stairs in silence as Mira fished her key out from the little purple velvet pouch she carried over one shoulder. She opened the door and led the way into the sun-soaked living room. She offered Septime a glass of sparkling water and sat down next to him on the ultramodern red couch that stood out from the antique design of the white room.

"Interesting décor," Septime said. It was obvious that he hated it.

"Tatiana wanted something original."

"Well, she got what she was looking for."

Mira took a sip of water and gazed down at Septime's leather shoes. They looked ordinary, but she knew they were worth a fortune. Septime was the only person she knew who insisted on wearing uniquely the work of the top designers of the moment and following every trend. That, just to be what he considered charming and seductive.

"So," Mira said, looking him boldly in the eyes, "what

happened with Cecile?"

"She left."

"Because she finally realized that you're a womanizer."

"That's a bit of an exaggeration, Mira…" Septime grinned and shook his head.

"If that's how you see it, you're fooling yourself… I've cooled down since the other day, Septime, but I still haven't changed the way I feel."

They remained silent for a moment, defiant eyes locked. Mira refused to back down from her stance. Finally, Septime looked away.

"You're probably right, Mira, but that's my life. I can't change it—at least not right away. I've changed enough… I'm not ready for something more."

He set his glass down on the coffee table and turned back to her.

"You know, Mira, if my behavior breaks the heart of a girlfriend, it's not your problem. You can't go around mending everything that I supposedly unravel. It's not going to erase what you went through with Antonio. Comparing the two situations is useless."

"Let's end this whole conversation," Mira said. "We can't agree. What's the point of trying?"

"To lie to ourselves, perhaps? That's what we all love doing, now isn't it? It's how we hide from the pain of our existence."

Mira glanced at him curiously out of the corner of her eye.

"I thought you were satisfied," she said.

"Until the next challenge comes along… Life is mundane without the new and unexpected. I guess that has been and continues to be my downfall… I'm constantly searching…"

"Well, when the next challenge arrives, I don't want to hear her name—or anything else about your relationships for that matter. I don't want to meet these women who are naive enough to fall for your act… Because that's what it is. For you, life is a stage, Septime. But that's not for me. I was curious this time and that was wrong. You were right from the start—I had no business meeting Cecile. We should stay out of each other's lives."

"No, Mira. I have to help you."

"What's that supposed to mean?"

"Look, I came here because I wanted to apologize. But I have a second motive as well."

Mira set her glass next to his and crossed her arms.

"What is it?"

"I know this artist named Laura who is planning an exhibit in a few months, and she wants a partner."

"If she's someone you're sleeping with, this conversation should stop right here and now."

"Of course not!"

"It's not that ridiculous of an assumption," Mira said, leaning back against the stiff cushion.

"OK, maybe it isn't. But this has nothing to do with me. I told her about you, and she's interested in a meeting."

"So that I can exhibit with her?"

"Yes, Mir… This would be fabulous for you! It's exactly what you need to get started here in Paris."

"It's wonderful that you're so knowledgeable about what I need at this point in my life, Septime, but it's best to keep your suggestions to yourself. I don't want any part of your friends."

"Mira, she's not a friend… she's someone I know. C'mon! Don't be ridiculous about this whole thing!"

He took her by the arms and looked at her in annoyance.

"Don't you realize how hard it is to get started in a new city?"

Mira stepped back as if she had been slapped. She never thought of herself as a novice. Her work met with quite a bit of success at home, so why not here in Paris as well? She wanted to strike out at him, but she stopped herself. Mira closed her eyes, took a deep breath and thought about Septime's words. There was a lot of competition in this city, and no one here had ever heard of her little gallery or quirky portraits. And it wasn't as if she had gobs of money to start a whole new operation on her own. She probably would be able to extract just enough from her business with Clara to start anew in Paris. Maybe Septime was right from time to time.

Mira felt heat rising into her face as she realized that she had been ridiculously naïve.

"I'll meet with her," she said, her voice a mere whisper. She had to wake up to reality and throw herself into her work if she hoped to survive in this place.

"When are you free? Tomorrow afternoon?"

Mira nodded dully, unable to completely shed her concerns. She hoped that she could at least trust her brother's instincts when it came to business.

Chapter 37

Rafael

The message on his voicemail was clear. Rafael had arrived too late. Wearily, he sank onto the unmade bed and played the recording once again.

"Mr. Mendez, this is Madame Pantin. I'm calling to let you know that Carmen returned to the apartment, packed her bags in a flash and told me she wouldn't be back. I asked her for a forwarding address, but she refused to give me one. She took everything this time—including the emerald ring—so I truly believe she won't return. I'm sorry if this isn't much help... Best of luck anyway."

"Son of a bitch!" he hissed, propelling himself off the bed and marching across the room to the door. He didn't know where he was going, but he had to get out of the cramped space within these four walls. He forgot about the fatigue of his trip and the drama of the past few days in his homeland.

As he opened the door, Hugo was walking up the stairs. He waved to Rafael.

"Where have you been? I thought you'd left for good..."

He shifted his tattered backpack around and shook Rafael's hand.

"Not without saying goodbye... I returned to Colombia to settle family business."

"That must have been quite a voyage..."

"You don't know the half of it..."

"How are you doing?" Hugo asked, wrinkling his brow.

Rafael leaned against his door and closed his eyes for a moment. His head was spinning. How could he begin to explain the pain and frustration that had been eating away at him? He looked intently at Hugo.

"Have you ever been so near to the end of a quest that you see it and taste it... And then suddenly, the floor collapses beneath your feet..."

"Are you talking about Carmen?"

Rafael nodded. "I met her in Colombia without realizing that she—this, strange young woman—was in fact the person I had been searching for... then I followed her to Paris only to find out that she returned to her apartment here one last time. She left before I could make my way over there. And now she's gone forever."

"Do you have any leads?"

"Nothing. My one clue is a fucking green stone that has given me nothing but grief my entire life..."

Hugo wrinkled his brow again.

"What is it?" Rafael asked, looking curiously into his friend's eyes.

"Carmen is involved with the emeralds then?"

"Yes, she knows the stones as well as my parents did, which at first was shocking to me. She learned her skills here—I'm sure from Marie. There's no other explanation."

"I know someone who might be able to help you," Hugo said slowly.

"What do you mean?"

"My mother's fiancé is a jewelry designer here in Paris. He knows a lot of people, and he works with emeralds... Maybe it's a long shot, but it's a risk worth taking."

Rafael grabbed Hugo's hand and shook it warmly. Feelings of hope resurrected themselves within his heart as he thought back to the one who had escaped him.

"You can't understand how much this means to me..."

"I hope we're not disappointed," Hugo whispered. "But I won't waste any time... If there's any way he'll see me today..."

"I can come with you..."

"No, don't worry about it, you just got back. I'm sure you have other things that you have to do. The shop is across town, and I don't even know if he's in. It could take hours to get some answers..."

"That's nothing compared to what I've gone through these past few weeks."

"If you don't get a message from me by tomorrow, come and see me at work. We'll be filming in that little garden we walked through together once. The one near the canal."

Rafael watched Hugo hurry to the stairs and then returned to the apartment for a quick shower. Finally, at least for the moment, he had managed to liberate himself from the quest for Carmen. It was time for a reunion with Laurel.

As Rafael hurried along the Rue des Martyrs, he saw nothing but Laurel's face, adorned with the sarcastic nonchalant expression that defined her personality. Nervous excitement was building up within as he thought of his escapade in a world that was odd and unlivable, far from her. He only hoped that she would understand why he had departed abruptly.

Rafael's determined footsteps quickened as he approached the door to her building. She couldn't turn her back on him. She had to accept the reason for this one last fight in the world of emeralds. A rush of adrenalin returned as he thought of the trek that had reunited him with a stranger. He squeezed his eyes shut as if to push away thoughts of Tigo, whose life ended so easily on the wooden floor.

He opened his eyes and took a deep breath. There it was right before him. Laurel's building. Sunlight warmed the brick façade and glistened in puddles left behind by early-morning crews who hosed down the sidewalks. The concierge pushed open the main door and dragged a broom behind her. Rafael's heart leaped. He darted between overheated cars and shouting drivers, and within seconds had slipped into the corridor.

This would be Rafael's first visit to the place Laurel never wanted to share with him. He climbed the stairs two-by-two until he arrived on the third floor. The apartment was on the left, with the chrysanthemum-adorned balcony overlooking the street. A narrow opaque window let some light into the landing that led to four separate residences. It seemed like a calm, quiet place—an ideal workspace for a writer like Laurel. Rafael rang the bell before his courage could abandon him.

A tired-looking man of about 50 answered the door. He obviously was Laurel's father. They shared the same light-green gaze, but his held a seriousness that Rafael never had glimpsed in hers.

"Hello… I'm Rafael, a friend of Laurel's…"

The man looked at him warily for a moment.

"She doesn't have any friends," he said gruffly.

He was about to close the door, but Rafael stopped him.

"Wait… I have to find her!" He could feel the desperation in his own voice and was ashamed of this sign of weakness. The man raised an eyebrow and crossed his arms across his chest.

"You've actually managed to break down the barrier?"

"What do you mean?"

"She trusts you…"

"Why wouldn't she?"

"You don't know?"

"Know what? Look… I have to see her."

"The easiest thing would be to go to see her at work…"

"But she doesn't…" Rafael knit his eyebrows together and studied the pale, worn-out face.

The man shook his head and held the door open for Rafael.

"Come in for a moment. I'm her father, Mr. de Champigny, and I think we need to talk."

Rafael nodded and stepped inside. Paintings in transparent blues and greens gave the apartment an aquatic air. Rafael felt grubby in his jeans and T-shirt as he followed this man in perfectly pressed gray pants and a matching sweater through such a well-kept home. Mr. de Champigny showed him into the living room, which looked like an underwater paradise with its blue velvet couch, fish tanks and silky lampshades. Rafael sat down gingerly opposite Laurel's father.

"Where can I find her?" Rafael asked.

"I'll tell you... but first I want to know something. What exactly has my daughter been saying about her life here?"

Rafael felt a shiver run down his spine. It was the type of sensation one feels right before everything goes haywire. He studied Mr. de Champigny's intense, perplexed eyes. It was obvious that he cared deeply about Laurel's well-being, yet didn't quite understand her.

"She said she was here writing a book—a university project," Rafael said tentatively, as if replying to a trick question.

Mr. de Champigny looked away and shook his head.

"What is it?"

The man returned his attention to Rafael and sighed.

"This is what I was afraid of..."

"What exactly do you mean?" Rafael asked, a feeling of discomfort rising from within.

"I thought the lies were over... These lies she uses to escape reality. This web that has entangled her and kept her from a normal life, from friends, education..."

Mr. de Champigny held his hands to his head and looked up to the sky as if to plead for some sort of divine intervention.

"I don't understand," Rafael said. "What does Laurel have to escape from?"

Mr. de Champigny's sad eyes returned to Rafael.

"There must be something special about you if you were able to break through the wall that has separated her from the rest of the world... She hasn't spoken of friendship with anyone in years. Of course she hasn't told you why... and I can't either. You have to discuss this with her. I can't get involved. It wouldn't be fair. The only thing I can say is this: Don't hate her for what she's done... It's self-preservation, that's all."

"Where can I find her?" Rafael asked, hastily rising from

his seat. His heart was pounding. He wanted to see Laurel. The Laurel he knew. Not a stranger who would only disappoint him. The jumble of her father's disorganized words made Rafael's head ache.

Mr. de Champigny sighed and remained silent for a moment as his empty eyes traveled well beyond the view offered by the window.

"You can find her at that rather offbeat bar on the corner—the one with the straw awnings and electric white lights. She's a waitress there."

Rafael, as if in a daze, followed Mr. de Champigny into the hallway.

"Maybe I shouldn't have told you," the older man said. "It certainly isn't any of my business... But I don't think keeping up a lie would have been to Laurel's advantage. I'm tired of lies in my house. I'm putting an end to all of them."

His expression was one of firm resolve.

"Thanks... for the information," Rafael said dully. He could hardly hear his own voice. He just wanted to see Laurel and find out why she had turned his already tipsy life upside down.

He raced down the stairs and retraced his steps south along the Rue des Martyrs. The bar was so close that he didn't have time to think before he pushed through the door and stood face-to-face with Laurel. Her eyes widened with panic, shame and excitement all at once, as she remained frozen, holding an empty tray in her hands.

"I have to talk with you," he murmured. He was blind to the customers, co-workers and the scenery around them as he faced the one who had driven his emotions out of control.

"I'm at work..." Her face reddened as she pronounced the words.

"It would have been nice to know that through you rather than from your father."

She glanced around nervously in a way that was unfamiliar to him.

"I have a fifteen-minute break. I'll take it now."

She set her tray down on the bar and pushed ahead of him to open the door and remove herself from the place where many pairs of eyes had been on them.

"Where were you?" she asked, turning to him. She took his hands and led him into a dim alleyway between two buildings. "I thought you had left me, Rafael!"

"I had an urgent matter to deal with in Colombia," he said.

"Why didn't you contact me? I was going crazy around here!" She reached for a cigarette and lighter in her hip pocket and lit up. "I took this stupid job as part of the research for my book…"

"Look, Laurel, I'm tired of your games!" he said, the frustration of his meeting with her father reaching a peak. He grabbed her by the arms and turned her to face him. "I know that you're not a writer! You're here waiting tables, and you couldn't even tell me the truth."

"Who told you that?" she snapped.

"It doesn't matter. It should have been you!"

"It was my father, wasn't it?" she said almost to herself. "Cecile would be the only other one, but she left him— hopefully for good."

"This isn't his fault," Rafael said. "It's yours, Laurel. How could you try to bring me into your life when it wasn't really yours? It was a fantasy. And what about Carmen? You told me you could lead me to her. That was another lie, of course. Don't you realize how important this quest is? I'm tired of these fucking games!"

"I do know of a Carmen, Rafael!" She wrenched out of his grip and turned away. "I was having trouble getting in touch with her… She used to live in our building, but she disappeared without a trace. I thought I somehow could find her… I need more time!"

"Is everything you told me a lie?"

"No," she said, softly, her eyes glimmering.

"Then what is this? This story about writing and being a student…"

"I didn't know what to say to keep your attention!" she said, throwing her cigarette to the ground. "You never would have stayed with me if I'd told you the truth… If I said that I'd spent the past few years in and out of mental hospitals and that my father brought me here by force because he was afraid of what would happen otherwise. If I said that I was waiting tables because this bar is the only place that would hire me. If I said that I didn't even know what I wanted out of life. And if I told you a lot of other things that I can hardly talk about... Would you have stayed? No!"

"You're wrong, Laurel! Nothing would have changed my feelings for you. I fell in love with you because of something within, but you can't see that!" Then he stopped.

She stared at him with widened eyes once again. He had told her he loved her, but in a way that was completely unlike how he had planned, and this disappointed him. Rafael turned away. Her tumultuous experiences didn't change his feelings for her. Nothing could. And that was what frightened him.

"I love you too," she whispered.

He didn't want to hear those words now. He forced himself to avoid those ever-seductive eyes.

"What else are you hiding, Laurel?" he asked. "Your father said you had been through some kind of ordeal..."

"That was long ago," she said desperately. She took his hands and squeezed them in hers. "It's true. Something terrible happened. I could only live through the lies, but I can't talk about what drove me there! ... I can't share it with anyone. Not now. But I've been honest with you, Rafael! I've been honest about everything that counts. I came here to recover... but it's difficult. I couldn't tell you that I was this tormented person who didn't know what she wanted out of life! This person who could only reinvent her life rather than live it."

"The problem is I don't know who you are, Laurel. Where do the lies end and where does the truth begin? We have to be able to share everything—good and bad—about our lives in order to have a relationship. If you don't want to do that, I don't think we have a future."

He felt as if his heart was breaking as he pronounced that very stilted speech. But he knew it was the right decision. Gently, he pushed her away.

"I have things to handle in my own life. I've found some answers. Finally, I'm moving away from the confusion that has hovered over me ever since my parents died. I have to fix one problem at a time, Laurel."

His eyes met hers for a split second. She was about to cry, and this twisted his heart. No longer was she the tough wiseass. Laurel, for once, was completely vulnerable. And this too scared him.

"I have to be on my way," Rafael said.

Slow tears trickled down Laurel's cheek, and Rafael brushed them away with his fingertips. She took a step back.

"Go!" she shouted hysterically. "Get the fuck out of my life! Like the rest of them—just leave!"

Before Rafael could say anything else, Laurel ran into the street and vanished from sight. He emerged from the alley and looked through the window of the busy little café, where Laurel's empty tray remained alone and unnoticed on the bar. Then he turned and walked slowly toward the place he was starting to call home and did his best to hold back the tears that he refused to let fall.

Chapter 38

Cecile

A knock at the door late that night startled Cecile as she tried unsuccessfully to read one of those novels meant to carry the reader to faraway places. The only destination that seemed far away to Cecile at the moment was her own true self. She shivered slightly in her fluffy, pink bathrobe and glanced at the old grandfather clock that loudly ticked midnight.

Cecile slipped out of the armchair and tiptoed across the hardwoods to the door.

"Who is it?" she whispered tentatively, hoping that maybe, quite possibly, it would be her daughter.

"It's Manu, Cecile... Please let me in. I have to see you!"

Cecile's heart pounded wildly. Viv had told him she was here, but she couldn't be angry with her daughter for that. Cecile still wasn't ready to see Manu, yet at the same time, she wanted to face him, to scream at him for all that drove her into Septime's arms. She flung open the door, expecting to find that calm person who would try to convince her to return home for the right reasons. Instead, Manu looked frantic. He wore an old sweatshirt thrown over a pair of jeans whose existence she had forgotten about long ago. He stepped inside and roughly pulled her into his arms.

"I've been trying to reach you for days, Cecile," he said. "I thought I never would find you!"

She closed her eyes and felt the warmth of Manu's chest against her cheek. His heart was racing in time with hers.

"It's a long story," she whispered.

He took a step back and looked at her with desperate eyes.

"You left, and then on top of that, tonight I got home and found this from Laurel."

He took a piece of paper out of his pocket and held it out to her.

Papa,

I can't stay here any longer. Thank you for everything, but I have to find the way on my own if I ever hope to make things work in my life. So, I'm leaving. I'll be in touch soon. I promise.
Love,
Laurel

Cecile read it twice before reacting. She swallowed hard and looked up at Manu. She didn't know what to feel. Of course, she didn't want Laurel living with them, but she didn't want this unbalanced girl to be on her own in the streets either. She could see the pain in Manu's eyes, and for the first time in a long while, it touched her.

Cecile led him into the room. Manu sat at the edge of the pear-shaped armchair, and she climbed onto the bed facing him.

"What happened?" she asked.

He held his head in his hands.

"I don't know, Cecile. You were the one who left me!"

"I'm talking about Laurel…"

"Let's start with us."

Cecile took in a slow, deep breath and looked into those eyes that still gazed at her with warm intensity from time to time. She had to know the truth.

"The letters," she said. Images of him undressing a woman whose identity remained a mystery flashed before Cecile's eyes. She couldn't count the number of times she awoke during the night after nightmares of Manu and his lover. "You were having an affair. I found those damn letters in the house, Manu!"

His face reddened, and he looked away.

"You know you can't deny it," she said. Cecile could feel the tears streaming down her face, but she didn't care. "I have the proof! You lied to me! What was wrong with our life, Manu? If anything, you were the one who calmed the passion! You were the one who didn't have time to go out or stay in for a romantic evening... You were too busy or too tired. Maybe you didn't find me attractive any more... But some men see things differently."

There, she had said it in the one fit of hysteria that she would allow herself. Cecile reached for a tissue and wiped her eyes. When she looked up, he was staring at her with sadness once again. Then he leaned forward and took her by the hands. His grip tightened.

"Why did you do it, Cecile?" he hissed in anger. "Why didn't you confront me instead of taking revenge behind my back?"

"That way you could say 'I'm sorry,' and everything would be fine. That would make it easy for you, Manu. Much too easy. Now you see what it feels like to be betrayed. To feel worthless..."

"Cecile, it was a mistake! It lasted two weeks... It started after that horrible story with Laurel. I couldn't handle it, Cecile. I felt as if everything was my fault... and then we argued constantly about the idea of her moving into our place. The whole world seemed to turn upside down. I'm not saying it was right, Cecile. I know it was the worst episode in my life. I regretted it, but didn't know what to do. I didn't want to ruin our marriage, so I retreated from you. I hoped you wouldn't notice, and instead it ended up driving you into someone else's arms."

He released her hands and rose to his feet. She stood up and followed him to the window.

"Why did you keep the letters?" she asked.

"I didn't realize they still existed," he said, turning around to face her. "I pushed them into the depths of my desk drawer and planned on burning every one of them. I suppose they ended up elsewhere when we started redecorating the apartment... Look, Cecile, I know that saying I'm sorry isn't enough. And I know that saying I didn't care about her isn't enough either. But you're the only one I've ever loved."

He touched her cheek, and she glanced down at her pearly pink toenails. She could feel the tears welling up in her eyes once again, but she refused to crack. She wanted to tell him that she loved him too. She wanted to say that she was sorry she had fallen like a silly schoolgirl for the artist who obviously had plenty of muses. She wanted to go home. But Cecile also was afraid of returning to the monotony of the life she knew too well. Maybe this was simply a trap.

"Please come home," he whispered.

"I still need time," she said softly.

"I won't take you for granted, Cecile," he said, wrapping his arms around her. She felt as if she had been transported back several years to the man who had seduced her so easily. But today, she would take things one step at a time. "I don't want to know the details of these past few horrible weeks. I want to look forward."

"So that means you don't want to tell me about her?"

"Ask whatever you want, Cecile."

"Do I know her?"

He shook his head.

"She was at the university for a symposium," he said. "Everything happened quickly, and I regretted it immensely afterward. She returned to her home in the south and after sending me those letters, which I didn't answer, she never contacted me again."

Cecile's heart ached from his infidelity and her own. She felt as if they both had irrevocably slashed a hideous hole through their relationship, yet at the same time, she desperately tried to convince herself that they could patch it up. She returned to her spot on the bed and looked at him intently.

"What are you going to do about Laurel?" she asked.

"I incessantly tried to reach you this weekend, Cecile, because I wanted to tell you that I was going to set Laurel up in a studio where she could start getting used to an independent life. I had found one for her and everything. It was going to be a surprise. But I was too late…"

"Just recently you didn't want to hear of her leaving our place…"

"I made this decision for you. And then I realized that it was the best thing for all of us. That's why I was calling… I thought it would bring you back to us, Cecile. I knew you were off somewhere with… him… and it was driving me out of my mind. I didn't know what to do to win you back…"

She smiled weakly.

"I'm sorry about everything… about what we've both done to hurt each other."

"We still have a chance…"

Cecile rubbed her eyes.

"I don't know… I have to sleep on this, Manu. I can't come back to you right away. Too much has happened…"

"That's what I expected, although I hoped that I was wrong."

"What can I do to help you find Laurel? I know our relations have been tense at best, but I don't want her wandering the streets either."

Manu shook his head sadly. "I already went to the place where she works, but she wasn't there… She walked out earlier today and never returned. Laurel will be lucky if she can keep that job. I'm going to try to find this boyfriend of hers, but I don't know where to start. He came by the house looking for her earlier. His name is Rafael, but of course I don't have his address… And he's about my only hope right now. Damn it, maybe they even ran off together…"

With that, Manu stood up and once again his gaze caught Cecile's.

"I can't lose you," he said.

And then he walked out the door, leaving Cecile with fresh tears in the corners of her eyes.

Chapter 39

Andre

A dark-haired young man pushed his way through the crowd of technicians and extras, and hurried toward Hugo and Andre as they stepped to the side to take a break from a long day on location. They were filming scenes in an obscure garden in central Paris, and what was supposed to be a two-hour shoot had turned into a several-hour one. Tension was high, and tempers were hot. Finally, the director ordered everyone to take a break and return with better attitudes if they hoped to continue in the business.

Andre took the whole thing lightheartedly, but he saw the nervousness creeping slowly but surely into his son's eyes.

"Don't worry about anything, Hugo," he said, tapping him on the back. "Nothing's going wrong on this shoot. Just relax."

Right at that moment, the young man slipped down next to them on the park bench amidst the colorful flowers that Andre was incapable of identifying.

"Rafael! Glad you found me…I couldn't break away."

"Does that mean you have news?"

Hugo nodded gravely, and then glanced at Andre.

"By the way, this is my father Andre Wren. Dad, my friend, Rafael."

"Nice to meet you, Sir," Rafael said, shaking his hand.

"Same here," Andre said, looking at the handsome young man whose smooth dark skin and almond eyes would have made him a natural on camera. Andre felt as if he had seen him somewhere before. *Most likely at an audition or something,* he thought to himself.

Hugo turned back to Rafael.

"I know where you can find Carmen," he said. "And that's why I'm saying this in front of my father—because she has returned to her original home at 120 Rue des Martyrs!"

"That's my building," Andre said. "Now whom exactly are we talking about?"

"It's also Laurel's address…" Rafael said under his breath.

Hugo glanced from Andre to Rafael.

"I spoke with my mother's fiancé, and he knew of a jewelry designer named Marie and her daughter Carmen. He wouldn't give me any other details about them. He just said that Carmen called him the other day looking for work."

"Laurel wasn't lying when she said she had heard something about a girl named Carmen… my half-sister." Rafael's voice trailed off.

Andre swallowed hard as he watched the young man digest this news that seemed to hit him almost unexpectedly. He did remember a woman named Marie, who lived on some other floor, but he hadn't heard her name mentioned in ages. It was true that Andre Wren hadn't been attentive to anything other than his own situation ever since his accident. He knew he wasn't the best possible witness to the goings-on in his building.

"Do you know anything about them, Sir?" Rafael asked.

Andre shook his head vaguely.

"I've heard the names before, but nothing more… You see I don't spend much time in my apartment and can't honestly say I know the neighbors. We've never had much contact."

"And Laurel?" Rafael asked desperately. "A woman about my age with long red hair… Do you know her or her father

Mr. de Champigny?"

"Ah, yes," Andre said, relieved that he did indeed recognize at least one family that lived in building. He hadn't realized how out of touch he had been with reality. "She moved in not too long ago… I've spoken with her stepmother —Cecile, I think—a couple of times. Sad story."

"What do you mean?" Rafael asked.

Hugo looked at Andre pointedly, and he got the message. At the same time, he realized why Rafael seemed familiar. He had seen him downstairs outside the front door holding Laurel's hand as she watched the night sky. Of course he couldn't uncover everything he had heard about the girl from her stepmother. He didn't know if the stories even were true. Cecile, or whatever her name was, seemed pretty disgruntled with her new little guest.

"Oh, one of those stories of the unwanted stepchild who moves in," he said, waving his hand in the air as if to dismiss every thought of the de Champigny family from his head. "And if you want the details, you can ask her. I don't remember everything people tell me, you know. I've got my own problems."

Rafael looked at Hugo, who had been intently watching Andre gruffly dismiss any connection with the residents of 120 Rue des Martyrs.

"Hugo, I'm going there," he said. "I have to find the truth. About my own family and about Laurel. I'm only hoping that is the place to find the answers."

"Good luck," Hugo said. "But you might not need it at this point."

"It's still too early to yell victory, but thanks… for being a friend." He smiled, nodded at Andre, and jogged down the path of crushed shells that encircled the lush grass. Andre and Hugo watched him disappear.

Hugo was the first to speak.

"Why didn't you tell him what you know, Dad?"

"How can you be sure that there's more to my story?" he asked with a sly grin.

"It's in your eyes."

"All right, you've got me… There are certain things that

one should find out on one's own, Hugo. The stories I've heard aren't the easiest to tell. And who knows if they are even completely accurate! It's not up to some stranger to inform Rafael about secrets of people whom he apparently cares for very much. I can't do that."

"That's what I thought," Hugo said quietly.

"Now you're worried that Rafael won't find out the truth. That's what you're thinking about, isn't it?"

"No, I'm thinking that you do know how to make the right decision after all."

"I guess I just haven't made enough of them in my life to make much of a difference," Andre said with an ironic laugh. He tapped his new pack of cigarettes until one fell out and then lit it.

"Better late than never," Hugo said. "I suppose that's life, now isn't it?"

Chapter 40

Mira

Mira walked boldly through the gallery door. The place was quiet and nearly empty at this early afternoon hour. Claire sat on the red, pink and purple striped stool in the corner and twisted a strand of hair slowly around her finger as she read one of those tacky romance novels that she kept in her handbag. She didn't seem to hear Mira approach, or at least pretended not to notice those soft steps squeak across the floor as music to be zen by played in the background.

"Hey Claire, is my brother around?"

"In there," she mumbled, nodding her head in the direction of the back room. It was set up as an office of sorts, but Septime used it as more of an area to relax. The owners of the gallery were never there at the same time that he was, so he had the run of the place. Mira rounded the corner into the pale, yellow room scattered with bright paintings of what seemed to be every variety imaginable.

Then her breath caught in her throat. Septime almost sank into oblivion as her eyes locked with those of Antonio. She wanted to turn around and run, but her feet were frozen to the ground. He and Septime had been having some sort of intense conversation. Septime's face reddened, and Antonio slipped off the edge of the desk and rushed to her.

"Damn it, Mira! Do you know how hard I've been trying to find you?"

He took her hands in his and tried to pull her close, but she pushed him away.

"What are you doing here?" she asked. "Didn't we already have this conversation? It's over, Antonio."

"You didn't hear me out, Mira. I have to talk with you. Clara meant nothing to me!"

"Then why did you do it? And why did it take you so long to come to this realization?"

Septime cleared his throat and touched her on the arm. She nodded and watched him slip out the door leading back to the gallery. Mira steeled herself as she stared into those eyes that once knew how to charm her.

"It's over, Antonio."

"This is craziness, Mira! I know there's someone else… you wouldn't be able to turn your back on us otherwise."

"Are you insane? You were the one cheating on me!"

"We were both drunk the first time…"

"And the second, third etc?"

"I don't have a good excuse, Mira. You and I have been together since high school… I was tempted by the idea of a new experience, and then it spun out of control. I regret everything that happened."

"It's too late for us now," she said. A small twinge of sadness pierced her heart as she glanced into his eyes and at the lips that used to grin at her mischievously when they would run around town late at night not so long ago.

All had changed in the past couple of months, yet she hadn't really noticed the deterioration of their relationship until discovering Clara in Antonio's arms. The separation allowed her to clear her mind and focus on what she truly wanted out of life. She needed honesty, but with Antonio that was impossible. She never would be able to trust him again.

"You're in love with someone else," he said coldly. "That's right isn't it?"

Mira swallowed hard. She looked at him steadily.

"It doesn't matter."

"You want another man to raise our child?"

"I told you that it's over."

He approached her and grasped her hand.

"Give it some time, Mira. You can't throw our relationship away! This is a mistake, Mira!"

She pushed him away once again and made her way to the door.

"If it is, then I'm ready to live with it!" Mira said. "I've made my decision, Antonio, and I won't change it. I'm not in love with you and haven't been for a long time!"

The words that seemed so hateful to her slipped out before she could consider containing them. Thoughts of Hugo made her heartbeat quicken. Finally, everything seemed perfectly clear.

"You can't convince me to accept the betrayal," she said.

Antonio grabbed the dark-green overnight bag that she knew too well off the floor. It was the one she had given him for his travels. He brushed past her and turned around only once.

"Don't think you can keep me out of our child's life, Mira."

"I never said I would."

He turned around in silence and walked out the door.

Mira didn't know how long she remained there, rooted to the spot, before Septime calmly returned to the office and jolted her out of her reverie.

"He was begging me for your address when you ran in."

"It doesn't matter, Septime. I'm not in love with him any more. Maybe I never was… Maybe he was right to cheat on me. At least it brought an end to a relationship that seemed all right, but never would have been spectacular. There were good times, of course, but it wasn't meant to last… It's better that we ended it now. A clean break. I have to move on… and so does he."

Septime was silent. He leaned against the desk and pulled open the window, letting a refreshing breeze into the stuffy room. Mira could smell the odors of butter and burned batter from the *creperie* next door and the scent of mixed flowers from the vendor across the way.

"Oh, if life could only be so sweet," Septime said, shaking his head.

"It can be."

"Who is he?"

"You don't know him."

"I know his face," Septime said with a sly smile. "You're painting his portrait. I'm sure he's the one."

Claire's voice rang out from the gallery. Laura had arrived and was eager to meet her new partner.

Chapter 41

Rafael

Rafael climbed the familiar staircase at 120 Rue des Martyrs, but he didn't stop on the third floor, where thoughts of Laurel would only overwhelm him with sadness. He couldn't think of that strange young woman who had stirred up his emotions and tangled him in her web of lies. He wanted to be angry, to hate her for it and forget her existence, but it was impossible. He hesitated for a moment on the landing, but continued. His priority for the moment was finding Carmen. Only one more flight and he was in front of the navy blue lacquered door. He reached out and pulled the tiny brass hoop that let out a ring much like that of a child's bicycle.

She was home. He could hear her footsteps tentatively approaching.

"Who is it?"

"It's Rafael."

Silence.

"Carmen," he whispered against the chipped paint. "Everything is going to be all right… I have to see you."

Slowly, a tiny beam of light appeared between the door and its frame. It widened until it illuminated her face. She looked at him with calm, steady eyes. Her hair hung in damp ringlets that sponged themselves in a thick, gray terrycloth bathrobe.

"You figured everything out," she said sharply. She turned around and walked across the plush, raspberry rug that covered the floor. Rafael pushed the door closed and followed her down the narrow hallway and into a large, cluttered sitting room with several windows overlooking the Rue des Martyrs. The walls were covered with old photographs of his father and a woman who he knew was Marie. Rafael swallowed hard as he approached one of the two of them holding hands. A girl of about five with long, dark pigtails was grasping his father's pants.

He turned to Carmen. She was that child. He could see it in her eyes. Rafael felt as if the floor was spinning beneath him. Marie was supposed to be his birth mother. And Carmen was supposed to be her child with some other man. Half-siblings. That was the scenario Rafael had been envisioning since the story of Carmen's life had unfolded. But there was much more to this tale. And he was certain that Carmen knew the details.

"I don't understand," he said, emptily. He wrinkled his brow and turned back to the photo. He had never seen his father look so carefree and young. Those tense lines between his eyebrows seemed nonexistent. That hardened expression was nowhere to be found.

"What's difficult to grasp, Rafael? Diego chose you and your mother over us. That's the bottom line. Mom was supposed to help Diego and Tina have a baby—you. But then Diego ended up falling in love—if you could call it that—with Mom. He wouldn't let her go, but everything had to be on his terms. And she loved him too much to walk away. That's how she was—a hopeless romantic, who never thought of herself first. And in the end, she was alone. Diego didn't even come back when Mom died two years ago… He said it would be too painful. But what about me? What about my pain?"

Rafael's heart sank. He looked into the eyes that now seemed to carry so much resentment. Carmen shivered and pulled her robe more tightly across her chest.

"I came here looking for you, for her…" he said dully. "I had no idea…"

"She was in a car accident," Carmen said softly. "I was only sixteen. She left me here alone… yet he still wouldn't come. My own father did nothing but send me money. Well, I didn't want money! I needed a family!"

Tears started to fall, but she brushed them away in annoyance with the back of her hand and continued.

"I was so damn jealous of you, Rafael Mendez," she said between gritted teeth. "A real Mendez. You had that happy family life. You were learning about the emerald business. And I was here, feeling worthless with only the memories of everything Mom taught me about the stones."

"He never told me any of this," Rafael whispered. "He was living two lives, fulfilling two dreams…"

Rafael didn't know whether he should be furious or forgiving. For the moment, he simply felt hurt for himself and for this near stranger who was his sister.

"Why were you looking for someone named Carmen?" she asked.

"Because as he was dying he whispered your name… He told me I had to find you."

Carmen's face whitened and she looked down at her slim hands twisting the belt of her bathrobe.

"He cared about you," Rafael said.

"Maybe… but everything got screwed up somewhere along the line. He wanted the best of both worlds, Rafael! That was his problem! You and Tina had the better situation because you didn't know about us. Diego's sister Mariana was the only one who knew, but she didn't want any part of us."

So that was why Mariana avoided speaking directly to Rafael ever since the murder. He thought back to her note. She finally must have realized that she had to do something to bring Rafael and Carmen together even though this second family was more of an embarrassment to her than anything else. The lies sickened him.

"We suffered," Carmen was saying. "We knew that we weren't the important family—the real family… We were the ones Diego was ashamed of. The ones hidden in this damn closet of an apartment that carries too many memories of Mom. I tried escaping, staying in Mom's work space across town. I moved all of her design equipment out of the place and transformed it into my own little apartment. But the walls seemed to close in on me. I had to leave."

Again, the tears fell. But this time she let them flow. Rafael leaned forward to touch her cheek, but she pushed him away. He closed his eyes and took a deep breath. He didn't want to drive her any further from him. Rafael only wanted to comfort this girl whose suffering seemed almost more profound than his own.

"Why did you come to Bogotá... and to Tigo?" he murmured.

"I went to see Diego. I showed up at his office one afternoon. He was furious when he saw me. It was as if he didn't care that I'd lost my mother. Right then, I realized that we were fun and games for him and nothing more... He bought me a ticket back to Paris and ordered me to leave. But I couldn't. I wanted to go to the emerald mines. I wanted to show him that I could make it in that kind of business, and I didn't need him to do it... I met Tigo in a café a few days later... He was looking for a partner and so was I. We were a perfect match."

"Why, Carmen? Why would you want to get involved in something so dangerous?"

"What did I know about danger, Rafael, and what did I care? I wanted to forget about the real world and live an adventure. And I did just that. Until the night of the murder."

"What do you mean?" Rafael's throat went dry.

"I wasn't simply aware of what happened after the fact, Rafael!" she said, staring at him intently with her glassy eyes. "I was there. I didn't know Tigo was going to do it. Everything happened very fast. That's when I knew it was over. I wanted to get out. But I couldn't. He threatened me. And for the first time, I was scared... but I never let him see it. That would have been fatal."

Rafael's mind flashed back to the horror of that night. He could hear his father's weakened voice and see the paleness of his face as blood flowed from his body. Rafael reached out to

Carmen and pulled her into his arms. And for the first time, she clung to him. He could feel her chest heaving as silent tears dampened his shirt.

"I hated you for having what I wanted," she whispered, choking on her tears. "But then when I met you... I realized I was wrong. It wasn't your fault. And you ended up miserable like me on that awful night. I'll never forget it... I've tried, but the nightmares haunt me..."

"Me too, Carmen," he said. "It's too painful to disappear. But at least we've both uncovered the truth. That's what Diego wanted, you know. He wanted us to find each other... It was his last wish. You were his final thought."

Rafael looked into his sister's reddened eyes as she sank back into the oversized cushions on the couch.

"What do we do now, Rafael?" she asked.

"I don't know just yet."

He held onto her hands, feeling the rough edges of what he knew was the ring Madame Pantin had showed him weeks earlier. He gazed down at it, sparkling against her golden skin.

"It was Mom's," she said. "Diego's last gift to her. I refused to wear it before."

"Why are you wearing it now?"

"Because I'm trying to accept all that's happened."

Rafael thought of his own hatred for the emeralds. They brought back too many horrible memories. But he knew that he and Carmen would have to find a way to live with them.

Rafael could have spent hours with Carmen uncovering the details of his father's other life far from Colombia, but he realized that it was too soon. He and his sister needed a couple of days to digest what they had discovered together. So they parted at the door to her apartment.

"Are you sure you won't disappear?" he asked.

Her half smile was a reflection of his.

"I don't plan on returning to Colombia anytime soon... I have a few decisions to make here."

"Me too."

He kissed her on the cheek and hurried down the stairs. He would stop at Laurel's place. Rafael was tired of being too late. Too late to save his father, too late to meet his birth mother Marie. He had to find out why Laurel had created her fantasy world, and why she was afraid of being honest with him.

Rafael rang the bell. No answer. He rang again insistently. Rapid footsteps and the door flew open. Mr. de Champigny, a haggard version of the well-dressed man Rafael had met once before, stood there with a look of desperation.

"Rafael! Where is she?"

A sinking feeling gripped Rafael.

"I came here to see Laurel," he said slowly.

Mr. de Champigny shook his head and ran his hands wildly through his hair.

"Oh, God I was afraid of this..."

"Where is she?" Rafael asked nervously.

"She's gone."

"What?" Rafael thought of Laurel wandering around alone and this terrified him. "Wait a minute, do you have any idea..."

"Of course not! The only thing she left behind was this note."

He thrust a piece of paper into Rafael's hands and walked into the living room. Rafael read it as he followed Laurel's father.

"This doesn't tell us much of anything," he said, setting the note on the coffee table. "I guess you went to the café where she works..."

"Yes, and she hasn't been there."

The two men sat down opposite one another.

"What happened to Laurel?" Rafael asked. "I mean, what traumatic experience did she go through? I have to know, Mr. de Champigny! Her disappearance is my fault... because I told her that it was over between us. I was wrong to act hastily, to jump to conclusions... I want to understand her..."

The older man was silent for a moment. He looked down at his moccasins and closed his eyes before returning his gaze to Rafael.

"Laurel's mother had custody of her ever since our divorce. They lived in the south, so I only saw my daughter on holidays. I knew her mother was unstable. She went from job to job and man to man... never had much direction. I tried getting custody of Laurel for years, but it was a losing battle. I wanted her here even though I knew my wife didn't get along with her. I felt that my daughter was in jeopardy, left alone half of the time... She fell behind in school, and her mother didn't care. And then, when Laurel was 14... her mother's boyfriend raped her."

Rafael's breath caught in his throat. He felt as if he had been punched in the stomach. He wanted to hold her close to him and beat the hell out of that bastard who had forced her out of reality and into that false, safe world she had created in her mind.

"At first her mother didn't believe her," Mr. de Champigny continued. "Can you imagine that? Anyway, after the DNA tests, it wasn't possible to deny. I spent a month down south with Laurel, trying everything to pull her out of the depression that had taken over her whole being, but nothing worked. And then she overdosed."

Mr. de Champigny took in a deep breath and shook his head.

"From there, it was a psychiatric hospital for months and months. She was in and out of that place. Her survival tool was the ability to lie and believe her lies. She created a world that comforted her. Her psychiatrist worked with her through that long and difficult period. And somehow she returned to reality and managed to finish high school only a year late. That's when I insisted she come to live with us. I told her there would be more opportunity here, and she could take a year or so off to decide what she wanted to do with her life. That was a few months ago."

"We have to find her," Rafael said, getting up from his chair.

"Where do you suggest we start?"

"Anywhere... everywhere. I'll walk up and down every street of Paris, but I won't give up."

Mr. de Champigny looked beaten by life's hardships as he

faced Rafael.

"The determination of youth," he said, shaking his head. "I hope it doesn't falter."

"It won't. It never has."

Rafael scribbled his phone number down on a scrap of paper he found in his pocket and handed it to Laurel's father. "This is in case she happens to return."

"You'll be the first to know," he said, patting Rafael on the shoulder.

Rafael ran down the stairs and into the street. He looked around at those unfamiliar faces and felt as if the world was closing in on him. And then he ran. As fast as he could. Away from the building. Anywhere. Hoping to bump into Laurel. Hoping, like a fool, to be that lucky.

Chapter 42

Cecile

Cecile had an idea. Yes, Cecile de Champigny, who had always profoundly disliked her stepdaughter, had an idea of how to find the one she for so long had wanted to drive away. For the first time in days, Cecile methodically pulled on a light, linen dress, dotted a few drops of Chanel No. 5 on her wrists, lined her eyelids in gray and her lips in pink, slipped on her patent leather heels and slammed the hotel door shut behind her. She was on her way to meet Viv at the ballet school. Her daughter was the key. She was Laurel's confidante after all.

Cecile hurried through the door and down the familiar hallway packed with other mothers, who had once seemed intimidating. But she wasn't focusing on them or what they thought or on herself. She saw Viv at the end of the hall, a peach towel thrown over one shoulder and her dance bag dangling from the other. They caught each other's eyes at the same moment and met in the middle.

"What are you doing here?" Viv asked.

"We need to come back to each other, Viv. C'mon, let's go outside. There's a problem we have to solve together. It's for your father."

"For Dad? What do you…" And then she stopped. Cecile saw the look in her daughter's eyes. She knew of Laurel's whereabouts.

The light of day made Viv squint as she faced her mother on the grassy patch on one side of the building.

"I'm sorry I disappointed you, Viv… sometimes it's hard to understand a teenager. I had trouble looking back to when I was your age, to my own experiences. If I had been able to, I would have realized you needed me."

"It's going to be OK, Mom," she said. "I promised myself I'll try for the program next year… I'll make sure I'm prepared. This year, there were just too many distractions."

"You mean that boy…"

Viv blushed and looked down.

"He's going on to the next audition… and hasn't spoken to me since."

Cecile tentatively put her arm around Viv's shoulders. It felt odd to console this girl who had seemed perfect and in control only weeks ago.

But it had been an outward display. It was her sense of pride. Viv's worries weren't different from those of any other girl her age, and Cecile finally was waking up to that fact. She was ashamed of her lack of motherly instincts, but she knew she had to face forward rather than look back.

"That means he wasn't good enough for you, Viv. There will be others more worth your time."

"I know… That's what Laurel said too."

"Speaking of which…"

Viv's eyes widened.

"I can't, Mom! She swore me to secrecy! She's OK, but that's the only thing I can tell you."

"Viv, we're not out to make Laurel's life miserable… Her father has found a solution that should work for everyone. Please listen to me. You know where she is, so please go to her and tell her this: Her father has rented a small apartment for her right down the street from us. It's a lovely little place. He wants her to stay there so she can get on her feet. He really loves her, Viv. This whole situation is making him suffer, and I'm worried about him."

"You mean you've forgiven him for the other woman?" Viv asked, scrunching her eyebrows together. "How can you accept that?"

"Because everyone makes mistakes," she said, looking away from her daughter and into the clear blue sky.

Viv took a deep breath and gazed steadily at her mother.

"How do I know you won't follow me?"

"I suppose you have to trust me, Viv… and even if you don't, can you imagine me running after you in these shoes?"

Viv smiled as she glanced down at Cecile's feet.

"OK… I'll do it. But I have one question, Mom…"

Cecile already knew what it would be.

"Are you coming home?"

Cecile had thought about her options all night long as she tossed and turned in that cold hotel bed. And finally, at daybreak, she had reached her answer.

It was too late to transform herself into anyone other than Cecile de Champigny. This was her life. There were some bumpy parts to it, but many of them were due to her lassitude.

She would return to her reality, but as a different person—as a woman who would no longer embrace disappointment. Gone were the days spent as life's bystander, sitting on a Montmartre bench and watching the world go by.

෨ঌ

Cecile saw Septime one last time. She didn't have any intention of meeting with him. He was the one who called out to her through the crowds milling around a lively square in the neighborhood. She recognized his voice, but pretended that she didn't. She hurried around the corner, but she wasn't quick enough. He caught up with her.

"Cecile!" He held onto her hands and tried to drink her in with the seductive expression that seemed to work well for him. But she was no longer vulnerable to his advances.

"You got what you wanted from me," she said coldly. "Move on to your next adventure…"

"Cecile, I'm sorry for disappointing you… I didn't mean for things to end that way."

"But they couldn't have ended any other way, now could they? I should have listened to your sister's little hints, but I was blind to the truth. I wanted to believe you were different. I learned my lesson. It's one I won't forget."

Septime touched her cheek, and she took a step back.

"You can't even say it wouldn't happen again," she said, shaking her head.

He was silent.

Cecile crossed her arms. "You must be leaving town soon…"

"Tomorrow," he said. "I'm returning home to start work on some new projects."

She nodded.

"Look, Cecile… I didn't want to hurt you."

"Don't worry about me, Septime Galino. I am perfectly fine."

Cecile turned around on shaky ankles and made her exit, as triumphant as she had ever been in her miserable little life.

Chapter 43

Andre

"Dad, wait…"

Hugo came running up to Andre as he was about to exit the studio for the last time. Andre's scenes were in the can. He felt both melancholy and relieved, as he usually did when he finished up such a project. But this time, the melancholy part was tied to the fact that his work with Hugo had come to an end.

Andre turned around in the dim, narrow hallway and faced the boy who had seemed to turn into a man before his very eyes these past few weeks.

"I wanted to say that I enjoyed working with you," Hugo whispered, almost timidly. "You taught me a lot."

Andre's grin was awkward. "I don't know if it's worth very much, Hugo. … But I was glad to… to spend time with you. And I'll tell you one other thing. I appreciate that portrait of you."

"Portrait?" Hugo raised an eyebrow and looked at him oddly.

"The one your girlfriend gave me."

"She gave it to you?"

"You mean you didn't know?"

"I had no idea..." he said with faraway eyes. "But I'm glad. If you like it, I'm glad."

"She's quite talented..."

"Yeah, I think so too."

"Well, I guess I'd better be on my way... I have to get back to my agent. There are several lousy offers waiting for my refusal."

"I don't understand it, Dad... I still think you should be getting the cream of the crop."

Andre smiled and shook his head.

"You have a lot of learning to do about this business, kid."

He swallowed hard, patted his son on the shoulder and pushed open the door into the blinding, late-afternoon light.

∽∾

It was funny how a Harley could be addictive, like a drug that torments one's system and leaves its mark there forever, as a reminder of those glorious days. The bad memories are forgotten. Only the ecstasy remains. That just about sums up what Andre Wren felt as he polished his Harley yet again in that dark garage with only one small bulb to illuminate the brilliant metal. He rubbed a cloth with abandon against each crevice, trying to forget about his frustrating conversation with Jack, who continued to throw him degrading offers. So he told him to go to hell. Andre Wren would never return to the career that ate through his life and ruined the best of it.

The bitter smell of his old leather jacket hanging from a spike above his head soothed him. He thought back to those rides through the countryside on a warm spring afternoon, those crazy races with some of the other Harley owners whom he hadn't spoken with in ages and finally that horrible conversation with the doctor. Behind those thick spectacles that most likely had never even seen a Harley, he ordered Andre never to ride again.

Andre buffed one last bit of metal and stabbed his cane into the cement ground to lift himself from his nearly crouched position. He gazed at that perfect bike and his twisted reflection in its shiny curves.

"Fuck them all!" he hissed.

He threw the stained cloth and his cane into the corner of the garage and poured gasoline from a little metal can into the pleasure that had been denied him way too long. Hoisting himself onto the seat was the most difficult, painful part of the process, but once he was there, he wondered how his doctor could have been silly enough to refuse him a motorcycle ride once in a while.

He revved the engine and rolled out of the garage, across the sidewalk and into the street. It was slow going all the way to the highway, but once he was on the wide expanse, he pushed that baby to its maximum. Andre didn't think about his leg or pain. He thought only of speed as he weaved from lane to lane. He slipped between cars and out again as if playing some kind of game. He admired the ability of this great bike to draw the attention of others, who let him take control of the highway. The rumbling beneath him and the engine that could be heard for miles were music to his ears.

He didn't have a care in the world. He didn't see or feel anything unpleasant. The wind rushed through his hair and chilled his cheeks. The scent of grilled rubber stung his nostrils. And then all of those sensations multiplied themselves by ten. Sudden, bright lights blinded him, and those wheels spun Andre Wren into never-ending darkness.

Chapter 44

Mira

Tatiana's hurried footsteps broke Mira from her reverie. She had set to work on a portrait that in the end would resemble Cecile de Champigny, the woman whose bland exterior hid many profound feelings. Mira would bring them to the surface, whether her brother approved of it or not. This would be the highlight of the show she and Laura planned to open in three months. She didn't need Cecile to model for her. The important elements of the woman's face and spirit would remain with Mira forever.

Mira adjusted the red scarf she had tied around her head to keep those unruly curls at bay and rose from her stool to face Tatiana. Her heart skipped a beat as she looked into eyes of panic.

"What's going on?" Mira asked, rushing forward.

"It's Andre Wren…" a soft, monotone voice came from her friend's mouth. "He's dead."

"What? Tatiana, what are you saying?"

"Look down there," she said, moving toward the ledge overlooking the Rue des Martyrs. "See those police cars up the street? And that mob gathering…"

Mira's eyes focused on the officers milling around and the hordes of people who lingered along the sidewalk whispering and craning their necks to see nothing. She turned back to Tatiana.

"What happened?"

"I don't know," she said, shaking her head. "There are several versions... It seems he took his Harley out last night and got into an accident on the highway. Some are saying it was suicide..."

"That's not true! He was getting closer to Hugo... becoming a real father."

"Yes, but at the same time he was realizing that his career was over. The theater was Andre Wren's life, Mira! He was an egomaniac."

"No! Not any more. He discovered something more. I really believe that... Oh my God, what about Hugo? Have you seen him?"

Mira brought her hands to her cheeks and wiped the tears that had started to flow.

Tatiana shook her head. "That's what I'm worried about."

"Well I have to find him!"

"Wait! Mira, calm down, think of yourself and the baby! I wouldn't have even told you if... if it wasn't going on right downstairs!"

Mira knew Tatiana was right, but how could she control her emotions at a time like this? As she hurried down the stairs, through the apartment and down the stairwell to the sidewalk, she told herself she would try to remain calm. But that was easier said than done. She ran crazily toward the crowd—forgetting those few extra pounds that had started slowing her down—and plunged into it. Mira pushed bystanders to her left and right until she reached an officer with a cell phone to his ear.

"Please,—tell me where I can find Mr. Wren's son Hugo!" she said desperately. "I'm a friend..."

"He's probably at the station, but I don't know if you'll be able to see him or not. There are a lot of reports to be filed."

"Where is it?" she asked.

"On rue Marcadet," he said, and then turned his back to

Mira to be swallowed up by the mass of people who days ago wouldn't have thought twice about Andre Wren. But today, in death, he had grasped their attention.

A woman named Clarisse let Mira into Andre Wren's apartment. Mira, who had missed Hugo at the police station, searched the neighborhood before returning to the place where she was sure to be successful. By this time, the bystanders had dispersed and she was able to sneak into the courtyard, through the inner door and up the stairs. Clarisse was leaving the apartment as she approached.

"Excuse me, but I'm looking for Mr. Wren's son Hugo," she said.

"You're his girlfriend, aren't you?"

She nodded.

"He's inside… I'm Clarisse—Andre's wife."

"Oh, I'm sorry," Mira held a hand to her mouth. "I didn't realize…"

"It's all right. I didn't expect you to know. We've been separated for months…" Tears shined in her eyes. She wiped them away. Mira opened her mouth as if to say something, but words refused to come out.

"This is life, isn't it?" Clarisse said. "It's too late to change things now." She tried to smile. "Go inside, please. Hugo needs you. But he's like his father, who never would admit to needing anyone."

Mira's feet treaded almost silently through the dim hallway and into the living room, where she was certain she would find Hugo. He sat there, at the edge of the couch with his face buried in his hands. The drapes were drawn and the lights turned off as if the apartment itself was mourning the death of its distinguished owner. Mira snapped on a small tea lamp and watched it illuminate the portrait of Hugo, which Andre Wren had hung over the fireplace. Hugo looked up, and his eyes—glassy with tears—met hers.

"He was proud of you," Mira said. She sat next to him and held his hands tightly in hers. She could feel him shaking.

"I'm sorry, Hugo."

He took a deep breath and slowly let it out.

"The most painful thing is the uncertainty," he whispered. "He didn't commit suicide, Mira! No matter what they say, I won't believe it."

"We know the truth. That's the important thing."

"But his memory shouldn't be tarnished by lies! He wasn't a has-been actor who wanted to end it all! Andre Wren wanted to live life to the fullest. That's why he took his Harley out on the road! Can't anyone understand that? I can... and I shouldn't be the one defending him. So he wasn't the best father in the world... but he had his reasons... and in the end, he recognized his mistakes."

Hugo shook his head and mumbled a few unintelligible sentences into Mira's neck as he leaned into her arms. They remained there in silence for what seemed like hours until Hugo pulled away and wiped his eyes.

"I found out something else today that made me understand how much my father regretted our separation..." Hugo said. "It was through Clarisse. She said Dad took the film role as a deal with the director to give me a shot at the lead. Dad didn't want to tell me because he thought I would be angry. And he was right... I would have been. I would have thought he didn't trust my talent. But now, I see it in a different light. He sacrificed the career that meant everything to him for me. For a few weeks, he was a father, Mira..."

"And a good one at that," she whispered.

"Are they still out there?" Hugo asked, nodding in the direction of the windows.

"The crowds are gone by now."

"Only there for the excitement, as usual."

Mira shivered as she looked around at the dark stillness to be found in this room, which already seemed lifeless without Andre.

"What's going to become of this place?" she asked.

"Clarisse is selling it... along with every reminder of Andre Wren. She said it's best that way."

Mira walked over to the fireplace, took the portrait between her hands and twisted it off the wall.

"Here," she said, handing it to Hugo. "I think he loved this portrait more than anything else in this old apartment, if I do say so myself... because it is you. Take it."

Hugo held the frame between his hands and stood up.

"I think we've spent enough time here," he said.

Together, they walked to the door without looking back.

Chapter 45

Rafael

Rafael Mendez turned away from the painful past and ran wildly along the Rue des Martyrs to 120. He would find Laurel there. Her father had called moments ago, whispering into the phone that she had returned—at least for the moment. Rafael didn't want to waste time. He couldn't let her escape him once again.

Out of breath, he mounted the stairs two by two until he arrived at the de Champigny's door. Mr. de Champigny, who had regained color in his face and life in his eyes, led Rafael into the apartment and quietly down the hall toward the staircase.

"She's in her room," he whispered. "The second on the left. She told me she wouldn't stay long—just enough to pack up a few more things. Maybe you can talk some sense into her... I don't know what's on her mind!"

But Rafael was hardly listening. He was already climbing the staircase and thinking only of Laurel.

The door with a "do not disturb" sign on the handle was shut. Lightly, he tapped the wood with his fingers.

"Papa, I told you I would be down in a few…"

"Laurel, it's me," he said.

The door swung open. She looked at him with wary eyes.

"What are you doing here? I thought we made things clear. It's over."

"Laurel, I know about everything that happened to you."

Her face turned scarlet, and she looked away. It was painful for him to see the ever-confident expression crack. Rafael pulled her into his arms, but she stepped back.

"He shouldn't have told you," she said. Rafael followed her into the room and closed the door.

"Why? Why shouldn't I know? I'm in love with you!"

Laurel leaned against the open window and gazed beyond the Rue des Martyrs.

"Don't say that, Rafael…You'll only say it and then walk away."

"I don't plan on going anywhere."

She turned around and looked at him with accusing eyes.

"You've found Carmen, haven't you?"

He nodded.

"So you'll go back to Colombia."

"No! You have it all wrong, Laurel. I came here on a quest for something. I've found it, but along the way, I've discovered many things that I can't abandon. My life is no longer in Colombia. I can't go back there. I've left behind too much sadness."

"Well, if you're going to stay, you're better off without me," she said. She pushed the window open a bit farther and deeply inhaled the air tainted by car exhaust.

"Why? Because you've had traumatic experiences in your life? Well, so have I."

"I know."

"We're both haunted by terrible images in the night…"

"Sometimes I think they'll never leave me," she said, turning to him with grief in her eyes.

"What do you plan on doing out there on the streets by yourself? Will that help your situation? I don't think so."

"My days of doing crazy things are over, Rafael, and I'm starting to get my life in order. I'm back in touch with my doctor. I can't stay away from my fantasy world, otherwise."

"Why did you decide to look for help now?" Rafael asked.

"Because I found a reason." Her eyes escaped his.

"And that is?" Rafael's heart was beating a mile a minute as he waited for her answer.

He reached out and took Laurel's hands, leading her to the white loveseat in the corner. For a brief moment, the familiar warmth coursed through his body as they sat side by side. And then, all at once, he could sense that she was slipping away from him.

He wanted her to say "you and me" and fall into his arms. But instead, in a soft voice, she said "Maybe I'll tell you one day. For now, let's take things slowly. It looks like you've found your way, Rafael... I still have to find mine."

"But we love each other, Laurel!" he said, a feeling of panic consuming him. He suddenly was desperate to hold onto her, to cast away the voice of logic.

"Everything has happened too quickly," she said, running a hand through her tousled hair. "I need more time... and so do you."

"I can help you... find your way," he said quietly.

"There are some things we have to do alone."

"That's what I used to think... until I started paying attention to encounters."

But he realized that insisting any further would be futile. He would have to accept Laurel's decision if he wanted to maintain even the slimmest chance of a future together.

"What exactly did you find out these past few weeks, Rafael Mendez?" she asked, interrupting his thoughts.

"That my father wasn't perfect, but he took care of his family in the best way that he could. And, as I said, I found Carmen—my sister."

Laurel glanced at him inquisitively.

"She's your sister?"

"And she lives in this building. Or at least she did before you moved in with your father. You were right about that. Now, she's returned... It's a long story."

"I think I might have time to listen..."

Laurel's gaze met Rafael's. And the look in her eyes, a

small glimmer that seemed to reflect all that they had experienced together, sparked hope in his heart.

A Note from Adria J. Cimino

Dear Reader,

Thanks for reading *Paris, Rue des Martyrs*. I was inspired to write this novel as I crossed many of the same people each day in my Parisian neighborhood, and yet they remained strangers. I thought: "What if our lives entwined?" And then I started to write.

If you enjoyed *Paris, Rue des Martyrs*, I'd love it if you left a review on Amazon. Even a few sentences can make a big difference! Reviews are so important; the more positive reviews a book has, the more promotion it gains through Amazon and other outlets. And the more others will want to read it!

I also would like to invite you to join my mailing list to stay up to date on my new releases and special sales. I send out a newsletter once a month at most, so I promise I won't bombard your inbox! You can sign up here: http://bit.ly/cimino-news

All the best,
Adria

P.S. Read on for a sneak peek at my novel *A Perfumer's Secret*. This story of love, fragrance and family secrets will transport you to the flower fields of Provence.

Acknowledgements

A special thank you to my husband Didier, for being there, always. I also would like to thank the great team at Velvet Morning Press for the editing, formatting and all of the faith in our project... And I can't forget to mention artist Cooper Copetas, for a cover drawing that captures the spirit of Paris. A big *merci* to all!

About the Author

Adria J. Cimino is an author of contemporary literary fiction and a partner in the boutique publishing house Velvet Morning Press. She lives in Paris with her husband and daughter.

To follow Adria's latest adventures in Paris or learn about her upcoming books and writing projects, visit AdriaJCimino.com. And get her short story *Flore* for free by joining her mailing list: http://bit.ly/cimino-news.

Other Titles by Adria J. Cimino

Adria's other books include:

A Perfumer's Secret: The quest for a stolen perfume formula awakens passion, rivalry and family secrets in the fragrant flower fields of the South of France.

Before Paris: a prequel novella to *Paris, Rue des Martyrs*.

Close to Destiny: Alternating between the reality of day and the mystery of night, *Close to Destiny* is a magical realism story of déjà vu and righting past wrongs.

The Creepshow: What does Wanda Julienne, recently back to the corporate world after maternity leave, do when faced with a glass ceiling? Fight back.

Read on for a sneak peek of *A Perfumer's Secret*...

An intriguing encounter at...

Flore

Apolline has tea at Café de Flore in her chic Parisian neighborhood every week with her mother and grandmother. But today, after the teatime routine, she dares to return alone... for an intriguing encounter.

"Flore" is the first in a series of Café Life stories by Adria J. Cimino. In this volume, it is accompanied by "Love Unlocked," one of the author's stories from the anthology *That's Paris*.

Get it for free! Join Adria's new release mailing list and she'll send you a free ecopy of *Flore*: http://bit.ly/cimino-news.

A Perfumer's Secret

A Novel

ADRIA J. CIMINO

Chapter 1

The photos of Lolitas licking glossy red lollipops and elegant young women gazing dreamily across Long Island Sound left Zoe uninspired. She had tacked the colorful series along one wall of her tiny midtown office, with the following sentence written in calligraphy: *We are seeking a perfume that would suit both F. Scott Fitzgerald's Daisy and Vladimir Nabokov's Lolita.* That was the assignment from the French designer Cherone, and Zoe was one of a handful of perfumers at fragrance companies from New York to Tokyo vying for the contract.

Crumpled papers with failed formulas and scented samples littered the stark white desk. Zoe abruptly swept them to the floor, twirled her long black hair into a knot and marched over to the window. She slipped out of her stilettos and pressed her cheek against the cool glass. Grand Central Station loomed large above her head, the trio of Hercules, Mercury and Minerva beckoning to her. She studied the statue without really seeing it. She was frozen, unable to churn out a submission offering the perfect balance of originality and comfortable familiarity that would grant her status as more than an ordinary up-and-coming talent.

"A woman attached to wealth and comfort. A precocious kid. There isn't a link. Why not be direct about it and ask for a guaranteed best seller that every woman on Earth will wear?"

Although Zoe said the words aloud, she meant them for herself alone. She jumped at the sound of a suave voice that she didn't want to hear.

"A designer once requested the simplest and most difficult of creations: 'a perfume for all seasons.' Now what could be more banal than that? The key was finding an angle, something unexpected. I did that. And I won the contract."

Zoe bristled, turned around, stepped back into her patent leathers and glared at Drew Hudson, the senior perfumer who had stolen her heart and then smashed it to smithereens. She knew he would have loved to see her intimidation, but she refused to give him the satisfaction. Zoe had become an expert at masking her emotions, hiding behind her teardrop perfume that everyone inquired about, but no one could identify.

She had only cracked once. She didn't exactly cry, however. Her eyes filled with tears that wouldn't fall as she packed her bags and slammed the door of the apartment she and Drew had shared for more than a year. He ran after her along West 14th Street as the rain poured down, drenching them. He caught her by both arms, but she pushed him away. She told him she didn't want his excuses. The rain drowned her words.

That had happened a week ago. Now, she was face-to-face with him once more, searching the depths of those eyes that still sought to work their magic, to draw her closer. She felt as if her heart was breaking yet again, but she wouldn't budge.

She had been aware of the risks. Getting involved with a fellow perfumer was a bad idea. There would be too much competition, too much at stake. From her colleagues, she had heard about the messy breakups and professional disasters that ensued. But Zoe didn't want to resist the temptation. There had to be a few exceptions to the rule. She used the same argument over and over: How could she possibly fall for someone who *didn't* share her passion? And that common passion is what had torn them apart.

"Are you here to celebrate?" she asked. Her voice remained neutral, concealing the rancor that boiled deep within. "Exactly one week ago, you snatched control of this project from my hands, and I walked out on you. That does merit recognition."

"Zo, I didn't take control. I was given control!"

"Because you told Veronica I wasn't capable," she said sharply.

"You need help on this. Why can't you admit it? You don't have the experience to deal with this one on your own!"

He pushed a lock of glossy brown hair away from his face and sank onto one corner of Zoe's desk.

"Look." He indicated the pile of scent dips at his feet. "You haven't gotten very far. It's always a struggle for you, Zoe. Admit it."

Zoe's eyes wouldn't release the hot tears of anger. She had lost the ability to cry years ago.

"Perfume is about patience." She pronounced the words through gritted teeth. "But I shouldn't have to tell you that."

"Try explaining that to a client," Drew snapped.

"You still haven't answered my question. Why are you here? To deliver a message from the client?"

"Cherone is asking for initial samples by next week. I wanted to touch base to see what you had in mind. We are supposed to be working on this project together in case you've forgotten."

Next week! Zoe's heart was racing, but she didn't flinch. She would come up with something. No matter what.

"Everything is under control," she said, even though it wasn't. Pressure never hurt anyone, especially when dealing with a creative project. She'd pull a few all-nighters, and that would do the trick. Even though she wasn't happy with the management of this project, she wouldn't abandon it. The designer was influential, making this an opportunity for her to shine. Or sink. But Zoe wouldn't even consider failing.

"What are you using for the juice?" Drew asked.

"Look through what's on the floor, and you'll know what I'm not using."

He picked up a scent dip, sniffed, and screwed his mouth into a thoughtful pout. He repeated the routine several times. Zoe glared at him with satisfaction in her eyes, as if to say "I told you none of these were right." She was back in the driver's seat.

"You need more synthetics," he said. "I'm finding the same flaw in each of the samples. You're too bogged down by naturals. What you've got is too heavy."

"Zoe?" A slight knock on the half-open door, and an intern popped her head inside. "I have the mail."

Zoe distractedly thanked her and accepted the slim envelope as she explained to Drew that the problem wasn't only with the scent's inertia.

"Jasmine doesn't work," she said as she opened the envelope with foreign handwriting. "It's too sophisticated and…" And then she stopped.

The document was written in French, the language of her mother, Barbara Rose Flore. A scent flooded her mind in one great burst: Barbara Rose's powdery homemade concoction with notes of bergamot and almond. Zoe coughed as if choking on the fragrance that escaped as quickly as it had overcome her. She scanned the letter. She was invited to the reading of the will of her great aunt, Marie-Odile Fontaine, in exactly forty-eight hours in Grasse, France. And she was to inherit "a souvenir of olfactory significance." The Fontaine perfume family. This couldn't be right. Barbara Rose didn't have family in Grasse or anywhere else for that matter. Her closest connection to Grasse's perfume industry was the lovely photo of a lavender field that Zoe had inherited. Zoe had carted the clunky frame all over the city as she moved from apartment to apartment over the past several years.

Barbara Rose was a Parisian, and that was where she first had dabbled in scents. A Parisian who became a New Yorker when Zoe was a few weeks old. Barbara Rose had followed her best friend, Joy, across the Atlantic to escape the loneliness. "Why were you lonely?" Zoe's small voice would ask. Barbara Rose never answered, but Zoe glimpsed the sadness that conveyed more than words. Then her mother's face would brighten, erasing any trace of unpleasant memories, and she would delight Zoe with her latest olfactory creations.

Zoe's eyes now remained riveted to the letter, but they only saw images of her mother: boarding a plane with a newborn in her arms, sharing a cramped apartment with two other young women, mixing potions in her makeshift laboratory.

As strange as this note from abroad seemed, Zoe couldn't

dismiss it as a mistake. The letter was clearly addressed to "Zoe Flore, daughter of Barbara Rose." And it would seem logical that Barbara Rose's extraordinary knowledge of flowers, plants and other raw materials came from time spent in the town known as the perfume capital of the world.

"Is everything all right?" Drew asked.

"Yes," she said, snapping back to the present with a look that surely would mask the sense of confusion building in the pit of her stomach. "A bit of personal business to attend to. I have to step out for a while."

"Zo, I can help if you need anything." He lingered in the doorway.

"No. I can take care of this and a lot of other things on my own."

He took a few steps backward as he made his way down the hall and shot her one last coaxing glance before turning away.

Zoe's hands shook as she stuffed the thick white piece of paper back into its envelope and the envelope into her already overflowing handbag

Find out what happens next... buy *A Perfumer's Secret* today!

$\mathcal{D}$iscover more by

ADRIA J. CIMINO

BESTSELLING AUTHOR

For new releases, deals and a free
ecopy of *Flore*, sign up here:
http://bit.ly/cimino-news

Printed in Great Britain
by Amazon